The Apple of Doom

by

Robert King

R King
17/06/05

Published by Aultbea Publishing, Inverness

Copyright details

Black Dragon Trilogy
Book 1: The Apple of Doom
by
Robert King

First published in Great Britain by
Aultbea Publishing Company in 2005,
106 Church Street, Inverness IV1 1EP

First Edition

ISBN 0-9549340-4-0

Printed by Highland Printers Limited
Henderson Road, Inverness IV1 1SP

For my parents: not because I couldn't think of anyone else, but because, without them, I wouldn't be where I am today.

Thanks to Gerry, Catherine and everyone else I met due to the Pushkin Prizes, for all the help and advice they gave, and for making me realise how fun writing can be. And also to Miss K. De Jonkheere, who gave me encouragement when I was at the first draft stage, and thank you to everyone who reads this book!

Contents

Black Dragon Trilogy

Book 1: The Apple of Doom

Chapter 1
The Broken Root

Gybes stared out of his hut window and yawned. Today didn't feel right. There was something oddly disturbing in the warm, moist air of the Tsabian Rainforest, though at first nothing odd struck his mind about this typical, early summer morning. It was the 1st of Potiton[1], and yesterday Gybes had experienced his eleventh Life-day[2]. It had been a fantastic day yesterday (the 33rd of Viraton), what with the fresh spragfruit juice, the soft, recently picked pacoo nuts and the games of hide in the jungle, go crazy, mushroom-hunt and splat.

Gybes stopped reminiscing and hopped out of his bed, putting on his white t-shirt, poncho, shorts, sandals and straw hat, then slipping out of the door. He was tall and thin, with dark brown hair and aquamarine eyes, the same as his Father's. His family had had a well-off life until they had moved to Tsabia when it had been conquered. The 'Land of Opportunity', as it had been advertised, turned out to be a land of poverty. Shortly after his family had arrived, a very honourable figure, Gybes' very own Great-Great Grandfather, Sir Gampolball of Goodport had succumbed to the temptation of gambling and gone bankrupt. The Gampolballs had changed to a more usual name, the 'Marronons', and diminished to a typical immigrant family.

Mother and Father were already up, preparing a breakfast, which consisted chiefly of a tender fruit called bhalop.

'Good morning, Gybes,' said his Mother. She was carefully removing the good part of an especially squishy fruit.

'Morning Mother,' replied Gybes, shielding his eyes from the sun

'Would you mind if you went to get me a couple of docef fruits from the forest?' she asked.

Before he could answer, Gybes heard someone shouting his name from the far side of the village clearing. 'Wait, someone's calling me,' he said.

'Hey Wizz! Wanna come play Mushroom Hunt?' came the voice

'Coming, Trudge', Gybes yelled back, forgetting quickly his Mother's request. All children in Lavos village had nicknames. Gybes' nickname

[1] The fifth Month in Greenworld's 10-month year. There were 329 days in the year of Greenworld, and 330 days in a Longyear, which occurred every five years.
[2] Birthday

was Wizz because he was a very fast runner, while Trudge, whose real name was Djok, was slower and rather chubby. The nicknaming originated from the ancient Aartan priests of Tuvak, the Capital of the Greenworld Empire. It had been brought over by the invaders in 1603, when religion was strong enough that the people were too afraid of the priests to call them by name. Some still believed the children's nicknames to be blasphemous.

Gybes ran over to the edge of the dusty open area where he found Trudge, Clamber (who was good at climbing), Mystica, and Gybes' best friend, Fiddles, whose real name was Dagtan.

'What are we playing today?' asked Fiddles, yawning.

'Mushroom hunt,' muttered Trudge. 'I'm timing.'

Someone walked out of a gap between two huts and yawned. She had long, blonde hair and turquoise eyes. She looked around at the rest, rubbing her eyes.

'I only just woke up,' she said. 'What are you playing?

'Mushroom hunt, Chleosa,' said Clamber and Gybes simultaneously.

The rules of mushroom hunt were very basic. All you had to do was run into the Rainforest and pick as many edible mushrooms as possible within the time limit. After ten minutes the players had to return and add up their points. Each type of mushroom was worth a different number of points. Forest mushrooms rewarded their finder with five points each, tree mushrooms fetched four, yellow caps gave you three and the common mini whites only merited one point each. Specialities such as yellow delights and goldfire tallcaps were valued at fifteen points each. Any toxic mushrooms, such as dusky nightcloths and rancid hoplongs deducted points.

Trudge held up his timepiece and began counting. Gybes, Fiddles, Chleosa, Clamber, Mystica and, unknowingly to them the bully Kicker, entered the forest. Gybes took a path to the west and then dashed off into the forest to the right. There were only fifty metres between him and the village when he spotted some mini-whites. He scooped up about twenty or so and shoved them into his woven bag. He continued hastily onwards into the jungle.

After another twenty metres or so, Gybes came upon a stream. It was not very wide, so maybe, he thought, he could *just* about jump it. There was a loud splash followed by a swear as Gybes' foot landed in the stream Shrugging, he carried on with one wet foot into the bushes ahead.

When he emerged on the other side, Gybes found himself in a clearing, overhung by shading branches. He caught something out of the corner of his eye to the left.

'Forest mushrooms!' he yelled, forgetting that other people might hear him. They could have them toasted for breakfast! He rushed up to the clump only to spot three more. He had never known forest mushrooms to be this prolific. He hurriedly picked as many as he could of the hoard and dropped them carefully into his bag.

'Think you're gonna get the best, eh?' came a voice from behind Gybes. He turned round. There was someone standing there.

*

Some way to the north and a little further into the forest Chleosa was not having much luck. So far she had come across only a small patch of yellow caps and a scattering of mini-whites, not to mention four clumps of execution mushrooms, a couple of small groups of devil powder mushrooms and one lone death giant.

She carried on, walking swiftly, kicking dead leaves and getting her poncho caught in the undergrowth. Deep in the jungle you didn't need a hat, as the leaves protected you from the ravaging heat of the sun. Today though, she thought, a hat would have been quite useful, because twigs kept getting caught in her hair.

Looking ahead, she caught a glimpse of yellow held momentarily in a ray of sunlight.

'Just more yellow caps,' she muttered to herself.

Looking closer though, she noticed that they had thicker stems and flatter tops than yellow caps. They were yellow delights!

She dashed over and plucked them delicately so as not to damage them, as they were a local delicacy and worth fifteen points each in the game. Once her bag was full she turned and went back on her tracks so that she could get back and show the rest. She was bound to get a nickname like 'Magnet' or something. Even 'Mushroom' would do. In the five years she had lived in Lavos, the other children had somehow never seen it fit to give her a nickname.

She passed unheeded under some tree mushrooms, a group of almost thirty yellow caps and even happily kicked a bunch of forest mushrooms. She heard Trudge calling in the distance, and realized that time was up. She hurried down the forest path and took a left turn. Suddenly she realised she didn't recognise her surroundings.

'Oh no,' she muttered. 'Where am I?'

Continuing onwards, hoping she would find her way back to the village, a tree up ahead caught her eye. It was a strange shape and texture for a tree in a rainforest. More like one perhaps, from Eastwood. It was mottled brown-green with a bent trunk and rough bark. It looked like an ancient oak from the city of Elmor, or maybe the western slopes of the West Border Mountains. Ignoring the black monkey that crossed her path in front of her, she rushed forwards to examine it closely, completely forgetting about the game and not noticing the root protruding from the base of the tree. She tripped and toppled forwards, her head knocking another tree.

*

'Kicker!' yelled Gybes, surprised.

'Wizz,' acknowledged Kicker. He smiled horribly, displaying surprisingly clean teeth. 'Hand me the mushrooms.'

'What mushrooms?' said Gybes innocently, hiding the glaringly obvious, bulging bag behind his back.

'You know what I mean, Wizz,' sneered Kicker. ' You yelled at the top of your voice, idiot! Did you think no one would hear? If there aren't any in your bag, then why are there loads of mushrooms behind you? Didn't you pick them?'

'Well I was just about to but...'

'Hand 'em over Wizz, or your face'll be so bruised your mother won't be able to tell the difference between you and a monkey!'

Gybes acted quickly. He ducked, which was lucky, because at that moment Kicker owned up to his nickname. Gybes ran at top speed through the thick trees towards the village, ducking under branches and jumping over roots. He leapt clear over the stream and flung himself forwards. Kicker wasn't going to catch him - he was the fastest person of his age in the area.

But Gybes had underestimated the speed of his pursuer. Kicker was three years older than Gybes, and just as fast.

'Come 'ere you little nutheed!' shouted Kicker from around twenty metres back.

Gybes heard Trudge calling from the distance. He hurtled the last thirty metres back to the village clearing and out onto the dusty earth.

Trudge waddled up and smiled broadly.

'Wotcha got 'ere, Wizz? he asked. 'Looks pretty good to me. I'll wait for Clamber - he's the one who's good at adding.'

Just at that moment Fiddles followed by Mystica came walking out of the forest. They ran up to Gybes and Trudge with bulging bags.

'Great!' said Gybes. 'Just Clamber and Chleosa to come now.'

Not a moment after Gybes had said this, Clamber walked onto the dry mud at the edge of the clearing, looking dishevelled.

'Ah, the counter,' cried Trudge.

'Clamber always adds the score!' protested Mystica. 'He's probably cheating.'

'Not likely today,' he mumbled. He opened his bag to reveal a squishy pulp. 'I fell out of a tree.'

After a few minutes, Clamber had finished counting all the mushrooms from Gybes', Mystica's and Fiddles' bags.

'In third place,' he pronounced with the air of a commentator, 'is Fiddles the Finder.' Everyone cheered sarcastically. 'In second place,' he continued, 'is Mystica the Magnet.'

'Huh, yeah right,' scoffed Trudge.

'And in first place... is Wizz the Wizard!'

'Yeah, great I won,' said Gybes distractedly. 'Where's Chleosa?'

'Dunno,' said Trudge. 'I think she went sort of north west, on that path Clamber got attacked by ants on.'

'Oh yeah,' laughed Clamber, remembering the occasion.

'I'd better go and look for her,' said Gybes.

'Don't be killed by wild beasts or knife bearing monkeys,' sniggered Fiddles. 'Or mad feather cushions, or killer vines with horned rats and poisonous mongooses attached to them. We wouldn't want that. No-one in the world would want that to happen to you.'

'Thanks,' said Gybes. 'Now I'll be terrified every time I see a vine, 'cause I'll be thinking "At any moment that could *eat* me!" ' He laughed and disappeared into the forest.

'Actually, that'd be pretty cool,' mumbled Kicker from behind the rest, so that no one could hear him.

*

Gybes was ten minutes along the path when he met a fork. He could see Chleosa's footprints heading along the smallest trail: to the right. As he ran along the dim, leafy path, it dawned on him that the footprints were going both ways. Realising what Chleosa had done, he turned back on himself to see if she had broken off from the main path.

Probably lost, he thought. She hardly ever came into the forest.

Sure enough, ten or so metres back on his tracks, Gybes found a small animal track leading off to the left, somewhere he had never been before, despite having lived in the area for eleven years. Chleosa had obviously mistaken this to be another path back to the village. He turned and strolled off down it.

After a while, the path began to slope gently upwards. It had been five minutes since Gybes had left the main path, and he was beginning to wonder just what *had* happened to Chleosa. He followed her footprints to the right and saw a strange tree ahead. Not noticing her figure lying face down behind a tree to his right he walked up to examine the tree closely.

'Strange,' he whispered to himself. 'I've never seen a tree like this in my life.' He turned and looked at Chleosa's bag.

'Leave my mushrooms, monkey,' said Chleosa dreamily.

'It's me, Wizz' said Gybes. 'What happened to you? Are you all right?'
'Yeah, I think I tripped on a root,' Chleosa replied. 'I hit my head on something.'
Gybes nodded and bent over the root, a look of puzzlement on his face.
'This root's got some weird symbols on it,' he said.
'Let's see?' said Chleosa. She peered over Gybes' shoulder. 'That's odd. Look, it's got a translation into our letters here,' said Chleosa.
'Translation, maybe, but I still don't know what *"Te B'ardkos uoth Krethak"* means.'
'Let's go back to the village for breakfast,' suggested Chleosa, changing the subject. 'I've found loads of yellow delights!'
Gybes didn't object, merely nodded and got up, but as he did so, he slipped the root into his pocket.
When they got back to the village the others were already eating breakfast.
'Womp fum mufwoomf?' said Trudge, who was devouring his.
'We'd love some,' said Gybes and Chleosa in unison.
Although it was the normal happy-chatty breakfast Gybes was used to, he was far too busy thinking to want to chat. Why was there an unusual tree lurking only a couple of kilometres into the forest, and what was the meaning of the inscription on the root he had in his pocket?

Chapter 2
Tombhadi

There was a knock on the door.

'Come in.'

A man with short brown hair, who was wearing a grey cloak boasting golden fastenings, strode through the door.

'Ah, Sarmon,' exclaimed a round-faced cheerful man at the desk. 'Please sit down. So, my dear friend, what is it that you wish to purchase on this fine, breezy morning?'

'I'm in a hurry and I'd rather not be delayed, Attabory Milson,' snapped Sarmon. 'I have no time for your fake hospitality.'

'What are you on about?' chuckled Attabory Milson. 'Of course you have time! Come through to my living room and have a cup of tea with me.'

'I mean it, Attabory - no time. Just tell me when you can see my master.'

'Hah! Master!' laughed Milson. 'So what's the job you've got now - are you on a ship?'

'No, Attabory.' said Sarmon, still standing. 'This is no joke. My master wants to purchase something, not I.'

'What would he want with my scrap metal, fruit seeds and old chairs, eh?[1] No boss of a firm buys anything off me, not even the poorest!' Even though Milson seemed cheery, he was daunted by the way Sarmon spoke.

'He isn't a boss of a firm,' said Sarmon impatiently. 'Give me a time.'

'If he isn't the boss of a firm and he wants to buy merchandise from me, then who is he?' asked Milson. 'A carpenter? An assassin?'

'Give me a time!' demanded Sarmon.

'Oh OK, if you must persist, tomorrow morning at ten,' Milson conceded, 'but if I'm still in bed, don't wake me. I don't like being woken.'

'My master will see you at ten tomorrow,' said Sarmon, 'whether you are awake or not.'

*

Milson was awoken the next morning by a loud bird outside his window. He looked at his timepiece. It was only nine o'clock. He got up and got dressed quickly, ready for this dubious 'master' of Sarmon's to see him. He ate his breakfast, cleaned his teeth, shaved and put on his best

---

[1] Milson was a merchant. He sold scrap wood and metal, as well as fruit seeds and, secretly, weapons. He was also a barber.

business jacket that he saved for *special* occasions. The moth holes, however, gave away the fact that it was very rarely worn.

Milson swelled with pride. He was going to have a deal with a big business man - even a millionaire. He swallowed his pride, however, when he remembered the fact that this man wasn't the boss of a firm, and also the trace of urgency he had heard in Sarmon's voice made him uneasy.

Nine fifty-seven. The man would arrive any moment. He straightened his short hair and made certain he could see his own reflection in his shoes.

There was a rapping sound on the door. Milson put on his best posh businessman look.

'Come in,' he said. The door didn't open.

Then it did.

Milson wished it hadn't. As soon as the door was wide, it felt like the air had suddenly become colder. A figure strode through the doorway. It was dressed in a black hooded cloak and dark shoes. The hands were gloved and only the chin could be seen of it's face - the rest was in an unrealistically dark shadow. The figure seemed to suck all the light out of the room. The candle flames on Milson's old, dirty chandelier flickered as the figure strode up to his desk. It lay a gloved hand down on the table.

'So you are Milson,' it said. The voice was deep and unnerving, but smooth. Milson just sat, still as a rock. The man seemed to survey his jacket. 'I see you are an accomplished businessman, Mr. Milson.'

Milson gave a nervous laugh, but felt, and looked, terrified.

The figure lay down the other hand and Milson could tell, even though he could not see them, that the figure's eyes were staring directly into his. 'I will require eighteen packets of your best quality apple seeds in three weekly instalments,' growled the man.

Before Milson could even consider being confused, sheer terror strangled him. He helplessly grappled for words. 'Why don't you... er - want them sooner... perhaps now... give seeds to you...

'I require them only at the dates I shall set!' said the man angrily. 'You *will* co-operate!'

'Who are you to boss me around?' said Milson, suddenly feeling more confident.

'I am much more than you think,' the man said smoothly. If you do not co-operate, then you shall have to suffer the... consequences.'

Milson sunk into the depth of his chair.

'The first installment,' continued the man, 'shall be on Slarday the 10th - in 6 days time. The second shall be six days from that - Cudday the 16th. And the last - the last, I will receive on Poriday the 22nd.'

'Anything else?' asked Milson, hoping the man would leave.'

'Only that I want the seeds at half price,' said the man. 'And there will be no questions asked.' He leaned closer. ‘No questions asked,’ he repeated in barely more than a whisper.

'V... very well,' muttered Milson, feeling too terrified to object 'I normally sell them at seventy buntas a pack, so all together they would cost er... seventy eights are five hundred and sixty... seventy tens are seven hundred... That means it would cost one thousand, two hundred and sixty buntas...'

'Twelve kroms and sixty buntas, idiot,' growled the cloaked man. 'At half price that's six kroms and thirty buntas. I want them at six kroms.'

'That hardly gives me any profit then,' protested Milson weakly.

The man pressed a gloved hand on Milson's throat. 'I will have them at half price,' the figure said in a rasping voice. 'And if you double cross me - Tombhadi never forgets.'

Tombhadi turned and left the room, slamming the door behind him.

Milson sat perfectly still, white-faced, open-mouthed, staring at the door.

He came to his senses.

‘Why is it,’ he grumbled to himself, ‘that whenever I think something good’s going to happen for my business, the opposite does?’

His kitchen tap began to drip.

*

Milson was having his lunch when he remembered that he needed to see someone about the seeds. His supplier lived and worked on the shore of the great city. In Tuvak, as the city was named, most people who ran their own shops or businesses lived and worked in the same place. Milson was one of these people. He was a supplier for small shops and markets - he even exported some merchandise to places such as the sandy beach resort of Riso for planting plum and alicarego trees along the promenade and even as far away as Myen, where scrap metal was used to make weapons to fight the Empire. If the Emperor ever got wind of this, Milson would be imprisoned for life, but this didn't bother him, because no one would ever discover that he exported products to a country the Empire was attempting to conquer. However, he would not be doing it if the penalty were death.

He finished his lunch, got up, walked over to the door and slipped his shoes on. He was only half a mile from the coast, so he wouldn't have to catch an Intercart. The door opened and he strolled onto the alley.

Soon he was making his way down a larger, sea bound road, where many tourist shops and market stalls could be seen. The shops were beginning to open after their lunchtime break, and some men were telling the few people who were walking around of their fabulous fruits from Greenforest and goat's milk from the herders of the hills around Westport. Others were chatting with friends or sipping tea under colourful awnings. Two old women were gossiping about the old days in front of a wool shop and to the right a crowd of teenage girls were boasting about their boyfriends' new race carts and flashy outfits. Other young women in their early twenties were showing off dresses and shoes while an old bearded man with a yellow suitcase attempted to scare some five-year old children who were giggling madly at his faces.

Milson spotted the sea ahead. It was a clear blue day and sailing ships were setting out on voyages from the main harbour onto the Bay of Tuvak. Other large boats were off for set destinations with passengers or cargoes of wood, diamonds from the Cohen Downs, tobacco and lipstick from the Tuvak Industrial Estate, bread from the bakeries of Field West and other splendid and humble things.

When Milson reached the waterfront, he turned to the right on the cobbled road. He stopped in front of the second building to the right, a white painted, three-storey affair, unlike Milson's house, which only had two floors. He climbed the stairs outside it, and walked through the open door at the top. He turned left along a short corridor. At the end he found himself facing a door. He knocked.

'Enter,' said a familiar voice from inside. Milson pushed open the door lightly. He was now in a room about twice the size of his small reception room, with white walls and rugs hiding the wooden floor, one of them with an imitation crogor's head on it[2]. Its head was complete with fangs and piercing glare. On the walls, several paintings of farmland, famous people, mountains and sailing ships were hung up on hooks and two elaborate chandeliers dangled from the ceiling, the candles giving off a dim light that felt somewhat comforting.

At the desk sat a medium sized, black haired, moustached man, smoking a large, round cigar. His name was Istfig Doran.

'Ah, good afternoon Attabory,' he said. 'I wondered when I'd see you. Are you here to buy?'

'No, I'm here to plead,' said Milson.

'Plead?'

'Yes. I need to have apple seeds by Slarday - six packs. And another twelve soon after that.' Milson knew he made no sense.

---

[2]A wild tiger-like cat found in the Forest of Shadows and Western Border Mountains. It nearly became extinct because of the fur trade, but thanks to make-lots-of-money-quickly business Companies with plenty of cheap (and mostly useless) products and loads of adverts, crogor hunting died down and people began buying cheap, gimmicky fake crogor heads to put on their rugs.

'Bit short notice,' said Doran, not seeming to think it odd. 'Could you wait until the weekend? I mean, Slarday *is* the last day in the week, so I could have them for you two days after that.'

'Tsuday?'

'Yes, in eight days time. All the churches are open then - I get my deliveries from the churches now, because they get the seeds for the churchyard to plant in honour of Aa and sell the excess at a lower price than the big merchants. They can buy the seeds directly from the farmers and aren't as interested in profits as the big companies. Anyway, Mercanto are bust - It's really hard to find seeds anywhere and I'm not getting any tomorrow because the church doesn't have any until Chauday. Everything is all mongo-bongo right now. Can't get any condoria spores 'cause the plantation's had a bad season.'

'Look, I know things aren't going well for merchants Doran, but I *must* have these seeds for Slarday!' said Milson desperately. 'Or else...'

'Or else what?'

'Or else I will have to "suffer the consequences", if the man who's purchasing them doesn't have the seeds before the times he was asking for them by. He'll probably kill me!'

'Kill?' snorted Doran. 'My dear Milson, no one outside the mental hospital would kill you for not giving them seeds. The "consequences" are probably him being a grouchy git!'

'This was different!' shouted Milson. 'The man was cloaked - I could hardly see his face and his hands were gloved! Maybe he *was* out of the mental hospital!' Even that thought felt slightly comforting, but Milson seriously doubted it.

'Well that rules out all the theories I had in mind,' said Doran. He frowned. Then he burst out laughing. 'Ha! This is a stupid joke, and I believed it! A stupid joke so that you can sell seeds to someone and get loads of money, or keep them for yourself, grow them into trees and sell them even dearer, or just so you can make fun of me! Isn't it?'

'This is serious, Doran!' yelled Milson. 'You haven't met him; you don't know what it was like! The room felt like it got colder!'

'So what's this dark ice demon's name then? Mr. Evil?'

'Tombhadi'

The smile vanished from Doran's face. 'You're joking,' he said.

'No.'

'Seriously.'

'Yes.'

'Are you sure?'

'Yes.'

'You *are* joking, really.'

'No.'

'Oh.'

*

It was only an hour after they had left Milson's home that Tombhadi and Sarmon reached the edge of Tuvak. They set their course for a path that was heading straight across a road into the Tuvak waste area, an area of hundreds of year's worth of rubbish ringing the city. As the two reached the edge, it could clearly be seen that most of the rubbish was now a brown, toxic earth, coloured green and yellow by algae. Many abstract objects were lying scattered on the earth: old clothes, rubber, teabags, rotting fish, paper bags and even someone's saddle from the Tuvak horse rider's club.

'So, my master, how long until you act,' said Sarmon, treading on an old ale bottle.

'If all goes well, then I will have control over the rebels by Milnday,' said Tombhadi. 'However, as I feared, the rebels are considering Dameid Uma as a candidate for their leader.'

'Dameid Uma is in league with us, Master,' reminded Sarmon.

'I do not trust him,' said Tombhadi.

'So who shall be chosen as an ally?'

'That is yet to be decided.'

'Bueno Castalaire?' ventured Sarmon.

'He will not suffice,' growled Tombhadi. 'He is an utter fool. However, he is extremely gullible, and would easily join us.'

'He is at a loss as to what to do with his new rank as Sergeant.'

'Yes.'

'Are you sure the plan is secure?'

'Of course I am! All shall go well this time, and I shall regain power. Now let's hurry up, we need to take some horses – I want to be at the Rebel base in two days time!'

For a moment however, both stood still and stared ahead. What would happen? Sarmon thought for a while as they continued to walk. He didn't know why he was helping this man. Tombhadi seemed to have an unnerving power over him. And there was the money, of course. Sarmon needed that. But he couldn't help thinking: had he been gullible? Had he been pulled into a trap?

Chapter 3
Motherton

It was Tsuday. As an ancient custom, Tsuday was the day of rest and play in The Greenworld Empire, but Gybes was not as relaxed as most of the rest of the locals. No one had told him that there was a strange tree in the forest not far away, with a bewildering root inscription at its base. His mother and father would have told him about it, but he didn't have a historical or geographical note[1] in his memory that they had ever told him such a thing. If the general public didn't know about it, then normally this meant it was either irrelevant or too dangerous for them to know about, without the possibility that someone might attain it or people might panic. Gybes hoped that it was because it was irrelevant, but somehow he suspected it wasn't.

'Cheer up Wizz,' said Chleosa. 'It's only a root.'

They were both at Fiddles' homely hut, where they had just told him about the root. He was just as amazed as either of them that no one had told them about it, but he shared Chleosa's view that there was nothing to worry about.

'Can I see it?' said Fiddles.

Gybes took the dusty piece of broken root out of his pocket and held it in the light. It was about ten centimetres long and three thick. The inscription had been carved in and filled with white, weather-resistant paint. Weather resistant paint hadn't been invented as far as Gybes knew.

'My Uncle Prongo said there were two hundred and forty-seven different languages in Tsabia alone!' said Fiddles.

'Oh that's a *great* help,' said Chleosa sarcastically.

'Surely its not all that hard to find out the meaning of a couple of words on a manky root,' said Fiddles.

'But it might be a lost language no-one's ever discovered,' said Gybes. 'Archaeologists have discovered over thirteen thousand languages from the last three thousand years, but they don't know them all.'

'My Uncle's got a book on the languages of the last three thousand years,' said Fiddles. 'All thirteen thousand of them! And this is a very distinctive alphabet - we should be able to find it in there, and then look for further information if necessary.'

'Convenient,' muttered Gybes.

---

[1] In Greenworld, Education was a private thing. There were no public schools, and mainly Parents would teach their children basic skills and the way of life, as well as writing, mathematics, reading and 'vocabulary development' along with a bit of historical or geographical information. Anything else was taught to children through experience or when the situation arose. Teenagers could study in a Royal Institute once they were sixteen, with an enormous variety of subjects on offer, but that meant going to Tuvak, and that meant money, and money was scarcely extremely scarce in Tsabia.

'Why don't we ask to have a look at it - he lives in Motherton,' suggested Fiddles.

'Good idea,' said Chleosa. 'Motherton's only just up the hill a couple of kilometres to the east. It shouldn't take us long to reach.'

'Let's go then,' finalised Gybes.

*

Gybes' home village of Lavos was very small, but as it happened, it and the neighbouring larger village of Hillside Riverton were just a couple of kilometres to the east of the second most busy route in the rainforest island of Tsabia. This meant that people frequently dropped in for a rest, and now it was Summer and the tourist season. Although Lavos was hardly what you'd call a haven for tourism, as Gybes and his friends wandered towards the edge of the village they could see a number of people they didn't recognise. One was obviously a native, with dark skin. Another to Gybes' right was an old Tuvakian gentleman with a lost look on his face, and farther to the right, a dark skinned immigrant from the Forest of the Sun in the south with a popadom in his hand he was drying chillies on a white piece of cloth laid out on the ground.

When they reached the other side of the village they headed up a track into the forest, just wide enough for a cart with one horse. Here there were few bushes, but the trees filtered the light so that it became a lazy glow, and the dim light made everything seem to glow yellow. Gybes looked ahead at the familiar surroundings. The dusty path continued along the flat ground and turning slowly to the right.

'Let's take the quick route,' said Fiddles. They took a turn to the left. This way was too steep for carts, and too difficult footing for horses. It was not much wider than an animal track.

After a few minutes, they came to a clearing. Brillos cycads, hulpane ferns, asteriona flowers and majestic celembar trees grew clustered around the edges. Many exotic insects flew around the pool in the centre of the clearing, while monkeys danced around the ferns, their young playing and rolling on the grass.

'Let's stop here for a moment,' suggested Fiddles. 'This is my favourite spot.'

All three of them walked over to a grouping of rocks by the edge of the pool and sat on them.

'What does this say?' inquired Chleosa, examining the rock beside her, upon which a message was chiselled.

'It says "Eth gloroth eth hultheth. Eth Galiradra Hoplorod."' said Gybes. He didn't want to know it, but unfortunately patriotism was virtually compulsory, and the famous patriots of the pre-Greenworld-Empire period sometimes jokingly called the 'Dork Ages' were taught to every inhabitant of the Empire.

'"For glory, for liberty. For Galipady Hopelrode,"' quoted Fiddles. 'King Hopelrode was an egotistic git. He blamed everyone for everything. He never blamed himself, of course.'

'Let's get to Motherton,' said Gybes. 'I want to be back for lunch.'

The next part of the journey involved climbing an even steeper slope, among ferns and horsetails. They scrambled up the difficult path, treading on the roots that were strong enough to hold their weight, acting as steps. Prayer flies were abundant here, and there was no avoiding the irritating mosquitoes that buzzed repeatedly round and round their heads and bit their bare arms.

After a while the path levelled out and continued horizontally for a while. They met the main track, which still gradually sloped upwards. The foliage was less dense here and the mosquitoes less suffocating. They took a shortcut again as the slope became too steep for carts and scrambled on upwards past numerous berry bushes full of tsabfinches, tough grasses scratching at their legs.

'I hope your Prongo's book proves useful,' said Gybes, feeling the root in his pocket. It was inexplicably smooth.

'I hope he's *in*,' said Fiddles. 'He normally goes hunting on Phomday.'

'But it *isn't* Phomday,' said Chleosa.

'Trust me to get the days muddled up like an old man,' said Fiddles. 'I'm only eleven!'

'You're ten,' said Gybes, stifling a giggle.

Fiddles put on a face of mock terror.

'We're here,' stated Gybes as the ground levelled and they joined the track again. Ahead on a small flat area a village could be seen, not unlike Lavos, with slopes leading up to forested cliffs and hills. Far to the right, in the distance were mountains, their peaks shrouded in cloud. In the centre of Tsabia, there was a mountain range, and Lavos was right on the edge of the very northern tip of it, but still only about fifty metres above sea level. Motherton was at least another hundred metres higher, though one hundred and fifty metres was not very high statistically.

The village itself was about the size of Lavos, with houses and a small inn. It was situated on the south side of a hill, which sloped steeply up to a staggering cliff one hundred metres high.

Uncle Prongo's hut was a small, circular building about six or seven metres in diameter, with two semi-circle rooms, a kitchen and a living room-bedroom. Fiddles looked in through the door.

'Hi Uncle!' he shouted.

A man in a brown poncho and brown leather shorts with shoulder length black hair and a face of stubble emerged from the hut. 'C'mon in

Fiddles,' he said. 'An' yer friends Wizz an' 'Leosa can come in too.' He was the only adult Gybes knew who called them by their nicknames. 'So, wotcha 'ere for? D'ya wanna 'ave a go on me ol' swing?'

'Actually we wondered if we could have a look in your book *Languages of the Last Three Millennia*,' said Fiddles with unnecessary formality.

'That's… odd,' said Prongo, obviously surprised. 'C'mon in an' 'ave a look, then!' They walked in through the door and sat down on the hearthrug. Uncle Prongo went the kitchen and started making some drink.

Meanwhile Gybes was looking at all the interesting and not-so-interesting books Prongo had on his shelf. There were titles such as *'How to grow cauliflower in Tsabia'* and *'The ancient city of Talmor - did it really exist?'* Gybes examined the hearthrug and noticed it was a woven picture of Prongo.

''Ere ya go,' said Uncle Prongo, ambling into the room and placing a jug of juice and a plate of biscuits down beside them. He proceeded to look for the book on the bookshelf Gybes had been examining. Prongo pulled a large, old, tattered book off the highest row and handed it to Fiddles.

'Now, do be careful with it 'cause it's the only book of it in the area, 'cept the library in 'Illside Riverton,' he said. 'Looks at it *every day*, I does,' he added with a voice laden with sarcasm. He went out the door into the intense heat of the growing summer.

'Let's look inside it,' said Gybes.

Fiddles opened the book on the rug. 'Let's see... Ancient Alphabets pages 576-643.' He turned to the first page of the section and started skiming the text with his eyes.

'It's nothing like any of those,' said Gybes, holding the root in his right hand and flicking his eyes between it and the book.

'Well, that's all the Tsabian languages,' said Fiddles. 'We must have missed it.'

'Maybe it was imported,' said Chleosa.

'Imported?'

'Well, you know what I mean, maybe it came from somewhere else. Let's keep looking.'

'But it was *growing* on a tree!' said Gybes. 'I didn't see any nails in the tree when I took this root away.'

'There's still a chance,' persisted Chleosa.

However, they could not find any alphabets or letters that looked remotely like the ones on Gybes' root. Even the first few legendary languages were nothing like what they were looking for.

'Look,' said Chleosa, turning the last page in the booklet 'This is a bit more like it.'

'Yes, that's from Blackness Island,' said Fiddles. 'It's the code they use to converse with the people of the Bay of Enchantment. Nobody lives in either place though – I suppose this is just legend.'

'Turn the page,' said Gybes.

'There's nothing there,' said Fiddles. 'It's on to the structure of languages.'

'What about the islands further south?'

'Too mystic, I suppose.'

'Ooh, mystic! Sounds int'restin' Find anythin' useful?'

Uncle Prongo had just entered into the hut with dry clothes off his washing line.

'No,' said Gybes.

'It's lethally boring,' said Fiddles. 'Where could we find information on the languages of the far southern islands?'

'Oooh, they's legendses they is,' said Prongo. 'No one's ever come back from goin' that far south. Yer might just find summat in the town, y'know, 'Illside Riverton. They's got a library, 'asn't they.'

'OK, good idea,' said Fiddles.

''S lucky I 'as kept that book,' said Prongo. 'I never looks at it. 'S just 'cos it's valuable.'

'Can we have a go on your swing?' asked Gybes.

''Course you can mate,' said Uncle Prongo. 'Follow me an' I'll show yer it.'

'What's your Uncle's swing like, Fiddles?' asked Chleosa as they walked out of the hut and headed to the edge of the village.

'I didn't know he had one,' said Fiddles.

They had come to the north edge of the village and were now following Prongo up the steep path on the hill. Birds were singing and rasping and making lots of different notes and weird noises. Different varieties were calling to each other from tree to tree and flying through the canopy. After a few minutes they arrived at a small clearing, with a tiny cliff about a metre high at the far side. There was an old, wizened tree on top of this cliff, and from one of its multiple branches was hanging a battered looking rope with a thin log tied to the end of it. It wasn't exactly what you would call 'safe' but it looked fun.

''Ere ya go,' said Prongo, indicating to the stick on the string. 'Tha's me swing, an' believe me, it makes yer dizzy, so 'ang on tight. Don't bash into the tree, mind.'

'You first,' said Fiddles to Gybes.

'OK,' said Gybes. 'This'll be fun…'

'Safe, too,' said Fiddles sarcastically.

Gybes scrambled up to the top of the cliff and jumped onto the swing. He flew through the air, whirling round and round. He could see the figures of Fiddles, Chleosa and Prongo on the ground a few metres away every time he turned around. It was exhilarating, but he was glad to get off.

'Great, isn't it!' said Fiddles when Gybes jumped clumsily to the hard ground.

'Can I have a go next?' asked Chleosa.

"Course,' said Prongo.

After Chleosa, Fiddles had his go, in which he fell off and rolled into a tree. Luckily, he was not hurt and got up laughing to give the swing to Prongo. Prongo, being by far the bulkiest, nearly snapped the rope and hastily got off when he heard a disconcerting sound. He told them that the swing was too unstable for them to use until he had replaced the rope with a stronger one, so they said their farewells and left towards Motherton.

They took the road back to Lavos and walked swiftly down the hill past kleya flies and mosquitoes, hearing the ever-present bird’s voices resounding through the trees. A young flightless kombough was calling to it's mate in a low, whining sound, while a blue haired sloth inched along a branch above them, so called because of the blue algae which grew in its hair. Small parrots fluttered around the understorey as they joined the main track again. The monkeys in the canopy called to each other, while countless species of butterfly extracted nectar from even more countless species of flower. Small rodents scuttled off the path as the three of them neared them, searching for beetles and grubs. Gybes was sure he could also hear whooping and yelling coming from the forest to his left. It wasn’t unknown in Tsabia for natives to escape from their reservations to hunt, but Gybes doubted it, because he hadn’t heard of it happening for years. They were harmless anyway.

They came to the clearing with the pool in the centre.

'Hey, it's my favourite spot,' said Fiddles. He sat on a rock beside the pool and the others followed suit.

'Let's not have a long rest,' said Gybes. 'I want to be back in time for lunch.'

'Let's go, then,' said Fiddles.

'No,' said Chleosa. 'I'm watching this frog.' The two boys turned round and noticed a small, blue frog hopping peacefully on the lily pads on the pond. As they watched, a dark shape appeared from underneath. There was a splash and the frog was gone. The fish swam back to the bottom of the pond.

'That's sad!' said Chleosa.'

‘ “Many things in life are sad, but we’ve all got friends! I said we’ve all got friends, yeah! Ooooooo-oo-ooh!” ’

'That’s the worst song in Greenworld, Fiddles!’ said Chleosa.

‘I cannot *believe* you actually *know* the words to a ‘Marionettes’ song!’ laughed Gybes.

'Oh come *on*,' said Fiddles. The three friends walked out of the clearing and down the path to their village.

Chapter 4
The Terrorists

The day dawned bright and, in almost all possible definitions of the word, beautiful on the Green Savannah. The locals were up already and about their work, herding their cattle out onto the pasture to graze contently. Various antelope were also feeding on the shortest grasses of the savannah, flicking their ears and tails to rid them of annoying biting flies. The luscious grass was fading, as was typical of the beginning stages of the dry season. Spotted cats were ambushing herds of strange, fat, hairless mammals and gigantic hoofed monstrosities were fighting and uprooting trees. There were also two figures making their way through the long, dry grass, one tall and wearing a cloak with it's hood down, the other slightly shorter with their face in shadow.

Sarmon kicked the grass and yawned.

'Master, must we travel by foot?'

'Yes, Sarmon,' replied Tombhadi. 'That is why we had to leave our horses back there. Of course, we needed them to get here quick enough, but it is too dangerous to travel by horse in this area, for we may be noticed, and I don't think the Emperor would throw a fancy-dress ball if he heard that I were still alive. No, this is definitely the best way to go about our business; small and insignificant; not noticed by the public and *certainly* not by the envoys and spies of the Emperor.'

'Is it far to travel yet?' asked Sarmon.

'Not at all,' said Tombhadi. 'Do you see that mound in the distance?' Sarmon nodded. 'Well, that mound is the rebel base. *Our* rebel base. Once we reach it, the Septagons, as they call themselves, will most gladly accept me as a leader. They are no more than simple fighters and peasants from Myen. None of those scum have the power to rule and lead their attack on the Emperor and Tuvak, whom they despise for keeping their people in poverty, so they are looking for a commander to lead them into battle. They *will* confide in me, I am sure of it, though they will not know my true name or purpose until it is too late to turn back.'

'What will happen to them once they have seized power, master?'

'Ah, if only they knew.' Tombhadi cackled to himself.

'But the possibilities...'

'Sarmon, they will never know. I will have complete control over them.'

'And pigs can fly...'

Tombhadi turned and stared sharply at Sarmon from underneath his hood. 'Do not give your worthless cheek to me!' he growled. I am a powerful wizard – and you know it. My… abilities will assure our safe passage – I will *make* them see that we come in peace. I will be their leader. There is no other possibility.'

*

Eathon turned around.

'How were the cleam fish eggs, Panothon?' he asked, 'I bought them at a very dear price from a northerner in Fulo-dibaté.

'Very fine, Eathon,' replied Panothon. 'How close are you to finding a leader to our group fighting the oppression of the Emperor?'

'It's not very easy, I considered Algian Trudoider for a certain time, but he's just been executed for treason, so I had to rethink. I came up with the possibility of Moss Make.'

'A woman? Are you out of your…'

'Chomothon is a woman.' Eathon reminded the older man.

'But as a leader? Ridiculous! Preposterous!' said Panothon stubbornly. 'I thought Dameid Uma might...'

'Have you gone insane? Dameid Uma is a traitorous fool! He's devilishly devious! Evil! Spewed from the mouth of Hell! He's not clever enough to realise that it's not a good idea to mass-murder thirty-nine women and children in front of a crowd of two hundred!'

'That is his downfall,' said Panothon. 'He doesn't trick us, we trick him!'

'Quite out of the question! He's cleverer than he seems at first sight, anyway. He escaped, didn't he?'

'But Eathon...'

'Under no circumstances am I a member of a rebel band led by Dameid Uma.'

'Very well, Eathon,' said Panothon. 'Our leader is harder to find than I thought it would be. However… what about you?'

'It's suicide! So is taking on Uma as a leader.'

'But…'

'Come on, let's go and see if our guard has sighted anything,' said Eathon, switching to comparatively trivial matters.

The two rebels walked out of the room and climbed a flight of stone steps to a stone trapdoor. Panothon opened it and a rock on the mound moved. They stepped out into the open air.

'Anything to report, Lumbos?' said Eathon to one of the guards, who appeared to be chief.

'Nah, nuffink at all,' said Lumbos, who had a strong Westport Accent, ''nless yer count a couple o' wild cat fings attackin' a gazelle.'

'Westerners,' muttered Eathon. 'Can't understand half the words they say!'

The guard tapped Eathon roughly on the shoulder. 'Wossat over there?' he said.

'It looks like two people,' said Panothon.

'*That's because it is*,' said Eathon, with ladles of irony.

Sure enough, Tombhadi and Sarmon were steadily getting closer to the Septagons' base. The revolutionary band was really a barbaric terrorist group, and therefore would seldom tolerate intruders.

'Don't let them in,' said Eathon.

'One's carrying a flag,' said Panothon.

'It says, "we come in peace",' said another guard.

'We shall let them in!' declared Panothon. The words spilled from his mouth as though they had been poured there by someone else before he had a chance to choose his own.

'They could be envoys of the Emperor!' shouted Eathon. 'We must trust no one.'

'We must trust them,' stated Panothon blankly.

'DIDN'T YOU HEAR ME?'

'Eathon, I have been searching for you for ten minutes, I have news!' said a voice from behind them.

'Ah, Chomothon, so you have joined us at last!' cried Eathon. 'So what is this news that you bring us?'

A tall, thin, brown-haired woman stood behind the rebel leaders. She was very beautiful, and Eathon used her as a substitute for 'what we're fighting for'.

'There is a rumour that the Emperor has wind of our existence,' said Chomothon, shielding her eyes from the sun. 'We must act quickly. Only this morning I saw a horse rider leaving the village of D'neru, heading north to Tuvak.'

'We shall,' said Eathon. 'but we have just spotted two men bearing a flag reading "we come in peace".'

'You are of course letting them in, aren't you?' said Chomothon, fixing him with a stare that turned his stomach to jelly.

'Of...of course,' said Eathon. 'We were just discussing it.'

'Good,' said Panothon. 'I like banquets. Let's have one of those.'

'Quite out of the que…'

'I'll tell the head cook,' smiled Chomothon. She turned and left.

Panothon looked at Eathon.

'Very well,' said Eathon. 'I'm beaten two to one. The strangers will be greeted… cautiously. A banquet looks inevitable, so tell the rest of the rebels. Ask Captain Tametathon if he'll take responsibility for the newcomer's tour of our base. But take full precautions.'

*

Tombhadi climbed the rocky slope on the northern face of the mound, closely followed by an ever-doubting Sarmon. He reached the top and stood, waiting for the reception. The rock moved and a tall, blonde haired rebel greeted him.

'What is your business at our base, strangers?' he asked. 'How have you come to know our whereabouts?'

'I heard you were here from several rumours, and came to support your cause,' said Tombhadi, staring Tametathon directly in the eye.

'Very well. I am Captain Tametathon. If you would follow me, I shall introduce you to our leader Mr. …'

'I am Shainodari,' said Tombhadi. 'And this is my colleague, Basron. I will be most... honoured as your guest. It is a privilege to be admitted to your abode.' He followed Tametathon down the stone steps and into a small, stonewalled room. A flag hanging on the wall read: 'The People Of Myen Shall Be Liberated.'

'So. Have you found a leader?' asked Tombhadi, knowing the answer.

'Not *really*,' said Tametathon. ' Eathon is as close to a leader as we have, but he's not much of a military Commander, so we're still searching. It's a never-ending process. No-one has really sprung to mind as a good leader - yet perhaps someone will just come along by chance.'

'Oh, quite possible,' said Tombhadi. He smiled wryly. 'You must find a leader soon. I suggest an election be called.'

'Who are you to tell us what to do?' questioned Tametathon suspiciously. 'How did you even know we existed? Where did your "rumours" come from?'

'I have heard that the Emperor is aware of your presence.'

Tametathon stopped in his tracks. 'Truly?' he said. 'Then the situation is more critical than I had at first perceived it.'

'But the election?'

'Very well, you may ask Eathon,' conceded Tametathon. 'But we only have two choices –Moss Make, who we don't really want as our leader, or Dameid Uma! Imagine having him as our leader! Both would be willing, but we want neither. Moss would be our leader by default!'

'You would have three choices,' said Tombhadi, 'if you allow *me* to stand for election.'

*

Tombhadi was shown everywhere in the base; the kitchens, the bedrooms, the banquet hall, the offices. He was introduced to countless rebels and terrorists, from cooks and cleaners to soldiers and secretaries.

Tombhadi realised that there were very few women Septagons, and no children. This made everything satisfyingly simple, because although Tombhadi would kill any individual, it would be easier for him to mass-murder men than children if it came to it.

When it was time for the banquet, Tombhadi and Sarmon were taken to the hall and shown their seats, Eathon at the head of the table and Tombhadi and Panothon at either side. Tametathon and a high-ranking rebel called Ovuthon sat opposite each other just down the table from Tombhadi and Panothon. Another fourteen top rebels, including Chomothon, sat along the sides of the table, as well as Sarmon, all listening intently to Eathon's pre-meal speech. He confided in them briefly the news that the Emperor knew of their presence, before introducing Tombhadi.

'It is my pleasure,' he said, 'to present to you to this cloaked figure here; Shainodari!' There was scattered applause. 'He has suggested to me that we find a leader, of all things, which I find quite a good idea potentially, and that's what we've been doing for the last year and a half!' One or two people laughed, another couple coughed loudly. Eathon continued. 'He suggested that we should have an election. The candidates, we decided are Moss Make, Dameid Uma and this here Shainodari. Of course, the other two could not be here today, so only Shainodari will be able to provide a speech.'

There were murmurs from the rebels. The unjustness of it was so obvious; it was almost unnaturally unusual that nobody objected more strongly. But it seemed to Tombhadi that they liked the look of him.

Tombhadi stood up, aware of all nineteen pairs of eyes on him. 'Greetings, Septagons,' he began. 'I am honoured to be accepted as one of your possible leaders. It greatly aggrieves me to see you all here with no leader willing to go into battle, no easy path to victory. But if you were to elect me, there would be a clear road. Revenge is sweet my dear friends, and you must fight back against the Emperor who has so viciously attempted to conquer your homeland of Myen. Vote for me, Shainodari!'

There was an outbreak of applause, which was silenced by Eathons voice.

'All those in favour of Moss Make, please raise their hand.'

One rebel tentatively raised his hand.

'All those who wish to elect Uma, please raise their hand.

A few rebels at the bottom of the table shot their hands up.

'And finally, all those who wish to elect Shainodari as our Commander for battle against this ridiculous creature the Emperor Alu IV, please raise their hand!'

Many hands shot into the air and cheers echoed off the roof. Tombhadi grinned evilly underneath his hood. It had gone exactly how he had expected.

The meal began. Antelope, beef stolen from a local village, dock spuds, which were similar to potatoes, and various vegetables, such as golbross, jiglista, buk-wedder and cabbage. There was wine from the extensive vineyards of Tasea and bread from Tuvak, the best baked bread in Greenworld, which was made from the tall sadron corn of Field West, a land crisscrossed with fields to the west of Tuvak, the largest agricultural producer in Greenworld.

After the meal, Tombhadi stood up for a second short speech.

'So, my dear rebels!' he proclaimed. 'Let us discuss all that is to happen. We must take immediate action.' There were murmurs of approval. 'The Emperor knows of our existence, as you have heard. I have evidence for this, and if you do not believe *me*, you will believe Chomothon. For you have heard this also, is that not correct?'

'By word of mouth, sir,' said Chomothon.

'Then let it be,' continued Tombhadi, 'that we are ready to defeat the Emperor on Tsuday the 19th of Potiton, in a fortnight's time!' Cheers of approval echoed around the hall. 'It will be on that day which we eliminate the Emperor's idiotic and democratic councils and regime! We shall triumph over the poor, ill equipped army with our firearms - your very own invention! And, I have a secret plan, one that will make the whole thing as easy as… very easy.' he finished uncharacteristically lamely. 'All shall bow before us! Before *me* as Supreme Septagon!'

To Tombhadi's surprise, the rebels did not applaud him.

'But it will be Eathon who is King once the Emperor and his family are dead!' cried a terrorist at the end of the table.

'It is true, Shainodari,' added Chomothon, backing up the first. 'You are military commander, not supreme Septagon, for Eathon has worked so hard to achieve this!' She gave him a radiant stare. Eathon blushed.

Tombhadi stood up and surveyed his audience. All of them were silently agreeing with the other two; Tombhadi could feel it. He would have to make sure Eathon was out of the way by the morning.

Chapter 5
The Swamp

It was no later than six in the morning when Gybes awoke the next day. He lay awake in bed for a time, wondering whether to get up or not. The sun was shining brightly over the Village, as usual, filtering through the windows of the huts. Gybes yawned and stepped out of bed.

Once he was outside, and realised that no one else he was well acquainted with was up, he decided to fetch some water from the well for the kettle. The well was a few hundred metres to the north of Lavos. He set out with a bucket and headed off along the dirt road.

The forest to either side was dazzling in the early morning sun. Bright butterflies, bees, flies and birds were flying in between the trees. Mosquitoes were congregating in great numbers around muddy pools of water on the track. There was plenty to eat in the vast Tsabian jungle, whether you were human or wild animal. For humans, thousands of fruit bearing trees grew alongside the track, perhaps fifty species of them, each tree bearing many fruits of all sizes, shapes, colours and tastes. Some were poisonous, but you got to know which if you lived in the Tsabian Rainforest. Some roots and leaves were edible, and wild sugar cane was used a lot in sweet meals. Honey, however, was used the most for sweet things.

Gybes reached the well and attached his bucket to the rope. He lowered it and shortly heard it hit the water and submerge. He pulled it back up and took the bucket of water off before heading back towards the village.

Today, he Fiddles and Chleosa were going to Hillside Riverton to find out whatever they could about the *very* strange root in Gybes' pocket.

He yawned and kicked a twig.

*

When Gybes returned to the village, it was nearly seven, and other people were up. His Father greeted him.

'Thanks for getting the water, Gybes,' he said. ‘It’s a nice gesture. If you're going to Hillside Riverton, be sure to be back for dinner,' he added.

'I will,' said Gybes.

'And be careful you don't fall into the swamp!'

Gybes grinned and headed towards an alley between two stonewalled buildings, where Fiddles and Chleosa were already waiting.

'Hi,' said Gybes.

' 'Pon my word, 'tis Gybes!' said Fiddles, sniggering. Fiddles, for some strange reason found it funny using people's real names.

'Have we got lunch ready?' inquired Gybes.
‘Have *you* got the lunch ready?’ asked Fiddles.
‘No.’
‘Good, because I have. First thing I did when I got up.’
'*Before* you got dressed?' said Chleosa jokingly.
'Shut up!’ saud Fiddles good-naturedly
'Oh come on, let’s go,' said Gybes.

Five minutes later they were strolling down the path towards Hillside Riverton. The much larger village was about four kilometres down the road, on the edge of the hills. Cycads brushed their straw hats and hornets sped through the air above their heads. The forest here, either side of the track, was more like scrubland. It consisted of sparsely spread palm trees either side of the track for ten metres or so, filled in between with murderously quick-growing ferns and cycads. This was originally a long pathway cleared for the native Tsabian army, so that they could travel in large numbers in the times when the Great Tsabian War had drawn thousands of brave soldiers from the only kingdom in Tsabia. Back then, it was in the south, to their site of defeat, which was in the north, where the Empire had attacked the small and defenceless tribal village of Gurug'uta. Now the pathway was overgrown, but still only the fast-growing trees dominated, as the slower growing giants had had no time to grow in a mere century.

'How long do you think it'll take us to reach Hillside Riverton?' asked Gybes.

'Dunno,' said Fiddles. 'If we walk fast enough, maybe we'll get there in three-quarters of an hour.'

'Look, there's the South Lavos Shrine,' said Chleosa. It wasn’t something anyone normally commented on, because everyone took it for granted, but today she just felt like mentioning it.

The South Lavos Shrine was a tall, dome-shaped memorial, resembling a massive bee-hive. It commemorated the loss of thirteen native men from a long-disappeared native village near Lavos who had died in the Great War. It was situated just to the left of the track, with a little path leading to it.

Not far ahead, Gybes caught the glint of sunlight reflecting off water in his eye. He knew immediately that it was Lake Forou. They came up to the edge and began to walk alongside the expanse of water. It was approximately one kilometre long and about half that from north to south. Being the only reasonably sized, sufficiently clean lake in the area, Lake Forou attracted people from miles around and adults and children alike were here collecting water for washing themselves or their clothes and even enjoying a quick swim. No one was any good at it here, but at least they tried. Gybes had never really cottoned on to how to swim. By trial and error he had discovered that he invariably sank like a stone.

The path headed away from the lake for a while, but came back to it shortly. Gybes and his friends continued round the south of the lake. Here they were nearer to Hillside Riverton, so many of the town's residents were washing or collecting water. Some groups of people were holding out large nets and trying to drive fish into them, which was proving very tricky. Soon the path turned away again to the south. Since it was closer to the water, the palm scrubland to either side was more overgrown.

'Wow!' said Fiddles. 'I thought these beetles were rare, but they're everywhere!'

The air was filled with unbelievable numbers of beetles, mainly with bright red wing cases, which made it look even stranger.

'Someone - get - me - beetle - insurance!' yelled Fiddles as the tiny, round, red balls bombarded him stubbornly and flew into his mouth.

Gybes was so busy to keep flies and beetles out of his face that he didn't notice when the track changed into wooden plank. In fact Fiddles and Chleosa had to dive forward and grab Gybes to prevent him from walking off the walkway.

'You nearly fell in the swamp!' said Fiddles.

Sure enough the swamp was now around them, its muddy banks behind. The mysterious, murky water rippled and glinted in the sunlight, and barely visible fish swam under the surface. There were few trees, as the water could be up to two metres deep in places. Those that managed to grow were often mangrove trees and there were not enough of them to keep out the light. Floating lily-pads were home to frogs and toads, and grass grew where sediment formed on the surface of the water around the trunks of the trees. Occasionally, curious dark shapes were visible underneath the water, larger than most fish.

They walked onwards along the wooden path. Although it was wide and strong enough for a cart with horse, it was not very safe. Thanks to the 'authorities', as far as health and safety were concerned in Tsabia, it was barely out of the Stone Age.

'I can't wait until we find out what's on the root,' said Chleosa.

'Yeah, it sounds *really* interesting, doesn't it,' said Fiddles sarcastically. 'Searching for a small sentence on a root which probably means "I love Norbella" or something.'

'It's not *that* bad,' said Gybes. 'We could visit the Temple of Au Crassig afterwards.'

'Good idea, I suppose,' muttered Fiddles dully.

'We could play a game,' suggested Chleosa. 'What about, "spot the frogs"?'

'That sounds rubbish,' said Fiddles. ' Let's play "catch the frogs".'

'That's not...' began Chleosa, but she stopped speaking and walking, because there were no longer any wooden planks in front of them.

'Do you think an animal did it?' asked Gybes, staring at the five metres of water seperating them and the continuing path.

'Yes,' said Fiddles. 'Look, there's a carcass in the water. It must have happened recently, ‘cause there were people at lake Forou from Hillside Riverton.'

'How will we get to the other side?' said Gybes.

'You sound like one of those brain-teasers,' said Fiddles. ' "Three children have reached a five metre gap in a wooden walkway across a swamp. How will they reach the other side? Please write your answer neatly in the box. You have ten minutes".'

'Look, why doesn't one of us go back to get some ropes and we can make a rope bridge over the gap,' suggested Chleosa.

‘Of all the people to suggest that,’ said Fiddles.

'We'd need someone to climb across the palm trees to our left to get someone on the other side to catch the ropes and tie them there,' said Gybes.

‘You gonna do that then?’ said Fiddles.

‘You’ve got to be joking,’ said Gybes.

'Very well,' said Fiddles. 'I'll go back to get some ropes. And Clamber.'

'We don't need...' began Chleosa

'I was only *joking*,' said Fiddles. ‘I’ll do it, seeing as Gybes is a wus!’ He ran back along the wobbly wooden walkway towards Lavos.

Gybes looked down into the murky water at the large, horned carcass of the pulpakker. Any slightly rotten part of the walkway would break under it's weight, as it could weigh over a tonne, and the walkway could only withstand two horses, which had still been known to break parts of the path.

Soon Fiddles had returned with four ropes.

'I think I can climb onto that tree, and from that to the next and then down onto the other side of the gap,' said Fiddles optimistically, gesturing to the two palm-mangrove trees growing out of the water to the left. 'Then you can throw me a rope and I'll tie it at that end, and another and so on 'till there's a path we can crawl across.'

Fiddles climbed the tree quite easily, but it proved a mean feat to reach the next. He had to judge which giant palm leaves were strong enough to hold his weight and which would tear. Finally, after nearly falling into the swamp numerous times, he made it to the other side.

'Great, Fiddles!' said Chleosa. 'You and Clamber should have a contest some time.'

'Hah,' he said. 'Throw me one end of a rope, will you, Gybes?'

Gybes picked up the rope and thrust one end towards Fiddles. He caught it, and was nearly pulled into the water, but let go just in time.

'Don't pull it like that!' said Fiddles. 'I could have got *soaked*! Throw it again, and this time, don't pull it once I've caught hold of it!'

Gybes threw the rope again. This time it was more accurate and Fiddles caught it in his right hand. Both of them tied the ends of the rope to the last planks on either side and Gybes threw the second rope.

'Good catch!' cried Chleosa as Fiddles captured the rope's other end in his left hand, holding onto a tree for balance with his right. Once it was tied down, Gybes picked up the next rope and cast it across the gap. It landed short and scared a frog off a lily pad. The second time it flew through the air but still, fell short.

'I got it!' yelled Fiddles as the rope travelled through the air, then 'OW!' as it hit his nose and rebounded back into the water.

'So much for third time lucky!' he growled. 'This had better work!' He was satisfied when he caught it well in both hands.

'Brilliant!' exclaimed Chleosa as Fiddles caught the fourth and final rope first time. 'Now what do we do?'

'Crawl along the ropes,' said Gybes and Fiddles simultaneously.

'Er...'

'I'll go first, if that helps,' said Gybes.

'No, I'd prefer to go first,' said Chleosa. She climbed onto the ropes and began to inch her way along it. As she drew close to the end, she almost lost her balance, and exclaimed as her shoe fell into the water.

'That was close,' said Fiddles 'It's lucky it wasn't a sandal. It would've sunk.'

Chleosa regained her balance and made it safely to the other side.

Gybes followed after. He placed his hands cautiously in front of each other and moved slowly along the ropes, watching for dark shapes beneath him. However, he also made it safely to the other end.

'Let's get out of here,' said Chleosa, picking up her floating shoe and slipping it on. They ran to the far bank of the swamp and onto dirt track again. Following the road, they soon came to a point where they could see Hillside Riverton fifty metres or so up a shallow slope. However, as they commenced the ascent, they could see someone standing at the edge of the town. Someone they didn't want to meet.

'Oh *no*!' exclaimed Fiddles.

'What–'

'*Alfid*!'

Chapter 6
Sir Fawning of Goodport

The older boy stepped forwards and confronted the trio.

'So, the little kiddies from Lavos have come to the Big Town,' sneered Alfid. 'I bet you've come to do some kind of boring thing, but I think I'll leave you to your little nerdy ways for the time being. However…' He leaned closer. 'What is it you're doing?'

'Er... going to the Library,' said Gybes cautiously.

'Little bookworms,' growled Alfid. 'Knew you were going to do something uncool. Libraries? You can't get any uncooler!'

'Shove off, Alfid!' shouted Fiddles.

'Weak insult,' sneered Alfid. 'What're you going to say now? Call me Poo-poo or La-la or something?

Fiddles made a rude sign with his fingers and pushed past Alfid. Alfid looked like he was thinking about kicking Fiddles, but he thought again when he saw a bunch of important-looking men coming towards him.

They had entered Hillside Riverton. The place was, for lack of a better word, quaint. The white-walled stone buildings reflected the sunlight with tremendous intensity, and everything looked scaled down, from the little old houses to the trees that grew on the main street. Even the people looked diminished by the sunlight.

'Have you brought a drink?' Gybes asked Fiddles. 'I'm parched!'

'Yeah,' said Fiddles, dropping his bag onto the ground. 'Why don't we have lunch now? It's nearly one already.'

The three friends wandered to the grass at the edge of the small town and sat on the disappointingly hard ground. Fiddles rummaged in his bag for the juice and food. They took it in turn to drink, and by the time their thirst was quenched the flask was empty.

'If we go back to Lavos via the Temple of Au Crassig after having a look in the library we could avoid the swamp,' suggested Gybes.

'Goob ibea,' replied Fiddles with a mouthful of pacu nuts. The lunch was delicious and revitalising after the walk from Lavos and the 'great ordeal' of the swamp. Gybes was especially hungry, as he had forgotten about breakfast after fetching water earlier.

After lunch they walked to the centre of Hillside Riverton. People were ambling around the dirt streets, exchanging chickens for vegetables and talking about the weather. A group of young men were boasting to several not-easily impressed teenage girls about their great mansions and golden chariots.

'Rich snobs!' muttered Chleosa.

Fiddles laughed out loud. 'They're not rich! I know them! They live in shacks somewhere a bit farther south near Ogginsplatter and don't even have any horses, let alone chariots! They're even in debt! There's no point making things up to girls just to make them love you. Anyway, it doesn't work.'

'I know,' said Chleosa. 'If you told a girl your Father was rich then...' She stopped. Fiddles had stopped listening and was staring at a crowd. More precisely, at a tall, brown haired girl standing at the edge of the crowd.

'What is it?' asked Gybes.

'Asila,' Fiddles murmured, mesmerised. Gybes watched as, as if in a trance, his friend walked slowly up to the girl, who was obviously much older than him. She was at least a head taller as well.

'My father's really rich,' said Fiddles hopefully.

Asila glared down at him and turned back to the crowd without a word. Behind him Gybes and Chleosa were in hysterics.

'Trying to disprove yourself?' Gybes asked.

'Worth a try,' shrugged Fiddles as they began to make their way towards the large, white, rectangular, building that was the library.

Inside the library it was dingy and cool. There were rows and rows of books on the walls, seeming to close in around them. If none of them had eyes, Gybes was almost certain that they were staring at him with something else. A round table in the centre, where there were no chairs and no stacked books, let alone any people, betrayed the fact that the library was rarely used, and probably empty at the best of times. To the right there was a counter with elaborately carved wooden panels on it's forward-facing side. However, the strangest thing was that there was no librarian.

'I'm sure it's open on Chaudays,' said Chleosa.

'Maybe today's an exception,' said Fiddles. 'But then the door would be shut...'

'Maybe the librarian has got bored and left,' said Gybes

'But they'd need to keep an eye on the library in case anyone came,' said Chleosa.

'This is Hillside Riverton,' said Gybes. 'People don't read books: they throw them.'

'They read newspapers,' said Chleosa.

'That's different. They need to know who in the world to hate, and what to be paranoid about.'

'Well we can look for the book anyway,' suggested Fiddles. 'We're not going to steal it.'

They wandered the rows of intimidating books and examined the various sections. There were many; history, mathematics, literature, sciences, the arts, geography; they soon found that they were all listed on a rather tatty piece of parchment pinned to the counter.

'Here it is,' said Gybes. 'Linguistics: second section. Right hand wall, third row down.'

'This is quite a small section,' said Fiddles.

'Well how much information can you get on languages?' said Chleosa. 'After a certain point it gets boring.'

'Languages are boring all the time to me,' said Fiddles.

It took them a long time to find the book they wanted, considering the size of the section. They were mostly very, very old.

'Here it is!' cried Chleosa. ' "Mystic Languages of the Far South".' She pulled the book out and let it fall open on his knee.

They began searching through it's worn and tattered pages, but Gybes soon realised it wasn't what they were looking for.

'It's got the languages from the Forest of the Sun and Blackness Island, but nothing beyond that,' he said. 'Not even Flower Island. It's only got one language from any island and that's the one from Blackness Island we found in Prongo's book.

'That's because historians don't think people lived on the islands in the Great Ocean,' said Chleosa. 'Maybe there's a more legendary-type-thingy book.' She began searching the shelf for something a bit more like a legendary-type-thingy.

'Looking for something are you?' came a soft, unnerving voice from behind them. Gybes jumped and turned around.

The librarian was plump, but somewhat elegant. Her black hair was tied in a bun behind her head. She wasn't the kind of person you'd like to meet on a dark night. She eyed them suspiciously.

'We... we were looking for... ' began Fiddles.

'Languages of the islands of the Great Ocean,' said the Librarian mysteriously. 'Right here in front of your noses.' She pulled a thick book out from the shelf and handed it to them.

'Th.... thank you,' stuttered Gybes. Fiddles took the book from the Librarian and began to flick through it. The reason he had to flick through was because, for some reason, the book had no contents or index.

'OK, this is it, the alphabets,' said Fiddles. 'Want to take a look, Gybes?'

Gybes took the book and scanned through the languages. He took the root out of his pocket and examined it closely. Most of the alphabets were very similar - sometimes only one or two letters were the difference between the language in the book and the one on the root.

'There!' exclaimed Gybes. 'This is our language - the one we've been looking for, I mean.' He held the book closer. 'The language is "Koronich" from the Island of Trees.'

'Let's see?' said Chleosa. Gybes passed the book to her and she searched for the Dictionary section. ' "This language is little known",' she read. ' "It was once..." '

'Just tell us what it means!' said Gybes.

'What what means?'

'Te B'ardkos uoth Krethak!'

'Wow, Wizz, you sound crazily obsessed,' observed Fiddles.

'I'm not obsessed,' said Gybes, lowering his voice to normal level again.

Chleosa began searching down the lines under the letter 'T'. 'Te means "The", ' she stated.

'Wow,' said Fiddles sarcasticly. 'What does "B'ardkos" mean though?'

'Er... "apple",' said Chleosa.

'*Apple*?'

'I'll look for "uoth", shall I?'

'*Apple*!'

'Yes!'

'*Apple*?!?!'

Fiddles burst out laughing. 'This is a load of nonsense!' he shouted. 'Apple! Someone was just scribbling on a root for fun! See Gybes?'

'Who would graffiti in some language that's been lost for thousands of years?' Gybes pointed out. 'I would like to find out what the other two words mean.'

'Well, "uoth" means "of",' said Chleosa, 'so it's all down to the last word.

'Be quick, the suspense is *killing* me!' said Fiddles.

It took her longer to find the last word than the others. When she finally found it she read the whole thing together.

'The *Apple* of *Mole*?' sniggered Fiddles. 'What's *that* supposed to mean?'

'Oh well,' said Gybes. 'You were right, Fiddles. It is just a load of nonsense. But it's funny how someone would write "Te B'ardkos uoth Krethak" on a simple...'

Chleosa stopped him. 'Was it "Krethak"? I looked up "Krathak".'

'Well, look up the *real* word this time,' said Fiddles. 'It might help a little.'

Chleosa searched the dictionary again until she came up with the real thing. When she finally found it she read it out in a confused voice.

'Well, the real translation appears to be, "The Apple of Doom",' she said.

*

After they left the library they walked over to the edge of the village and stood in the shade of a bottle tree, so-called because of it's thick lower trunk. The sunlight filtered lazily through the bottletree's drooping leaves and relieved Gybes, Fiddles and Chleosa from the burning heat of the afternoon summer sun.

'I'm thirsty,' said Chleosa.

'I think I've got some water for us to drink,' said Fiddles, 'but no more spragfruit juice.'

'Thanks,' said Chleosa, as Fiddles handed her the leather flask. After the three of them had finished with it, he put it back in his woven bag.

'What's the Apple of Doom supposed to mean?' said Chleosa.

'I still think it's a load of rubbish,' said Fiddles. 'But all the same…'

'It's odd that it's an apple,' said Gybes.

'Too right it is,' muttered Fiddles. 'Evil fruits! Whatever next?'

Gybes thought he heard a distant noise. Perhaps it was clapping, but he couldn't think of who would be clapping. He listened intently. It was hoof beats, and they were coming from somewhere to the north.

Suddenly a horse rider rounded the corner of a building. He was notably wearing a brown leather jacket as opposed to a poncho, and instead of shorts he wore smart trousers. His sombrero hat was well made and his boots were as shiny as beetles' wing cases. The man had straight, straw-like light brown hair, slowly turning grey and a short, neatly trimmed beard and moustache. His chestnut horse neighed and beat the ground with its hooves.

The rider spotted them and trotted over. 'Excuse me,' he said. 'Do you know where the mayor of this fair town resides?'

'No,' said Gybes, unsure.

The man adjusted his hat. 'Seeing as I'm here to serve the public… is there anything you require?' he said. His accent was very upper class. Gybes suddenly became conscious that he had been staring at the man.

'Er... not especially...' said Gybes, taken aback.

'Ah well, not to worry,' said the man. 'But if you've got a message, I'll jolly well deliver the thing *Auki Erikumethus*.'

'What does hawky ikkymeethas mean?' asked Fiddles.

'*Auki Erikumethus*,' corrected the man. 'It means "The instant". Oh, and by the way my name is Sir-ish Waltoron Fawning of Goodport. And who are you?'

'I'm Gybes,' said Gybes. 'And this is Fiddles and Chleosa.' He paused. 'Why exactly do you want to help us?'

'Just trying to build up a reputation.'

'Er... Sir-*ish*?' said Fiddles.

'Well you see,' said Sir-ish Fawning, 'they only ever gave me seven eighths of a knighthood.'

'*Seven eighths of a...*'

'Well, you know what they're like these days - cant just give you a straight knighthood. "Oh no, that wouldn't be reasonable, old bean, we can't go giving him another eighth of a knighthood *just* for that", that's what they said. I only got the first half knighthood because my father is Sir Sir Conor Fawning of Tuvak. *The* Sir Sir Conor Fawning of Tuvak.'

Gybes gasped. 'He's the Duke of Kappleham,' he said, amazed that the man in front of him was the son of the man highest in the Empire's hierarchy apart from the Emperor himself and his family.

'Was the Duke of Kappleham, may I point out,' said Sir Fawning. 'He had two knighthoods, and shall, I rather hope, until his dying day.'

'Did he resign?' asked Gybes.

'Yes, a year ago,' said Sir Fawning. 'His chief servant was sentenced to death but escaped. He got new servants for a few years, but he really wasn't coping that well. Anyway, he was eighty-three. Then that egotistic blubber mountain Snofflington came and took his place. Sent all the helpless homeless people out of Tuvak, the son of a...'

BANG!

Gybes jumped. Sir Fawning had punctured his water bottle with his penknife. It spilled all over the floor and was swallowed up into the dirt.

'Dear me,' he said. 'I thought I saw Snofflington's snuffling face on my water bottle! What a jolly… strange mistake to make! How I was waffling on. Anyway - if there is anything you require...'

'No,' said Fiddles abruptly.

'Wait a minute,' said Gybes. 'Could you find some information in the Goodport library?'

'Indubitably, old fruit!' exclaimed Sir-ish Fawning. 'I'll be leaving for Goodport via Aurawey today - just tell me which book or what piece of information you desire, and I'll fetch it pronto. *Auki Erikumethus*, in fact.' Sir Fawning jumped down of his horse and took out a notepad.

'Do you know if the library might have something on "The Apple of Doom"?' asked Gybes.

'The Apple of... Doom?' queried Sir Fawning. 'Never heard of such a thing. Sounds like a load of old tosh, if you ask me. Apple? Probably someone's idea of a joke. But all the same, I'll have a look. But I'll need your name and address, so that I can find you again.'

'Gybes Marronon, hut 26, Lavos, Hillside Riverton, Aurawey District, Tsabia,' said Gybes slowly so that Sir Fawning had time to write it down.

'What about us?' asked Fiddles quietly.

'Shhh,' said Gybes. 'More than one address would confuse him.'

'He can't seriously be that stupid can he?'

'No but it's just common sense that I only give one address, unless you want to get a third of a book in a package.'

'But why you?'
'Because I found the root!'
'Chleosa tripped on it. If she hadn't...'
'Shut up! What does it really matter?'
They turned to Sir Fawning who mounted his horse and bowed to them.
'Thank you,' said Gybes.
'No problem,' said Sir Fawning. 'Well, ta ta, children,' he said. He stared at them for a moment. 'How did you get past the broken bridge?'
'We lay those four ropes down,' said Fiddles.
'Jolly good!' exclaimed Sir Fawning. 'I had to lay down a couple of planks for my horse - but you got there first. Well done young persons, and fare thee well!' He turned on his horse and galloped out of sight down the street, which was virtually empty.
'Odd fellow,' said Gybes. 'Who just wanders up and asks if you want anything?'
'He probably wants his other eighth of a knighthood,' said Fiddles.
'Don't you think he'll be a while?' said Chleosa. 'I mean, he went west to Aurawey, and Goodport's to the north. He might be a fortnight, for all we know. He might even forget!'
'So much for your Seven-eighths-of-a-knighthood Fawning,' said Fiddles.
'Come on, let's go to the temple.' said Gybes, hoping to end the debate; because he felt like he was losing. They turned their backs to the direction in which Sir Fawning had gone, and headed for the east side of the town - towards the hills and the Temple of Au Crassig.

Chapter 7
Dictatorship

Tombhadi opened the door to Eathon's bedroom cautiously. It didn't creak, which was lucky, but swung open smoothly. Tombhadi was careful not to let in any light as he crept swiftly through the thin gap. He trod quietly on the rug with immaculate technique, knife in hand, advancing slowly on the sleeping figure. As he drew close, he clapped his left hand suddenly to Eathon's mouth and stabbed him swiftly. The deed was done. Now he had to dispose of the body.

Tombhadi made as hastily to the entrance of the base as he could, carrying Eathon's surprisingly light body over his shoulder. He made sure with a little magic that the guard dozed off before he stepped out onto the mound and began to cross the savannah. After a few hundred metres he came across a clump of trees. He crept into the chilly depths of the darkness and concealed the body in bush. The vultures and cats would eat it before any human found it. Tombhadi made his way to the edge of the trees and realised that it was nearly dawn. He needed to be back soon - or else someone would spot him.

He also wanted to dispose of Sarmon.

It took him a while to reach the Septagon's base and, as he drew near, he was glad to see that the guard was still asleep. He opened the hatch and silently climbed back down the stone steps, passed through the first chamber, walked the length of the entrance corridor and opened the doors to the banquet hall.

When he finally reached Sarmon's bedroom, he opened the door carefully, as he had done before. He looked around, but there was no one to be seen. Sarmon had fled.

*

Tombhadi strode down the hallway smugly. Now that Eathon was out of the way it was going to be much simpler to conquer the terrorist rebels. But Sarmon - why had he fled? Would he betray him? Would he, if he returned (which Tombhadi doubted), tell the rebels that 'Shainodari' was really Tombhadi? Would he tell the world that the former servant of the Duke of Kappleham, who had successfully fled execution, was alive; that wolves in the Forest of Shadows had not after all brought his life to an end? He knew Sarmon had never trusted him, but he had always trusted his own ability to crush will power. Now that he was no longer within his sights, and therefore no longer within his power, for his own safety, Tombhadi knew he would have to hunt down and kill Sarmon.

He was making his way to the banquet hall for his second evening meal with the Septagons. He was hoping to meet the remaining top rebels and finally rise to the status of their overlord.

'Shainodari!' called a voice from behind him. 'I have something to tell you!'

'What is it,' said Tombhadi, spinning round and eyeing with suspicion the person he recognised as a Septagon named Ovuthon.

'I have noticed,' said Ovuthon, 'that overnight...' Tombhadi knew what was coming, '...you may think this sounds like irrational fear, and perhaps it is… but it seems that Eathon has disappeared.'

'How is this evident?' asked Tombhadi.

'I have not seen him at all since last night, and his room is empty.'

Tombhadi knew that he wouldn't be able to pretend that nothing had happened. 'I shall explain that at the meal tonight,' he said.

'It has been delayed, Shainodari,' said Ovuthon. 'The cooks were waiting for Eathon's opinion on the meal, but I suppose they would accept yours instead.'

Tombhadi grinned evilly under his hood. He was already beginning to manoeuvre himself into Eathon's position.

*

In a room to the side of the entrance Hallway, Panothon and Tametathon were discussing important matters.

'I don't trust this Shainodari,' said Tametathon. 'He thought *he* should be leader once we kill the terrible Emperor who has kept the race of Myen in poverty for centuries, not Eathon!'

'That is certainly unreasonable,' agreed Panothon. 'We may, however be able to come to some agreement.' He paused. 'Perhaps we could organise a Triumvirate - Eathon, Shainodari and I.'

'I haven't seen Eathon since last night,' said Tametathon, brushing his blond hair out of his face with his hand. 'I hope this Shainodari explains the reason behind his disappearance.'

'I fear we may be cornered here,' said Panothon. 'Cornered into taking the only choice. Accepting Shainodari's leadership. Remember what he said about the Emperor hearing rumours of our presence?'

'But of course he may be deceiving us,' stated Tametathon. 'There may be some dark plan behind this.'

'I do not believe that is so,' said Panothon. 'I believe that Eathon will turn up soon and he will make the *final* decision. And there will be a perfectly legitimate reason for his brief disappearance. Shainodari does not show any evil feelings or desires. He seems just sort of *right* for the part of our leader.'

‘He does not show any evil feelings or desires, but he may be hiding them.’ objected Tametathon. ‘Many evil rulers have achieved power by taking control of a group such as us. They normally hide it to begin with and fool the rebels into thinking that they are only there to help them and only reveal their true purpose when they have full and unchallengeable control of the rebels. Remember when Dameid Uma massacred that tribe of Maibats from Eastwood?’

'A very good example,' said Panothon. 'But that was… a bit *different*. The Maibats were brutal and unintelligent, so they wouldn't have guessed anything was going on with their peanut brains.' He stopped and stared at the door for apparently no reason. ‘So that’s that,’ he concluded, ending their discussion. He looked at Tametathon, as though expecting him to add something.

'I think dinner will be ready by now,' he said simply.

Dinner was indeed ready. By Tombhadi's recommendation, it was antelope steak with rice and assorted vegetables. As Eathon was absent, Tombhadi rewarded himself with the head of the table, and, to his delight, was unchallenged. This raised his spirits, as in this position he felt more like the Septagon’s leader than ever.

After the meal Tombhadi announced that he would make a short but important speech.

'I assume that all of you who are privileged to be present at the table have noticed one absence - Eathon's,' he began slowly. There were a few nods and murmurs. 'I do not wish to alarm you, but I am afraid the circumstances are not … the fact is that, by a most unfortunate accident, Eathon is dead.'

Many heads turned towards Tombhadi, their faces showing surprise and shock. The silence that followed was deafening. No one spoke for several minutes, although it seemed like several hours. Then a man started laughing quietly to himself, covering his mouth with his hands.

Suddenly the whole hall erupted into laughter. Fools, thought Tombhadi. They think that I'm lying. He picked up a fork and brought it down hard on the table, creating an ear-piercing noise.

'Don't do that, you'll damage the lovely, priceless table,' said a rebel, trying to stop himself laugh. The terrorists slid into uncontrollable hysterics again. When it had subsided, Tombhadi left a dramatic pause and then spoke quietly and seriously.

'I know you think I am lying, but Eathon *is* dead,' he said politely, in a convincingly chilly voice. He tried to slide in some sympathy.

'So what was this "accident"?' said Tametathon, unconvinced.

'He slid into an unseen hole and cracked his head.’ He left an especially long pause as all the rebels looked around in incredulous dismay. Chomothon and two other rebels had broken into tears.

‘Now that he is dead, I suppose it would be fitting that I propose to take over,’ said Tombhadi carefully. ‘Surely you shall accept me as true leader?'

But what came next was completely negative. Sadness and despair was transformed into pure rage. Angry yells bombarded Tombhadi from every direction.

'Never!' yelled Panothon furiously.

'Do you think we're fools?' shouted another terrorist.

'Down with Shainodari!' roared a third, standing on his chair. The rest of the terrorists followed suit.

Tombhadi had not been expecting this. Over the commotion he muttered to himself, 'So this is what I get for coming all this way. To think that I finally have the chance to lead the Septagons and they do not accept me. So be it. They shall know my true power.'

Tombhadi thrust something small and blue towards the centre of the table. The noise of the ranting terrorists continued despite the fizzing sound now emitting from the sphere. They didn't even notice the noise growing louder. They did, however notice the explosion that came from the blue object not long after it was thrown.

Smoke engulfed the table and collided with the ceiling. The rebels fell backwards in their chairs from the blast as the remains of the table collapsed inwards. As the smoke subsided it was clear that someone was lying sprawled on the table. Panothon was dead. The handiwork of the magical explosive was devastating.

An atmosphere of despair and terror engulfed the room. It was all Tombhadi could do not to be caught up in it. He churned his doubt up and used it to fuel his anger. 'Now,' he growled, 'If this is the way you want it, I am not to be your leader but your Master. You are not to be my followers but my slaves.'

'You'll never become our Master!' yelled a terrorist near the other end of the table. 'You killed Eathon and we know it! And now you kill Panothon.

Tombhadi felt for another blue object in his pocket and held it up threateningly. The Septagon sunk back into the relative safety of his chair and remained silent.

'Now if there are any more objections, I will be swift and unforgiving in dealing with them,' growled Tombhadi calmly. 'From now on you shall call me Master. You will travel with me where I go and you will carry out my plans without question. For I am Tombhadi, your overlord.’

'Tombhadi!' yelled Ovuthon. 'So you are the mysterious one! But you still haven't got control of us fully. We would rather die than serve you!'

'So be it,' growled Tombhadi. 'If you wish for death, it shall be granted. The *others…*' He looked around at the rest of the terrorists. ‘You will help me. You will not perish, if you take this path. You don't want to suffer the same fates as Eathon and Panothon, do you?'

Slowly, still with tears on her face over the deaths of her fellow rebels, Chomothon walked forwards, and fell to her knees, because she didn't have the will to stand. Tombhadi grinned. She didn't have the will to stand up to him. Nor would the rest. Indeed, soon Tametathon had followed suit, and was groveling, mutters of 'master, master' drifting to Tombhadi's ears.

'That's better!' he exclaimed. He turned to the rest. 'Don't you see him? He is of the highest rank in your rebel band left! Come before me and show me your loyalty to serving me. I, Tombhadi, your master order you to bow before me!'

One by one the Septagons came forward and bowed. Some, however, were still reluctant, as they all knew somewhere inside them that what they were doing was wrong. Once the final terrorist had bowed, Tombhadi addressed the them.

'I have decided,' he said, with an intense air of authority, 'that this society is to be named Black Dragon!'

*

Sarmon had fled only a few hundred metres from the base when he saw a dark shape in the distance. It seemed to be dragging something and was wearing a cloak.

Sarmon cursed. It was Tombhadi. So I was right, he thought. Tombhadi *was* going to kill Eathon, and probably do away with me too! Sarmon hid in a clump of bushes and watched as Tombhadi stepped into a patch of trees and came out again without the body. He walked back towards the Septagon's base and entered through the secret door underneath the rock.

Sarmon slid cautiously from his hiding place and continued into the savannah. It was growing lighter, and he wanted to be a fair way from the rebel's base by the time the guard could see him. He made for a higher area of ground on the horizon, hoping that he would be safer once he was over it. The grass was wet in the morning dew and Sarmon's feet were soaking by the time he reached the top of the rise.

The land sloped steeply downwards from here to a small village on the border of a large wooded area. The land then rose again, higher, into small, rolling hills about five miles away where the river valley ended. To the left of the village, several farmers were already up and herding cattle.

Trying to remain unnoticed, Sarmon descended the slope and crept swiftly around the right side of the village. Almost silently, he ran into the woodland and continued at a steady pace.

The floor of the forest was leafy and there was little grass, and Sarmon had to avoid muddy patches. Hoping to reach the river and buy a boat with the little money he had, he continued without stopping for a rest. Every now and then he had to empty his boot of a stone or leaf, which slowed his pace.

He was a couple of miles from the village when the woodland gave way to marsh. Looking ahead, he saw the river itself, glinting in the early morning sun. Undoubtedly, Tombhadi would track him down, and he needed to be far away by the next morning. Hoping to somehow find a boathouse somewhere down the river, he took the money out of his pocket and headed downstream.

Chapter 8
The Mayothan

Gybes, Fiddles and Chleosa ate dinner at Fiddles' Grandad's[1] house on the hill not far from the Temple of au Crassig. Their visit to the old Temple had encompassed the discovery that the crypt was flooded, and they had seen no one else at all.

After waving goodbye to Fiddles' Grandad, they headed along the track that would eventually lead to Lavos. The evening air was warm and still as they entered more familiar surroundings and reached the village itself. Laughter from the communal fire floated gently between the mud and stick huts and stone houses.

There was candlelight coming from Gybes' hut as he approached it with his friends. It flickered eerily and the light danced around his feet. He stepped inside.

'Hello, Gybes,' said his Mother. She was kneading bread on a desk in the 'corner' of the cylindrical hut. 'Your Father's away at your Uncle's,' she added as he looked around.

'Porloke's?'

'Yes,' replied Gybes' Mother. 'He's getting the axel fixed on our cart with Porloke's magic. Would you mind getting me some choz seeds for a cake I'm baking tomorrow?'

'Not at all,' replied Gybes. Choz seeds were bitter but tasty, often used in Tsabian baking, and they grew on strange plants with fern-like leaves, which grew only in forest clearings.

'We'll come with you,' said Chleosa, when Gybes stepped out of his hut and informed them of what he had to do. Fiddles nodded at her side.

Making tracks through the rainforest to the west, Gybes, Fiddles and Chleosa could hear crickets chirping from somewhere in the intense blackness around them. To the right Gybes heard the distinct, eerie cry of the night demonbird. Navigation was difficult, but, holding a small bag for carrying the seeds in, Gybes found his way along the path with ease. He knew this way well.

'Why do you think the language on the root we found came from the Island of Trees?' asked Fiddles.

'Perhaps the Apple of Doom came from there,' suggested Gybes.

'Yeah, and someone's going to be *bothered* to bring an Apple all the way here,' said Fiddles sarcastically.

'Maybe it's not here,' said Chleosa.

---

[1] The word 'Dad' was only used in Westport, where the word 'Mum' was also commonplace. So were the phrases 'Gordon Bennett!', 'lovely-jubley!' and, for some strange reason, 'cheese-monkey!'.

Gybes didn't reply. He was deep in thought. What on earth *was* The Apple of Doom? It sounded like a joke, but who would bother carving a piece of pointless information on a root in thousands-of-years-old language that might not have ever existed.

They turned to the left along a vague path in amongst tough rainforest grasses and horsetails. The ground was muddy and viscous from recent rain and it was easy to spot paw prints on the path, or it would have been, has it not been for obvious the lack of light. At night, this part of the forest was a paradise of its own kind. Nighttime creatures scuttled around, trying to avoid or hunt others. Pygmy bushpigs, half a metre tall, dug for roots around the bases of trees and shadowsnakes, the only Tsabian reptiles to be active at night, hunted rodents among the undergrowth. Gybes saw an unexpected flash of gold as a creature ran swiftly through a patch of moonlight. He pointed.

'That was a meat cat!' said Chleosa. 'My father said he caught one of those.'

'I heard a story of a *giant* one,' said Fiddles in a spooky voice. 'It JUMPS out of the forest at you and rips your…'

'Shut up!'

They came out into a clearing. The encroaching trees overshadowed most of it, but the moonlight lit up tall plants growing everywhere, swamping the clearing. Or at least, they would have been, usually.

'What's happened?' said Gybes, staring around at the choz plants. 'Most of them are destroyed!'

'…Said Wizz, stating the obvious…'

'They look like the seeds have all been eaten!' said Chleosa. 'What can have done this?'

'Dunno,' said Fiddles. 'Probably elephants escaped from a circus or something. Or knife-bearing mongooses…' Fiddles cleared his throat. 'There's a couple of seed pods over here, though.'

'Wahéy!' said Gybes. He picked one of them and emptied its contents – small, black, round, beady seeds – into his bag.

They were walking back across the clearing when they heard a strange noise.

'What was *that*?' asked Fiddles.

'Sounded like something crossed between a cat and an eagle,' said Gybes. 'It's coming from the other side of the clearing.'

They turned and walked towards the noise. If Gybes had been able to write it down, it would have come out something like 'EEEEEAAAAUUH!' They entered the dense forest on the other side of the clearing. The moon had craftily concealed itself behind a cloud and it was almost pitch black – the path was barely visible. The children kept on stumbling over roots and walking into bushes. Still the odd noise came from ahead.

They came out onto a flat area of ground and found themselves at the edge of a main road. It was cobbled and there was a sign standing beside it. A few moths flew across the front of Gybes' face.

'The north-south road,' stated Gybes. 'My Mother said I wasn't allowed to cross it alone.'

'Well, you're not alone,' said Fiddles, as the noise came again from not far ahead. 'You're with us.'

'I think she meant I had to be in the company of an adult.'

'Stuff that!' scoffed Fiddles. 'The weird thing isn't very far away. Although it may be extremely dangerous. But I like taking risks.'

Gybes felt a tingle down his spine. It had been a while since he had ventured into the dark this far – and he had never heard anything like the strange noise emanating from the rainforest in front of him. He tried not to admit to himself that he was a little scared.

They crossed the cobbled road and followed a thin, little used, overgrown path down a small slope to where it split. They took the straight on path, as the noise's origin was still directly ahead. It was growing louder now.

'Where is this creature?' said Fiddles, wondering. 'I'd like to turn around soon.' He couldn't keep the fear out of his voice.

His question was answered before any of them could decide to turn around. They came out into a small clearing, where the creature itself occupied a log in the centre. It was weasel-like in appearance, but much larger, and with a mane.[2] It had long, sharp claws and a slender tail. It opened its mouth widely and moaned pitifully, revealing disturbingly sharp teeth.

'What *is* that?' said Gybes, but before he had a chance to see any more of it the moon slid behind another cloud. He turned around and glanced up at the sky

'It's going!' cried Chleosa. Gybes span around. The strange creature had vanished.

'Odd,' said Gybes, and no more, as he was beginning to wonder if he had really seen the creature at all.

'Let's go back,' said Fiddles, in a small voice.

*

[2] If it had been light they would have been able to tell that the mane was a stunningly bright orange.

The three children spent the next morning at Chleosa's hut, looking at a book called 'Mammals of Tsabia' by A.T. Rimmis. They were trying to discover the identity of the strange creature they had seen.

'These aren't right!' said Chleosa in frustration. 'They all *look* like weasels, but none of them are like that... weird thing.' She shrugged. 'I'll try further ahead.'

Chleosa continued to flick through the pages of the book. After a few pages she dropped it accidentally and swore loudly and noticeably.

'Chleosa, language, please!' snapped her Mother from outside.

'Sorry,' apologised Chleosa. She opened the book again. After barely a second she pointed at a creature on the right hand side of the page. 'That's it! That's the one we saw! But it's related to the otter. Look, it says *Mayothan: reference page: 102.'*

Within a very short time, Chleosa had found the right page, illustrated with a pencil drawing of a Mayothan looking much more benign than the one they had seen the night before. She began to read the text.

' "The Mayothan is a genetic creation of Professor L.C. Clark, who lives and works on the northwest peninsula of Tsabia. So far it is only found in captivity." But that's wrong,' she said, looking up from the book. 'It's found here too.'

'Maybe it's an escapee,' suggested Gybes.

'Wait, I haven't finished reading,' said Chleosa. ' "When in danger, the Mayothan has been known to flee its home, and will travel to more secluded areas." Here it says "In 1603, the year of the great war, a group of Thans six hundred strong fled from their home where the initial battle took place to where L.C. Clark's laboratory is now located. In 1674, when he began work on genetic altering, as it later became known, he found his chosen site inhabited by the Thans. There, he bred the Mayothan, a cross between the danger sensing Than and its close relative, the tame mayocha, a hybrid creature that he hoped would warn people of danger and remain loyal in captivity. He finally succeeded in 1682, aged 53. Present day, Clark works on introducing a new type of Mayothan called the Monthan to Eastwood".'

'This book's old,' said Fiddles. 'My cousin Fasil told me he had introduced Monthans to Eastwood. Let's see the date.' He turned to the first page and swung his eyes to the bottom. 'This book was made in 1698! No wonder it's out of date. It's seven years old. So Clark would be... seventy six.'

'But why does the Mayothan have to turn up just when we find out about the Apple of Doom?' said Gybes. 'The book said that it flees its home when there's danger near! Does this mean there's an evil force coming from the north?'

'Stop being so paranoid!' said Chleosa. 'Whatever it is, it's nothing to do with us. It could even have run away from one of the other creatures on Clark's land! And if it's anything to do with the Apple of Doom, then it should be running *away* from here, not *to* here. Unless…'

'Unless what?'

'Oh, nothing,' she said dismissively, and continued reading. ' "The Mayothan has a golden brown coat and lurid orange mane. Its whiskers are short, but sensitive. The Mayothan has poor smell and quite good hearing, but its main asset is its excellent eyesight. It has large claws that it often uses to pull away bark from the trunk of a tree, underneath which it feeds on sap. The Mayothan is a semi-aquatic creature but normally will only use water to hide in. The Mayothan also feeds on the choz plant and is often found…" '

'So *that's* why all those choz plants were destroyed!' interrupted Fiddles.

'But one of them couldn't have done *that* much damage, could it?' said Gybes. 'There must be a whole tribe of them here!'

'That means they must be running away from something!' said Fiddles, clapping his hands together.

'Yeah, it really takes a genius to work it out,' said Gybes sarcastically.

'You are so stupid, Fiddles,' yelled Chleosa to their surprise.

'Would you *mind*!' yelled Chleosa's Mother.

'Sorry!' said Chleosa. 'Only joking,' she added apologetically to Fiddles.

'I hope you are,' came the reply from outside. 'I'm socialising with a gentleman of considerable importance here!'

Chleosa turned back to the conversation. 'There seems to be something strange going on here,' she said. 'The Apple of Doom, the Mayothan…'

Gybes recalled what Sir Fawning had said about the Apple of Doom. "The Apple of… Doom? Never heard of such a thing. Sounds like a load of old tosh if you ask me…" He relaxed a little and said, 'Why don't we go to the fire[3] for lunch?'

They stepped out of the door, only to find Chleosa's mother speaking with the Gentleman of Considerable Importance. He had short, grey hair and with a bald patch and a rather untidy moustache for someone of the considerably important persuasion.

'Ah *there* you are!' said Chleosa's Mother. 'Mr. Inkwell, this is my daughter Chleosa. She was eleven a couple of weeks ago. And these are her friends, Gybes who is also eleven and Dagtan who is ten.'

'Wizz and Fiddles, Mother,' Chleosa reminded her Mother quietly.

---

[3] 'The fire' was a communal area in the centre of Lavos. It rarely had a fire going, because no one could be bothered to start, which everyone else considered a decent excuse, seeing as they made it too.

'Oh, I don't bother with nicknames,' came the retort. 'It's enough trouble trying to remember real names.' She gave a high-pitched laugh. 'Anyway, this is Mr. Synley Inkwell, who is here representing a new newspaper called "Reporting Greenworld". He's looking into a murder case in Koglor, but he's dropped in for a rest, and I've offered to let him stay the night. But if there's anything you want to add – perhaps a small article you might want him to include, he'll be glad to add it in his newspaper somewhere.'

Gybes stared at Fiddles and Chleosa. They nodded at him. 'Well,' he began. 'Last night we heard a screeching noise in the rainforest. We followed it and found a strange creature. This morning we found out that it was a Mayothan'

'Ah, one of L.C. Clark's creations,' said Mr. Inkwell. His voice was deep and gruff as a result of the pipe he smoked. 'I'll mention that.'

'The whole clearing of choz seeds was ruined!' said Gybes impatiently. 'There must be a whole tribe out there!'

'Oh, children have such vivid imaginations,' said Mr. Inkwell, waving his hand. 'A whole tribe!' He laughed. It was a rowdy, raucous guffaw that reminded Gybes of a drunkard in Hillside Riverton. 'If there was a whole tribe out there, Lanran Clark would have told *me*.'

Gybes sighed.

'Oh, come *on*, let's have lunch!' said Fiddles.

'Very well,' said Gybes. They turned and walked away, Gybes catching the sound of Mr. Inkwell's unmistakable laugh on the wind.

Chapter 9
The Investigation Team

Milson moved lazily. He was on holiday – one of those package tours. They were touring the sandy expanses of beach some way to the northeast of Tuvak, near the town of Bermill, and he was lying in t-shirt and shorts on the coarse sand. The sun beat down hard and gave him sunburn. He rolled onto his front and began reading his tourist guide. It seemed to consist mostly of pictures[1] of young women in bathing suits running into the sea and was only about ten pages long. The last two pages were full of adverts; holidays, boats, restaurants, cafés, jobs, assassinations up for grabs; the whole lot. When Milson felt a cool breeze blowing from the sea he closed the booklet and sat up. Slipping a shirt on, he looked at the sky, observing the dark clouds slowly accumulating on the horizon and swiftly travelling towards the beach.

Milson ambled towards the dunes behind the beach, as he noticed other people doing the same. The breeze grew stronger, and waves began to appear on the sea. Boats sailed swiftly with the breeze to the nearest harbour, and seabirds flocked in, fleeing from the storm. He wondered whether Doran had brought the apple seeds he needed for him. Doran was also on the trip, along with his girlfriend Sashlea and good friend Coron Awaffling, the searcher[2]. Doran had said he would meet Milson in the dunes near to the Tourist Information Centre, a mile or so along from where Milson was at the time.

As he walked towards the Tourist Information Centre, Milson realised that he had lost his wallet along the way. He turned around and began to think about Tombhadi again. He wasn't even sure who Tombhadi was, seeing as he kept forgetting to ask Doran. He was sure he'd heard the name somewhere. There was still one question that Milson kept asking himself over and over. Why would this Tombhadi want *apples*? He thought it for the seventh time that day. Having recently had an apple with lunch, it was hard to get it out of his mind.

He reached a small dip in the dunes that he had previously passed through and began to search the ground for his wallet. After twenty seconds or so he spotted it lying on a small tuft of grass. He turned around and headed for the Tourist Information Centre, hoping to find Doran there with Sashlea and Coron.

When he reached the Centre, he found Doran, Sashlea and Coron lined up casually against one wall. Doran, wearing a hat, was smoking a cigarette, while calculating his bills for fruits he had purchased at the

[1] Taken by the magical 'kammara'
[2] The Greenworld equivalent to a policeman

Annual Fruit Show in Bermill. Sashlea was chatting with Coron Awaffling about his job.

'There you are!' said Doran, accidentally dropping a piece of paper. 'I've been waiting for you for some time. It's been a while since the time you agreed to meet us.'

'I lost my wallet on the way,' said Milson. 'I had to go back to find it.'

Doran nodded. 'It's not far back to the cart-park,' he said, holding onto the brim of his hat lest the wind steal it. 'We could go back to the holiday hut, as it's a bit stormy. I'll tell you about the trip I'm going on.'

They began to walk along the path towards the cart-park, talking quietly, Doran smoking his disc weed and drinking a bottle of nettle beer.

'So exactly what is this trip you and Sashlea are going on?' inquired Milson. Doran had said a couple of days ago that he was doing something, but he had failed so far to inform Milson what exactly.

'Well,' began Doran. 'The Emperor has heard rumors of a terrorist organisation which is said to reside in the Green Savannah, so he's sending an investigation team to, well, investigate. There was a meeting on Tsuday to decide who was going to be part of it, and I entered as Chief defence man.'

'Chief defence man?'

'Yes, I'm a good archer,' said Doran. 'They wanted me for long range defence.'

'Since when were you a good archer?'

'Since I studied at The Tuvak Royal Institute for Young Men Looking for Careers in the Armed Defences.'

'Never!'

'Why don't you believe I studied at The Tuvak Royal Institute for Young Men Looking for Careers in the Armed Defences?'

'Oh, I *believe* you studied at The Tuvak Royal Institute for Young Men Looking for whatsemys, but I thought you failed!'

'Oh, the first time I did, but I passed on the second try. The Tuvak Royal Institute for Young….'

'What about you, Sashlea?' interrupted Milson, not wanting to hear the tediously long name again. 'How did you get to go on the trip?'

'I'm a fast runner,' she said. 'And a good food collector. My mother used to teach me how to find mushrooms in the forest around my house. Also, I'm a painter. Because we can't afford a kammara, I'm going to draw some sketches along the way for the *Daily Emperor*, you know, the newspaper. There's a lot of competition between it and the new *'Reporting Greenworld'*, but the new one's only selling well in Tsabia and Gonithea. You'll never guess how much trouble I had at art school, being left handed. They tried to force me to use my right hand, so I left. I hope I did the right thing, because I also use my left hand to write.'

'You're right,' said Coron. 'There's nothing left in these art schools to write on.'
'Will you stop going on about left and right!' shouted Doran. 'It's enough to drive anyone round the twist!'
'All *right*, we will. You won't be *left* behind.'
'*Shut up*!'
'Very well, we'll stop *tormenting* you, Doran,' said Sashlea with good-natured sarcasm. 'I'll tell you more about why I'm on the trip. Last Slarday I heard that there was going to be this investigation team setting off on Cudday – that's tomorrow, and decided to enter for it. I think there are eleven people going, but all I know is the number – I don't know *who* they are.'
'I do,' said Coron. 'I know these sort of things, being a searcher, though these days there's a lot more secrecy around: there's a lot of things that only the Emperor and his council of Dukes seem to know. There's a lot of conspiracy going around too – there are rumours that there are people who dig secret passages into gold stashes for the Emperor and then mysteriously disappear…
'But I was sidetracking a bit there. You were asking about the members of the team. I know that one is called Pom Thukru – he's from Greenforest, and that from Eastwood there are Ani and Sampané Buhrokk – they're brothers. There is also Valisar Uma, the son of Dameid Uma, who is somewhat more respectable than his father, or so we are told, and two Sisters, Senira and Taka Rujeketa from Field East. Then there is Madley and Madsley – Conorrad Madley from Tuvak and Jolwin Madsley from Riso. And I think Synley Inkwell will be leading the team, representing the *Reporting Greenworld* Corporation.'
'Well, that sounds like a friendly team,' said Doran.
'What's your definition of "friendly"?' asked Coron. 'It's a rather unusual one if you think they're *friendly*. Apparently Senira's a bit *radical*; if that were the word you would use to describe her. She combs her hair with twigs and, well, put it like this: she wakes up in the middle of the night sometimes and howls.'
'So she's a bit on the wild side then,' said Milson.
'She's been in a mental institution three times and in jail twice,' said Coron. 'She says nobody understands her. I've heard that Valisar Uma is quite a good fellow though, despite his Father. And the rest are normal… ish.'
'Changing the subject slightly,' said Milson, 'where are these seeds you were going to give me, Doran?'
'I left them back in my cart,' said Doran. 'We're nearly there – I'll unearth them for you when we arrive.'

Shortly afterwards they came to a spot in the dunes where the ground had been levelled and cobbled. Several carts were lined up along the side of the cart-park, all of them holiday carts. Twenty of so other holidaymakers were standing in the shelter of the stables, because now the wind was almost gale-force and the rain was lashing down harder than ever. Milson and the rest joined them and sat on the hay on the stone floor.

A man was standing up and staring at a sort of register. He called out the names of the holidaymakers one by one.

'Coron Awaffling.'

'I am here,' said Coron from beside Sashlea

'Jorna Brown.'

A tall, slim woman in a leather suit nodded. She had dark make-up above her eyes and black, high-heel boots. She looked very out of place.

'Istfig Doran'

'Here,' yelled Doran a little too loudly from behind Milson.

The register man cleared his throat. 'Marzin Gottack,'

'All present and correct, Mistah,' said a scruffy man beside Jorna who was smoking a cigarette. 'How 'bout a fag yerself?'

'It is not someszing I desire,' growled the man.

'Sure?' said Marzin. 'You could 'ave two for alf the price o' three! Is that a deal or what?'

'You,' growled the man again, 'had better vatch it.'

After he had finished the register he laid the paper down and addressed the holidaymakers.

'Now you shall go to your carts and ve vill begin to move avay,' he bellowed, his attempt to make his voice heard over the howl of the wind and rain sounding all-too-military.

They formed an orderly line and began to manoeuvre out of the barn into the vicious weather. Milson, Doran, Sashlea and Coron made their way to a particularly grubby looking cart with a holed roof and climbed into it. Doran began rummaging in his bag for the apple seeds as the cart set off.

'Here you are,' he said, handing them to Milson around the waterfall of water that was pouring through he largest hole. 'I hope that Tombhadi is satisfied.'

'What are you on about?' said Sashlea.

'Oh so you're still trying to get people to believe *that*, are you?' asked Coron stiffly. 'You tried to tell me that hoax not long after it allegedly happened. Of course, I didn't believe a word of it. Nonsense. A load of old twaddle about him wanting apple seeds by Slarday. And I can see you're trying to live up to the joke as well! Giving Milson the seeds as if it's all real!'

'But...' began Milson.

He stopped. The man who had organized the trip was standing up in his cart and bellowing something. He was red in the face and looking completely furious. Milson pricked his ears.

'How dare you insult me!' the organiser was roaring at Marzin. 'Vot do you take me for? A fool? You vill be punished! *Get out you idiot and come into my cart*! I svear you vill be flogged ven ve get back to the city!'

'But this is an 'oliday, mate!' yelled Marzin. 'We ain't gets punished for just that!'

'You will get punished for vot I say you will get punished for, you slimy vermin!' roared the man.

'Go back to your wine and biscuits, nerd!' snapped Marzin.

'HOW DARE YOU!' roared the man. He whipped the horses viciously and was almost sick with fury. The horses reared and sped off so fast that he lost his balance and toppled off the side of the cart. He rolled down a steep muddy slope to one side of the road and flew into a thicket.

'Do you think he'll be OK?' asked Sashlea worriedly as the carts eased to a halt.

'Of course he will,' said Milson. 'Anyway, who cares?'

'Milson! That's disrespectful!'

'Don't worry. The medical people are seeing to him.'

'Talking of medical people... I *know* barbers aren't medical, but anyway, they want a barber on the investigation team, according to this newspaper,' said Coron.

'Why on earth...'

'Apparently there's been a replacement for Senira Rujeketa...'

'The mad one?'

'You could say so. Anyway, the new man's also a bit, well, crazy, and he wants a haircut on the way.'

Milson kept his expression blank. Most things lately had been *very* confusing for him, so this latest information didn't come as a huge surprise. 'Well, I'll probably enter for it,' he said

'Do what you like,' said Doran. 'You won't get in. It's probably just a joke anyway.'

They sat back into the cart as it began to roll onwards towards Tuvak. The organizer was laying in one ahead of the other carts, looking more angry than Milson thought anyone unconscious possibly could.

*

'What did Marzin actually do?' asked Milson.

'No idea,' muttered Doran.

Milson, Doran and Sashlea were sitting in a bar late at night. Milson hadn't drunk much, but Doran and Sashlea were slumped against each other, almost finished their third bottle of between them of a drink that had a label reading 'alcohol content: uncertain'.

'Wosh the time?' asked Sashlea, hiccoughing.

'Twelve thirty-three,' said Milson. 'I'd better get going. I've got to get to the contest at half one – odd how it's at night time – and I need to be at my Aunt's tomorrow to collect some carpets for my office.'

'Me an' Sashlea are going to shtay on a 'ittle bit longerer,' said Doran in a slurred voice.

'Well, goodbye then!' said Milson, finishing what was left of in the glass in front of him. He made his way out of the door and onto the dark street. He walked along to the right, away from the dingy 'Harbour Inn'. His shoes clattered on the cobbled road as he walked along it and the sound echoed emptily around the harbour. There was a surprising amount of noise for after midnight; fishermen docking, cargo ships being unloaded, the odd stowaway creeping onto or off a ship and the slow clip-clop of the hooves of the horses pulling a merchant's cart. Fireworks exploded in the distance

Milson walked for a few hundred metres down the practically deserted road, past the dry docks and fishing harbour. It was a couple of miles to the contest still, and even further to his home. Milson noticed the Tuvak 24-hour Public Seafront Library to his right. He walked up to the window and stared in. It was empty, apart from the man at the counter, who, dutiful to the cliché, was asleep. A small sign on the window read, 'All visitors after 12PM must enter the library.'

'Odd sign,' muttered Milson, as he made his way through the library door. A chime clanged and the man at the counter jerked awake, attempting to straighten his scruffy hair.

'Er, hang on a mo', he said in a breaking voice. Ai've got nao reason to be asleep at this time o' night.' He sprang up from his seat. 'Hi, the name's Bruce! Ai come from the desert bit of Wangoolie, ai doe! Well, *all* of it's desert, really. Folks call me "Desert Brucie". Ai had too much trouble huntin' kengeros[3], so I came to live in Tuvak.'

'I just wanted to have a quick look in a recent history book,' said Milson.

'Recent history?' said Desert Brucie. What might you fella be lookin' for in that? Never really been one for the past meself, so I don't know nothin'!'

'Just direct me to the section, would you?'

'To the right of the geographical section in the corner.'

---

[3] This isn't bad spelling. Kengeros in Greenworld were much larger than the Kangaroos of Australia, and roamed the out-the-back scrubland of Wangoolie.

Milson crossed over to the bookshelf and began to search among the rows for a particular book that might be useful. He picked up a likely looking one and began to search through the index for 'Tombhadi'.

'Page fifty-three,' he muttered to himself. He turned to the page entitled 'Tombhadi – the rise and fall of a true villain'.

He scanned down the page for information, and was bewildered to find out that Tombhadi had been the servant of the of the Duke of Kappleham, but had been sentenced to death for treason before fleeing, and that he had supposedly been killed by wolves in the Dark Forest. The most interesting fact was that he never showed his face – and had never been asked to, even by the Duke of Kappleham, or at least if he *had* been asked, he had refused, and no one had done anything about it.

He walked out of the library alone into the dark street and made his way towards where the late night contest was being held.

*

The man at the door was *fussy*. He didn't normally care what sort of things people wore, but he was annoyed when people weren't the neatest and smartest they could be (e.g. for a tramp, this was a few rags, for a businessman his best suit).

Milson approached slowly.

'Name, please,' said the man, handing Milson a scrap of paper

Milson scrawled his name on the piece of paper and handed it cautiously back to him, as if he thought the man would bite him.

'Neater, please,' said the man in the same droning, monotonous voice. He handed the paper back to Milson.

'What do you mean "*neater please*"?'

'I think it's perfectly clear what I mean,' growled the man, handing Milson another piece of paper.' 'I suggest you write your name on this if you want to enter.'

'Very well, if you insist,' sighed Milson. He wrote his name quickly, but neater, on the second piece of paper and handed it back to the man.

'Thank you,' he said, giving the next person a piece of paper, who quickly rejected it, because they wanted a *neatly cut* piece of paper.

Milson filed in with the rest into an amphitheatre with steps around its edges instead of seats. The rest were only five. He hadn't realized how few barbers would apply. They all sat down in the small amphitheatre and a man walked into the middle, holding a pot with the six names in it.

'Tonight,' he began with an air of great importance, 'I will pick out of this pot the name of the barber who shall accompany the Investigation Team setting out in no more than nine hours time…'

‘I thought there would be a contetht!’ yelled one barber with a lisp. ‘I don’t think thith ith fair!’

“Neither do I!’ shouted another, a man with an unnervingly high voice. Both stood up and marched from the room. There were now only four people left, including Milson.

‘Any other objections?’ asked the man. ‘No? Then I will pick the name.’

He stuck his hand into the pot and fished out a small piece of paper (Milson knew immediately it didn’t belong to the man who had been behind him, because it wasn’t ‘neatly cut’) and called out the name loud and clear.

‘Mr. Attabory Milson!’

If he had been on a chair, Milson would have fallen backwards.

Chapter 10
'Reporting Greenworld'

Gybes returned from another excursion to collect choz seeds from a separate clearing, thankfully unaffected by Mayothans. He handed them to his Father as he came out of their hut.

'Thanks, Gybes,' he said as he took the seeds from him. 'Did you meet Mr. Inkwell? The newspaper man?'

'Yes, I met him at Chleosa's,' said Gybes.

'Well, he left this morning, but I'm aware that he dropped off a competition – or something – in the Hillside Riverton Hall. Your friends have gone in to see what it's all about.'

'Well, I'll be off then,' said Gybes. 'Bye.'

'See you later,' said his Father.

Gybes began to walk in the direction of the hall, wondering what exactly this 'competition or something' could be. Despite its name, the Hillside Riverton Hall was actually in Lavos. It represented the entire Hillside Riverton district, from Yabbu and Troston in the north to Flasga and Nudabella in the south. It was a white, rectangular building, and was rather huge – at least, compared to the rest of the buildings in Lavos. It was quite new, and occasionally drew in small crowds for official meetings. Today however, it was more or less empty. As Gybes entered, he heard sounds coming from the reading corner and headed over.

The reading corner was a small area of the hall that was similar to a library, walled off on two sides by the main wall and on another by an insubstantial wooden board. It had a few small rows of books and was only accessible on weekdays. During the weekend it was kept out-of-bounds by a wooden door, which, uniquely for the village, could be locked. There was no librarian, but every now and then a person would come in and check that no books were missing.

Gybes entered the reading corner and noticed a large pile of papers, obviously the competition sheets. He pondered for a moment or two on why there was a slight smell of mustard.

'Hi,' said Fiddles. 'There are sort of these competition thingys here that Mr. Inkwell left, but I haven't started one yet, 'cause I was waiting for you and Chleosa.'

'Why does it smell of mustard?' asked Gybes, ignoring Fiddles' statement.

'I think it's that security guy who comes to make sure no books have been stolen,' replied Fiddles. 'I think his name's Mr. Davidson. He looks like a rat with acne.'

Just as he finished speaking, Chleosa rounded the corner of the flimsy wooden wall.

'Hi Chleosa,' said Gybes and Fiddles in perfect unison.

'Hello,' Chleosa replied, almost laughing. She pointed at the pile of papers. 'So these are the competitions?'

'Yeah, that's right,' said Fiddles. 'Shall we start one?' He picked up the question paper on top the pile and began reading the instructions.

' "This competition is for children only and no-one over the age of fourteen is permitted to help complete one which is to be entered. Simply answer the following questions and sent the competition to Pewter House, Reginald Avenue, Goodport, and you could win an exclusive once-in-a-lifetime trip to L.C Clark's amazing laboratory and see his ingenious creatures along with two friends!" '

'Cool!' shouted Fiddles. 'We can all help each other and we'll have triple chance'

'It says "no copying one another or conferring with each other to enter more than one competition".'

'I suppose so,' said Fiddles. 'But we could *cheat*. No one would *know*.'

'No!' said Chleosa. 'It's dishonest!'

'Whatever, Your Majesty Queen Perfect,' grunted Fiddles.

'We can all do one co-operatively,' suggested Gybes.

'S'pose so,' mumbled Fiddles. He looked at the first question and pretended to puke. 'Who the hell's gonna know that?' he spluttered.

Gybes peered over Fiddles' shoulder.

> Q1: Who was the third and most famous emperor of the Zing Dynasty in the ancient Empire of Xinchu-Hai?

'Wait a moment,' said Chleosa. 'I think I know it.'

'Sad girl,' said Fiddles. 'Lord have mercy on thy soul, ye doth be a Queen Perfect indeed!'

'I'm not a queen perfect, it's just my Mother told me once... or something like that...'

'You don't sound too sure,' said Fiddles.

'Come on, let's get on with it!' said Gybes. 'What's the answer, Chleosa.

'Zinguchi-on,' said Chleosa, producing a pencil from the pocket of the shorts she was wearing. [1]

'Write it in then, Kli-oh-sa, oh humble Empress,' said Fiddles.

---

[1] In Tsabia, skirts were very unpopular. At least, they were in 1705. In the 1660's however, to the shock and horror of old-fashioned citizens of the Empire, large numbers young women across half of Greenworld wore *very* short 'micro-skirts'. They were banned for a short period from 1671-75, and no one really got back into them in a big way.

With amazing speed they rocketed through the competition. They finished all the questions apart from the very last one, which they were stuck on.

> Q16: Who escaped from being executed for treason in 1698, but was killed by wolves in the Forest of Shadows?

'I *think…*'

'Here we go; Princess Brain saves the day again.'

'What do you think?'

'I think it might be Tombhadi,' said Chleosa.

'Who's he?

'Just an invention of the Quiz Queen again,' drawled Fiddles.

'Go on,' said Gybes. 'Who is he?'

'He was the servant of the Duke of Kappleham, who retired two years ago – that's Sir Fawning's father. He was involved in a plot to assassinate the Duke and was sentenced to death for treason. On the day that he was meant to be hung, he fled across the farmland of Field West and the Cohen Downs to the Forest of Shadows, where he was killed by a pack of wolves. My Aunt told me.'

'You've got an aunt?'

'Well, write it in then, and put it in the pile with the completed…'

'There was a completed pile?' said Fiddles. '*I've been robbed*! We could have copied them!'

'They could be wrong… too,' said Chleosa

'Well, whatever,' said Fiddles. 'But use my name and address.'

'That'll mean using "Dagtan Unthies",' said Gybes.'

'No way!'

*

After a hasty lunch, Gybes made his way to the clearing to participate in a game of grid hop, which was similar to chess, although the people were the pieces, and they all moved simultaneously. Some people said it was needlessly complicated, but that was only if you played by the rules. Mayhem was much simpler.

About halfway across the clearing they saw a man riding a horse coming from the track to the north. He was wearing a red and blue top. He dismounted and began hesitantly to advertise newspapers.

'Hey, kids, er… you lot!' he yelled, 'There's, um, newspapers up fer sale if ya wants ter – s'rry – if you want to buy 'em. Er, special… special offer, I think… Just thirty-four Fralli![2] 'S not fair!' he muttered to himself audibly. 'Up in Goodport I gets an 'ole ninety-seven Fralli… Um… Extra! Extra!'

'I'll buy one,' said Fiddles, walking up to the man.

'But you don't have any money!' said Chleosa.

'Yeah I do,' said Fiddles. He smiled, handed the man some money and took a paper.

'Ta mate,' said the man, slipping the small coins into his pocket.

'Let's go and sit down somewhere to read it,' said Gybes, eyeing Trudge, who looked like he wanted to eat it.

'Where?'

'Over there beside that building, in the sun.'

Gybes, Fiddles and Chleosa wandered over to the main water storage hut and sat down. Gybes began to look at the paper.

'It's called "Reporting Greenworld",' said Fiddles. 'Hey, this looks like the main headline. "Investigation Team to inspect rebel rumours". You read it, Wizz.'

Gybes peered over the newspaper and read the text.

> *An official Investigation Team has been commissioned to ascertain the truth about several rumours concerning a rebel force that may be collecting members in the Green Savannah. Some military experts believe that this is nothing more than a superstition of the villagers of D'neru, although many worried citizens of Tuvak are much less certain, as indeed is His Majesty Emperor Alu IV himself.*
>
> *On Tsuday there was a meeting to decide who would be participating in the operation. Those privileged to be members of the team will be leaving on Cudday. At 1.20 this morning, due to a hectic schedule and several mistakes, there was a second meeting to decide who would join the other eleven members as barber. Several reputable people called the organizers 'obsessed lunatics', although this was not really their choice, but was indeed, as they said, the fault of Arakkanidd Hirsuto, who replaced team member Senira Rujeketa.*
>
> *It has come to light that Senira, distraught after her cat's death, murdered her neighbour with a piece of flint, while dressed only in illegally imported wolf skin. The new member of the team expressed concerns that he would only have time for a haircut on the trek, which he was apparently*

[2] This was Tsabian Currency. There were one hundred fralli to a goni.

desperate for. Synley J. Inkwell will lead the trip, and compose a conclusive and in-depth report on the Investigation Team's discoveries.

Jakid Slemabot, 'Reporting Greenworld'.

'Mr. Inkwell again, eh?' said Fiddles. 'I wonder what else is in the paper.'

Chleosa took the paper off Gybes and began to scan through it, muttering sentences such as 'Tsabia to have free rule within ten years – oh good!' and 'Pet thief trial on Phomday –what the...?' Finally she found something that looked interesting.

'Look at this,' she said. ' "Is it a 'Bhad' Hoax?" It's got a report on it here.'

'Go on, read it then,' said Fiddles.

Chleosa began to read the report out loud so that they could hear her.

Mr. Attabory Milson and Mr. Istfig Doran today informed the press that that the supposedly dead man Tombhadi walked into Mr. Milson's shop last Phomday. Mr. Milson insists that Tombhadi demanded to have eighteen packets of apple seeds at half price. Yet there is no evidence apart from the words of Mr. Milson and Mr. Doran. It is presumed to be a poorly organised hoax.

Jakid Slemabot, 'Reporting Greenworld'.

'Strange,' said Gybes. 'I wonder if it's a hoax or not?'

'Of course it's a hoax,' said Fiddles loudly. 'That's all a load of waffle! Chleosa says he was killed by wolves in the Forest of Shadows and that's good enough for me.'

'It doesn't mention Mayothans,' said Chleosa. 'Mr. Inkwell said he'd mention it in his newspaper.'

'Maybe he hasn't had time,' said Gybes.

'Maybe he didn't *want* to mention it,' said Chleosa.

'Let's go and play grid hop with Trudge, Clamber and Mystica,' said Fiddles. 'There's one thing I'm sure about, and that's that the Tombhadi story is a hoax.'

*

As the sun began to set, Sarmon docked the boat by a tree and made his way up the steeply sloping riverbank, hoping to come across something in the way of a settlement. He hadn't eaten anything for quite some time, and was becoming extremely hungry.

The young man travelled over a flat piece of land for a while and then climbed a gentle slope up a small hill. He crept over the summit and found himself confronted with three bowmen.

'What are you doing on my land?' demanded the largest one, who wore a crimson robe and a polished, silver helmet.

'Er, nothing… I mean no harm!' said Sarmon. 'I didn't know it was your land, sir.'

'There was a huge fence in the way with "no entry" signs on them! And you *just happened* not to notice that, eh?'

'I came down the river,' said Sarmon desperately. 'There were no fences there.'

'That *is* true,' said the bowman. He brightened significantly, and almost became a different person. 'Anyway, as you are here, you are my guest! Come, and I shall show you my house.'

'House', however, was rather an understatement. As Sarmon neared the trees surrounding it, he could tell from the obtrusive turrets that it was more castle than house. They passed under a copse, the last rays orange sunlight shining on the ground, giving it a copper feel, and came out onto a large cart park. Ahead of them was the building. The double doors were reinforced with iron bars and were made of redoak beams. A stone gargoyle leered at Sarmon from above the doors, its wide eyes and sharp teeth making him feel like he was about to enter some kind of ominous lair. There were eight windows facing forwards and three floors, not counting two towers. To the right stood the outbuildings.

'Fetch in some wood for the fire,' the man commanded the other bowmen, who obediently took off their equipment and hurried towards one of the outbuildings. The owner of the house turned to Sarmon. 'I haven't introduced myself,' he said. 'My name is Winlow, and I am here by the border of the Empire to guard from any rebels. Come in, and tell me your business here.'

'I don't mean to impose…'

'Oh, it's nothing!' cried Winlow. 'What's your name, lad?'

'Oh… Sarmon.'

They walked into the impressive 'house' and Winlow showed Sarmon to the dining room, where he took a seat at the table, and gestured for Sarmon to follow suit. The walls were made of wooden panels and a large window looked out over one of the stables and a wide, green lawn, with a pond and shed, although Sarmon could hardly see this anymore due to the diminishing sunlight.

'Oh there's lots of things I'd like to tell you about this place!' said Winlow. 'I don't know where to begin…'

Sarmon wasn't listening. He felt uneasy. There was something that was telling him 'get out' inside him. He felt as though the air was trying to run away too. It was dark outside, and the wind was rushing through the trees.

There was a knock on the door, and then the sound of the doorkeeper rushing to it.

No… thought Sarmon

Suddenly there was a strangled yell as a gust of cold air rushed through the half-open door.

'Goodness me!' yelled Winlow. 'What on earth just…'

The door burst open fully, letting cold air rush through.

Someone was standing in the doorway. Sarmon didn't even need to look up to know who it was.

Tombhadi.

'Get out of my house!' shouted Winlow. 'You have no right to be here!'

'Sarmon,' said Tombhadi calmly, ignoring Winlow. 'What a pleasant surprise.'

'You're not going to kill me, Tombhadi,' said Sarmon as calmly as Tombhadi had addressed him, lifting his eyes to meet where he knew the cloaked man's were.

'Not yet,' said Tombhadi. 'But if I do not dispose of you, you will scuttle off blabbing to everyone about me. Tell me; where is your weapon? You must at least have *something* to defend yourself with? No, of course you don't. I remember now, you were never prepared.'

Sarmon stared defiantly at Tombhadi but said nothing. It was indeed true; he had no weapon for defence, but he would not admit it to Tombhadi.

'What is this devilry you have brought to my house?' yelled Winlow, turning now to Sarmon. He turned back to Tombhadi as he picked up an enormous crossbow.

'Put that down,' growled Tombhadi, pointing a metal stick at Winlow.

'What are you going to do with that little stick?' asked Winlow, half laughing. 'That's a ridiculously weak weapon! What do you call it? A throwing stick?'

'The inventors call it a "pistol",' said Tombhadi. 'Stand up and leave the room and no harm will come to you.'

'You are an utter fool,' said Winlow, tightening his grip on the crossbow.

'Do as he says,' muttered Sarmon. 'I warn you; if you don't the consequences will be devastating.'

'You're both as stupid as each other,' said Winlow. 'One of you is pretending to be Tombhadi! Well, nice acting, *Tombhadi*: goodbye!'

There was a sudden echoing bang and a puff of smoke. As it cleared, the body of Winlow was visible, slumped to the floor and still grasping the crossbow in both hands.

'So,' said Tombhadi, lowering the pistol he had just fired and turning to Sarmon, his voice chillingly calm. 'You *fled* from me. Why is this so?'

'You were planning to kill me!'

'Nonsense, Sarmon!' said Tombhadi in a fake 'kind' voice that could fool no one. 'I wasn't going to kill you! Come, and tell me your story!'

'My story?'

'Stand up, fool!' yelled Tombhadi suddenly. 'Did you believe I would forgive you for you treachery? You will pay for this, Sarmon. And don't think for one moment that I need you! I have thirty men behind me, and several hundred more where they came from! You cannot win any fight.' Tombhadi grinned as several fully armed soldiers carrying other guns stepped into the room behind him. His voice became unnervingly smooth again. 'Your time has come,' he said.

He raised his own pistol so that it was in line with Sarmon's head.

'Now,' he said slowly, 'you will die.'

Chapter 11
The Shadow and the Stone

The Investigation Team was on its first day travelling, and Milson's horse was already tiring, lagging at the back of the group alongside Doran and Sashlea.

'Hurry up you three!' yelled Mr. Inkwell from the front. Milson made an attempt at getting the horse to move faster and moved closer to the rest of the group. He'd never been on a journey as long as this in the saddle before.

They had not yet reached the Green Savannah and were traversing fields of giant sadron corn in the south of Field West. The corn provided protection against the wind, which, by the look of the swaying tops of the corn, was quite strong. The road that the group was using was the main trade route between Tuvak and the west coast, winding up eventually in Westport. Little did they know, it had been the road that Tombhadi had used to navigate by.

A cart trundled by, full to the brim with hay and driven by a short, square-jawed man with grey hair.

'How far is it to the Green Savannah?' Mr. Inkwell asked the cart man.

'Just round the corner,' he replied. ' Perhaps half a mile.'

'Thanks,' said Mr. Inkwell. They continued to trot onwards at a steady pace.

Sure enough, after half a mile the scenery changed suddenly and dramatically. The team emerged from the fields of corn and out into the open Green Savannah. The breeze rippled Milson's hair as he looked around at the vast expanse of grass dotted with trees that lay in front of him. Far to the right, about a kilometre away, the tall heads of the sadron corn could be seen swaying in the breeze. He had forgotten that the border was so clearly defined, as it had been years since he had last gone this far west.

He waited for Doran and Sashlea to catch up. 'Do you think these rumours about the rebel band are true?' he asked.

'We'll soon see,' said Doran. 'Did you leave those seeds in your office for Tombhadi?

'Yes, I left them on my table with a note which said…'

'I've heard that the bedding will be good in the tents,' interrupted Sashlea. 'It'll be quite dry in the savannah anyway, and that's… good, because there won't be any swamps to accidentally pitch camp in. Yesterday I asked Mr. Inkwell and he told me that the tents are going to be adequate accommodation. We'll be sleeping in the same tent,' she added with an odd smile.

‘Why did she change the subject as soon as we mentioned Tombhadi?’ Milson muttered to Doran under his breath. Doran merely shrugged.

A horse came suddenly up from behind them. ‘Hey Mister Miylsun,’ the part-time barber was greeted by a scraggy, hairy man[1] who was occupying the steed. ‘I’d a-like-a-my hair cut a-fore I go mad from the nits a-livin’ in it. Mah name is Arrakanidd Hirsuto, an’ I replaced Senira.’

‘I’ll… cut it as soon as we stop,’ said Milson uncertainly.

‘You’re mad enough?’ Doran laughed.

‘I’m not sure I’m brave enough,’ said Milson. ‘This is the Final Frontier of barber…ness. But I am willing to take on… The Challenge,’ he finished boldly, pronouncing it in a way that meant capital letters were compulsory.

*

The sun was red and setting when Emperor Alu IV’s official Investigation Team finally pitched camp in a sheltered hollow. Sashlea commented in an impressed voice that it was *not* a bog. The antelope, and the team’s horses were settling down and the nocturnal predators were creeping out of their abodes. A speckled waterbird screamed alarmingly as Milson pitched the tent with the help of Doran and Sashlea. As soon as the tent was fully erected, Milson, Doran and Sashlea went to the campfire to join the rest of the team for dinner.

‘Tonight it’s mutton casserole, Forshamer’s spuds and good old greens’ said Taka Rujeketa, the lately convicted Senira’s sister. ‘Conrad Madley’s a really experienced cook.’

‘This will be good for try,’ said Pom Thukru from Greenforest in an accent Milson had never heard before[2]. ‘I have never tried the cooking from other parts of, how you say, Green World. At home we have to eat only what there is in easy, er… reach. We are eating beetles and fish eggs, and sometimes we are having some meat, but meat is no find easy, how you say, er… rare. Although, the fruit from Greenforest is best in world, apart from, say, Rabfruit from Tsabesch – I mean Tsabia.’

‘I am used to delicious, succulent meat and home grown vegetables,’ said Ani Buhrokk of Eastwood. ‘In Eastwood there are so many animals to hunt that we can’t eat all we catch. Some of the meat is exported to Tuvak, and that is why out country is so rich and prosperous.’

‘I once had a gu-u’ta chop from Eastwood,’ said Milson. ‘It was delicious! I think it was coated in seg-egda herbs.’

‘Thanks for the compliment,’ said Ani’s brother Sampané. ‘Pardon my brother’s boasting, he is very patriotic.’

---

[1] In an accent anyone from Earth would associate with the stereotype of a mid-American yokel.

[2] Distinctly oriental to earthlings.

At that moment Connorad Madley appeared followed by Mr. Inkwell. 'Well, here's the food,' he said, handing out a plate to everyone. 'Traditional of the cottages and farms of Field West.' He poured out some red wine into glasses. 'Red wine from Tuvak anyone?'

'I only drink white wine,' said Pom Thukru.

'I jolly well don't drink alcohol, dear boy,' said Jolwin Madsley. 'Stuff for the inexperienced, or the mad. No offence, old fruit.'

'None taken…'

Most of the others wanted, or, as Valisar uma put it, 'required' wine, apart from Arakkanidd Hirsuto, who claimed his old Ma had forbidden him to drink, because he went completely insane whenever he consumed too much alcohol.

The food that followed was some of the best Milson had ever tasted. Even Ani and Sampané from Eastwood complimented on the meal.

'Absolutely scrumptious, what?' said Jolwin Madsley, from Riso. 'Most deliciously cooked. How did you did you do it, old bean? Is it talent, or was it the food?'

'Well…'

'It must be talent,' said Valisar Uma. 'He is obviously an accomplished cook. I would consume such a delicacy on multiple successive occasions and never tire of its taste.'

'I think I'm gonna have to have another glass o' wine,' said Arakkanidd Hirsuto, who had already, despite what his 'Old Ma' had said, drunk four glasses of the wine. He swallowed his fifth glass and quickly called for more.

'I think you've had enough,' said Mr. Inkwell. 'Anyway, we'll be rising early tomorrow and heading off.'

'Is tha… Is that so?' said Arakkanidd Hirsuto in a slurred voice. 'I'm havin' more an'… an' there's n… nah… nutt'n you can do 'bout it!' He got to his feet unstably and threw his glass at Mr. Inkwell narrowly missing. He violently splashed another glass into the barrel of wine, pulled it out and downed it in seconds.

'Why you…' began Mr Inkwell, and then stopped. Arakkanidd stood like an ogre, wine dripping down his front, his face contorted and his eyes swivelling from side to side.

'He's going mad,' muttered Milson to himself. *Mad.*

Milson was right. Within seconds, Arakkanidd knocked over the barrel of wine, spilling its contents onto the grass and threw his empty glass in the fire He swung a kick at Doran, only to discover that the man had had the sense to move moments before.

Arakkanidd screamed in rage and leapt onto a tent, ripping the thin cloth and landing on Mr. Inkwell's bedding.

'In the name Lord Aa, what do you think you're doing?' roared Mr. Inkwell.

'My only Lord is alcohol!' yelled Arakkanid. He attempted to lick the wine from the grass, and when this failed ran aimlessly, still screaming, into the darkness.

'Come back here this instant!' shouted Mr. Inkwell, but it was no use. After a short time Arakkanidd's yells were barely audible.

'Bed, everyone,' growled Mr. Inkwell. 'This is outrageous!'

Milson went into the tent with Doran and Sashlea and lay down thankfully in his sleeping bag.

*

Sarmon stood perfectly still as Tombhadi raised the pistol. He could see the intimidating dark hole in its end. It was all he could do not to yell out in fear.

'Goodbye, my dear Sarmon,' said Tombhadi calmly.

'Master! Master!' came a call from behind Tombhadi.

'What is it now?' he growled, turning around, his gun still pointing at Sarmon.

'We have heard that Basron knows of some secret route on the Northern Peninsula of Tsabia,' said Tametathon, entering the room.

'He does not – *I* do!' said Tombhadi impatiently, involuntarily dropping his arm. 'Have we not…'

'Basron is escaping, master!'

Sarmon had used the opportunity and ran towards the window. He smashed a pane with the corner of a light table and attempted to escape through it. The glass caught and cut him, but he persevered, knowing that he needed to be through before Tombhadi could fire.

'STOP HIM!' Tombhadi yelled.

There was an echoing 'BANG' and another cloud of smoke, but Tombhadi was too late. Sarmon had leapt from the first floor window onto the tarpaulin that was the stable roof, which gave way beneath him. He fell into the darkness, and felt a horse beside him.

Behind him, the diamond-tipped arrows of Tombhadi's anger shot down to the stable and struck Sarmon on the ears. He urgently tried to climb onto the horse, but was unsuccessful. He heard the slam of the front door, and shouts coming from what sounded like at least twenty people. He had forgotten Tombhadi has brought so many! He attempted to get onto the horse again and, this time, succeeded. He tapped it on the side with his feet and it obediently trotted out of the stable.

'There he is!' yelled Tombhadi.

There were six gunshots and Sarmon heard the bullets whistle past him. He was amazed to find that neither he nor the horse was injured. He heard something like 'more practicing' and 'useless' from Tombhadi as he sped onwards into the darkness. Where would he go now? He knew that he was on the run, but where to? Then it dawned on him where the most sensible place to go to was. He had to warn people of what Tombhadi was going to do, and he knew where Tombhadi was going.

Tsabia.

*

It was dark when Milson awoke to the sound of a distant thump. He felt around in the darkness until he found the door of the tent. He peered out. It was cloudy, and almost pitch black.

'Thump.' There it was again. It sounded like someone had dropped something. Milson crawled out of the tent and stood up. He could hear nothing but the rustling of the leaves on the trees.

He listened more intently. He *could* hear something else. It sounded like…

'Footfalls?'

'Sorry?' said Sashlea from inside the tent. 'What are you doing?'

'Nothing,' said Milson. 'Go back to sleep.'

Yet he *could* hear them, very quiet, but quite close. Maybe it was just his imagination.

But then he spotted a shadow – someone skulking around what had been last night's campfire. It was probably just someone getting water, he thought.

The figure stooped to pick up something. Then they began to run.

Nothing to worry about, thought Milson. It's just someone running.

Running?

The shadow was rapidly disappearing into the darkness. 'Oi!'; cried Milson. He ran after the person, into the savannah, but as soon as he was just outside the camp, he tripped on something and fell flat on his face.

'Hey, come back you!' he panted, still lying on the ground.

But it was no use. The person, whoever they had been had disappeared into the blackness of the night. Milson swore loudly and turned back towards the camp. He was not far from the campfire when he tripped again, on what turned out to be a large stone.

'Strange,' he muttered. 'There aren't normally any rocks here. They're further south.' He turned to look at it, though at first sight it seemed nothing more than a typical rock.

He tried to pull it out of the ground, but it was stuck fast. He sat down, puzzled, and felt it. It strangely resembled a tombstone. But, he thought, you would never find a gravestone in the middle of the savannah.

He walked around to the other side of it. If it had any letters on it, then he could feel them.

It did.

Remembering that he had a tinderbox in his pocket, he rummaged around in his coat and brought it out. With the new light he could read the writing on what was indeed a tombstone.

In the light of the tinderbox he could see four words on the grave. What Milson saw absolutely amazed and baffled him.

Rest in peace,

Tombhadi.

Chapter 12
The Fruit's Tale

Gybes, Fiddles and Chleosa were glancing back at the previous day's newspaper when Sir Fawning returned. Fiddles was still exclaiming profoundly that the Tombhadi story was a ridiculously obvious hoax. Gybes refused to be certain, and Chleosa was sitting a little away from them, not getting involved in the argument.

'Are you two ever going to stop?' she said, as Fiddles laughed at Gybes who was putting on a straight face.

'I'm just trying to get it into Gybes' peanut brain that the Tale of Tombhadi is utter fantasy!'

'We don't actually *know* though,' said Gybes stubbornly.

'You're as thick as a mule's backside!' shouted Fiddles. 'Tombhadi died ten years a…'

'Can you hear horses hooves?' interrupted Chleosa.

'I think…'

'Tally ho!' said a familiar voice from behind them. They turned around, only to see Sir Fawning on his horse behind them.

'Sir-ish Fawning!' cried Gybes, relieved not to have to continue the pointless argument.

'Great news, young fellows!'

'You've found the book?' said Fiddles.

'I've received another eighth of a knighthood! Now I'm *Sir* Fawning instead of bally Sir-*ish* Fawning!'

'That's… great!' said Gybes.

'But do you have the book?' asked Chleosa.

'Oh. Yes.' said Sir Fawning in a quieter voice. 'I was quite amazed when I discovered that the Apple of Doom was real after all!' He opened his jacket and produced from within a tattered-looking book, with golden letters etched into it's green cover spelling '*Greenworld's Legends*'. 'Here's the book. It concerns various myths and legends as well as the one you're looking for. I hope you find it interesting. Well, at least, I found it interesting. Intriguing, I'd say! Fascinating! But you'll have to decide on it yourselves.'

'You read it?'

'Yes I jolly well did! On the way it was, too. It made me rather jolly worried, I can tell you. Such a terrible thing, the Apple of Doom: I can only hope it doesn't actually *exist*. I don't have a bally idea why it came into being, if it truly did. Pure spite, I suppose.'

'Why, what is it?'

‘Find out for yourselves!’ said Sir Fawning, his voice becoming much more cheerful. ‘I’d better be off. I have to visit someone in Hillside Riverton before going north again, but I’ll be back to pick the book up! See you!’

‘Bye!’ chorused the trio.

With that, proud-to-be-Sir Fawning tapped his horse and trotted towards the south.

*

‘So, what is the Apple of Doom?’ Chleosa wondered, sitting on the corner of Gybes’ bed at one side of the cluttered hut.

Fiddles opened the book *Greenworld: Legend*. ‘You read it, Chleosa,’ he suggested, handing it to her.

‘Very well,’ she said, taking the book from him. She turned to the index. ‘The Apple of Doom – Page 184.’ She flicked through the pages of the book, careful not to damage them.

‘This is it,’ said Gybes, widening his eyes and holding his arms out as if to still the very air. He couldn’t help smiling at the mysterious atmosphere he had conjured up.

Chleosa stared closely at the minute text and began to read it out aloud. “According to legend, 5,000 years ago something called the Apple of Doom was created.” It’s got a sub-title, “The Story”.

‘Well that’s what we want, isn’t it,’ said Fiddles.

‘ “On the Island of Trees, there dwelt three ancient civilizations, each as magnificent as the others, and each with a culture of great splendour and brilliance. The great Emperor Mayvir, who was renowned for his cleverness and impeccable strategic genius, ruled the Mayvon, who inhabited the northwest of the island. Then there were the Kyron of the northeast, led by the subtle King Kyros, who, although not humble, was kind and charitable as far as kings go. And finally, there were the Pilon from the south, led by devious Lord Pilihsp, who was kind to those who worshipped him as a god. All three had a sufficiently kingly ego, but none as overblown as Pilihsp’s.

“All three monarchs agreed on holding a grand contest to see who would be Supreme King of a triumvirate of the new, adjoined kingdom. The contest was to be held on the eve of the New Year, coincidentally full moon. The Magi of the three civilizations were to compete against each other on a dangerous and trying magical racecourse in the sky, for the leaders would never compete themselves, as they needed to remain alive to become part of the ruling trio. The Magi’s course would be obstructed by levitating objects, curses and ferocious, mobile fire-rings, which they would have to dodge or extinguish.

"However, Pilihsp, devious in his ways as he was, devised a plan to win the competition. He would cheat, and frame the other wizards. His Mage would use illegal curses without being caught, and the other two Magi would certainly die before the end of the course by 'accident'. Pilihsp gave his Mage a special staff, which could be used to conjure illegal curses without the Ref-ari, or referee, noticing." '

'Is this going anywhere?' Fiddles droned.

'There's quite a lot more,' said Chleosa. 'Hopefully…'

'I'll read a bit if you want,' offered Gybes.

'No. I'm fine,' said Chleosa. 'I'll carry on. "On the day of the contest the Magi took off upon their broomsticks and sped daringly and confidently into the racecourse, ducking under enchanted tree trunks and accurately dropping gold coins in cauldrons, to stop them from following them and emptying their boiling contents on the hapless wizards. The Magi used their staffs to divert flying rocks called Kanars and propel them into the paths of the others.

"Pilihsp watched intently from a precipice as his Mage dived towards Mayvir's, using an illegal curse to knock him from his broomstick. The startled Mage fell to his death, but the Ref-ari noticed nothing, due to Pilihsp's magic. His Mage then approached on Kyros' Mage, who was flying underneath a cauldron of boiling monkey fat. The Mage cursed the cauldron, and its scalding contents fell towards his opponent. But Kyros' Mage was more powerful than he had reckoned, and he diverted the boiling fat towards Pilihsp's Mage, who didn't have time to curse it. He dived to the side and avoided death, but found himself travelling at an unstoppable speed towards a ring of fire, which was rising to meet him.

" 'Curse it you fool!' shouted Pilihsp as his Mage got steadily closer. But the Mage's staff was faulty, and the blue, three-metre wide ring of fire exploded into thousands of pieces as Pilihsp's Mage collided with it. He fell to the ground, burning in blue flame.

"Enraged, Pilihsp, with his arm outstretched, aimed the most deadly and illegal curse possible at Kyros, who at the same time was struck by Pilihsp's Mage as he rocketed out of the sky. It is said that at the time, Kyros was eating an apple, but this may just be to make sense of the ensuing confusion. When both curses struck Kyros, he burnt into a small pile of ashes, which writhed on the ground like worms. When all Pilihsp saw was an apple, he laughed at his enemy's defeat with the utmost glee and picked up the apple. But the power of the Apple was immense, and Pilihsp was killed instantly. He was thrown backwards over the precipice where it is said his bones still lie today. Mayvir became King of The Island of Trees and he and his family ruled the Korons, as the new tribe was named, for many hundreds of years, until the legendary Terrorisation of The Island of Trees".'

'That's a strange way to make an apple,' said Gybes.

'Yeah, what are they going to come up with next?' asked Fiddles. 'The Banana of Peril? The Orange of Devastation? The Pineapple of Despair?'

'Don't be stupid,' said Gybes. 'We are the fruits of life – we are great! We don't need any evil fruits!'

'So – are you the Mango of Ego or something then?'

'We still don't know what the Apple of Doom *is*,' said Chleosa.

'Er… an apple?' suggested Gybes.

'It's a myth,' said Fiddles.

'But – if it does exist – there must be something special about it,' said Gybes. 'I want to know what that is.'

'Well you read it then,' said Fiddles.

'Whatever,' said Gybes, picking up the book. ' "After the Terrorisation of The Island of Trees, the Apple of Doom was taken to Tsabia, where it was hidden underneath a tree. It is said by certain seers that one root of that tree has upon it an inscription, and when that root is snapped, danger is near. For a more detailed description of the Apple, see the end of this chapter." So we're in danger, then! But from what?'

'We're not in danger!' said Fiddles. 'It's just superstition. Anyway, I'm in as much danger as a little frog sitting on a lily pad.'

'Yes, like that one on the way to Motherton on that pond,' said Gybes. 'At your favourite place. Remember? The fish…'

'My point is, we're safe,' said Fiddles.

'Maybe,' said Gybes. 'But why are there Mayothans nearby, and why is there that story about Tombhadi? I mean, why would they lie?'

'Stop it!' said Chleosa. 'I don't *want* to believe it. I mean it's not as if… But…'

'There's no point believing in it,' said Fiddles. 'It's all nonsense.'

'Let's just get on with reading this,' said Gybes, trying to stop everything fall to pieces because Chleosa looked more worried than she let on and Fiddles was, well, being Fiddles.

'I'll read it,' said Fiddles.

'Go ahead.'

Fiddles began reading the next part of the book. ' "If man or woman were to touch the Apple, they would instantly die, unless they were a wizard. Even then, they would need to have drunken a special potion, of which the content will not be mentioned in this book, for obvious reasons. Once the Apple of Doom is within the grasp of a wizard or wizardess,[1] the owner becomes all-powerful. The legend goes that they would have total control over all Greenworld, and that they would be granted eternal life and a certain degree of invulnerability".'

---

[1] 'Witch' was thought of by some in Greenworld to be derogatory term.

'No wonder it's hidden!' said Gybes. 'Any wizard could steal it from somewhere obvious.'

'But it's a bit stupid to say *where* it's hidden,' said Fiddles.

'Under a tree in Tsabia? And how many trees are there in Tsabia?'

'Is it defended, though?' said Chleosa. 'I suppose it must be defended, mustn't it? Something as dangerous as that?'

'It's a little under defended, if this root is all there is between it and a greedy wizard full to the ears with potion,' said Gybes, fishing the root out of his pocket.

'Let me finish reading,' said Fiddles. ' "The Apple of Doom is thought to be indestructible. This explains why no one to date has attempted to destroy the"…'

'WATCH OUT TRUDGE!' Gybes yelled, suddenly spotting him running, a vine in front of him at ankle-height. But Trudge wasn't listening. He tripped on the vine and flew forwards; faster than he could ever have run otherwise, and staggered straight into his own hut wall. But he didn't stop there. His weight carried him straight onwards.

'WHAT ON EARTH DO YOU THINK YOU'RE DOING?' roared Trudge's Mother. 'YOU JUST MADE A HOLE IN OUR OWN HUT! YOU'RE FIXING IT, AND YOU'RE GOING ON A DIET, TOO!'

'Oh sausage,' said Trudge. 'Diets are pointless and…'

'DON'T YOU GIVE CHEEK TO ME, DJOK!'

Through Trudge's stammering apologies, Gybes read the next part of the book.

' "Several ancient scriptures agree that the Apple of Doom shall be stolen some time at the dawn of the Ogurian age, beginning within a decade after the year 1700. This has been confirmed by seers".'

'Does that mean we're in danger?' questioned Chleosa.

'It's nonsense!' said Fiddles. 'Seers are just money-makers. They'll do anything to get extra tips. They charge you *fifty* goni to have your palm read! That's two days wages of a decent job!'

'They need it,' said Chleosa. 'Seers are very hardworking, even if they're… weird.'

'They *need* it? Look, the way I see it…'

So, the Apple of Doom is a couple of kilometres away from here. thought Gybes. And we're all doomed. I think. Maybe. Hopefully not.

His head was spinning. Things were changing, fast, and he didn't like the direction they were taking. Nothing much had actually happened, but he suspected that things were going to start happening shortly.

'I said, Where do we put the book?' said Chleosa for the second time. Gybes re-entered reality.

'Right here,' came a voice from behind them, before he had a chance to answer.

‘Sir Fawning!’

‘Yes, I’m back already. My friend was out, I’m afraid to say. Was the book good?’

‘Er, yeah,’ said Fiddles hurriedly. ‘Yeah, great. Here you are. Thanks.’

‘Always a pleasure to help someone,’ said Sir Fawning, steering his horse away to the north.’

‘Well, that’s settled, then,’ said Gybes, trying to think of things Fiddles’ way. ‘Lunch time! Does anyone want an apple?’

‘No thanks, Wizz,’ said Fiddles. ‘I’m sick of apples.’

Chapter 13
Mabé-Mabé

The wind gently rustled the leaves of the akaria trees as Synley Jenkis Krybald Inkwell led a group of riders, now only eleven strong, across the extensive savannah. Peaceful gazelles grazed nonchalantly on the gradually yellowing grass, flicking their ears to rid them of mosquitoes and biting flies. Above them, a vulture circled, riding the wings of freedom on its never-ending search for carrion.

The Investigation Team was now at the fringe of the rocky centre of the Green Savannah. Today they were heading towards the small native settlement of D'neru – the village that had first alerted the presence of the alleged rebels to the Emperor.

They didn't know that they were being watched.

As the village drew near, Milson could see that it had walls of wood constructed around it, with a ditch dug around the outer perimeter to act as a second deterrent. Upon the top of the wooden wall there were wooden stakes pointing outwards, with barbed wire strung roughly around the top of them, like a deer fence. He wondered what they were so scared of, before realizing it was probably the same reason that they has been sent there.

'Remember, we are the guests,' Mr. Inkwell reminded everyone. 'They are the locals, and we should respect their authority – well, the Emperor doesn't, but that's beside the point. My point is, don't make fun of anyone, all right? Show them that we are a worthy race.'

'Races,' corrected Pom Thukru.

'It should be a jolly splendid occasion, meeting the natives, what!' exclaimed Jolwin Madsley. 'In Riso we always make everything a splendid occasion. All must be a jolly good show is what I say!'

The team arrived at the gates of the village. A tall, thin, dark-skinned man was standing behind the gate.

'What do you want here?' he asked in a quick voice, but not impolitely.

'We are the… investigators from Tuvak,' said Mr. Inkwell. 'We're here to discover the secret of the rebel base.'

'I'll tell the Chief,' said the guard 'He has been expecting you. He dashed off to what was presumably the chief's hut, a large, circular, mud-and-stick construction in the centre of the village. They could hear him speaking to someone inside the hut, probably the chief, thought Milson.

Moments later the guard re-appeared outside the hut and jogged up to them. 'The Chief tells you to come' he said, 'but leave your horses in the stables.' He pointed to a ramshackle building just inside the village.

The group followed the man to the stables and dismounted inside, before walking over to the Chief's hut and entering it warily, two by two. The hut was the second largest in the village and the walls were bedecked with hangings. There were three tables set around the edges, covered in pots and ornaments. The windows were fitted with curtains made of a fine material, and hanging from the roof were several chandeliers. But this wasn't what Milson noticed first.

What Milson noticed first was directly in front of him. The Chief was over two metres tall and about half a metre wide. He was bald and wore a white shawl and a wide grin.

'Welcome,' he boomed in a deep, resonant voice. 'You are here to see the dangerous men.' The statement erupted out of his mouth like a volcanic explosion.

'Er… yes, the rebels,' said Mr. Inkwell.

The Chief nodded to the visitors. 'I am Cudombaté,' he said. 'Many call me the big man, for I am the tallest in the surrounding ten villages.' He paused. 'You are the one they call "Inkh-huel"?'

'Very true,' said Mr. Inkwell. 'I am Synley Inkwell, and the men and women you see behind me are my team.'

'You are my honourable guests,' Cudombaté declared.

'That is very kind of you.' said Mr. Inkwell. 'There are less problems than I had perceived there would be. At least you speak our language.'

'We were forced to learn it when we were invaded.' said the Chief.

'Would you be kind enough to show us the rebel base?' asked Mr. Inkwell.

'We will show you,' Cudombaté promised Mr Inkwell in a way that left no doubt that he would not break it. 'But first, we must eat! You must be hungry. We will go to the big food hut. I am going to call all the men to the feast. Women are away at the next village right now, and so are the children.'

'Do you want a cup of tea?' asked a man to the right of Milson.

'Er, yes please,' said Milson, distracted from the discussion with the Chief.

'You will have a drink?' the man asked Doran.

'I'd like a cup of ordinary tea, please,' replied Doran.

'What do you mean, *ordinary*?'

'The tea with milk in it, not that herbal junk,' said Doran as though he thought the man should know better.

'We only have gégé tea,' said the man.

'For Aa's sake!' said Doran. 'Oh, I suppose I'll have plain water. Plain, that is. No additives, no rotting buffalo teeth…'

The man laughed and turned away to fetch the teas and, of course, one water.

Meanwhile, on the other side of the room, Mr. Inkwell had reached an agreement with Cudombaté, they would be taken to investigate the rebel base tomorrow, shortly after sunrise. They would, as the Chief insisted, have a meal immediately.

'The Chief has kindly offered to take us to his feast hall for the evening meal,' said Mr. Inkwell to the team. 'I am sure that you shall all be extremely polite, as we are *their* guests.'

Cudombaté stepped past them and began to make his way towards the largest hut in the village, situated on the far side. It was twelve or so metres in length and about seven wide. Above the doorway, an antelope's severed head hung motionless, long since dead and stuffed. Outside, the air was hot and full of intoxicating numbers of flies. The wind picked up and ruffled Milson's short hair, wrecking his neatly combed side parting. He looked at the building, the 'food hut', which seemed to be slowly crumbling.

'We definitely need to do some repairs on this hut!' said Cudombaté in his loud, deep voice.

Inside the hut, the walls were in much better condition than they were on the exterior. Like the walls inside Cudombaté's hut, they were decorated with vibrant hangings of men hunting antelope and crocodiles. One scene seemed to depict someone extracting a buffalo's tooth, dropping into a bowl of water and watching it decompose. The hut was full of other interesting items such as drums, spears, miscellaneous clothes piled up along the side and boxes of what looked like dried meat. A long table was set in the centre, surrounded by stools. On the rough, wooden table three stone platters held vast amounts of food for the meal.

'You will eat good food here,' said Cudombaté. He walked slowly to the head of the table and sat down. The rest of the team took seats around the edge of the table, which was soon packed with other villagers.

After a short time, several people holding trays of the gégé tea came through the door and supplied everyone (apart from Doran) with the hot drink. Finally, one man carrying Doran's glass of buffalo-free water appeared and placed it on the table. Doran looked embarrassed at having caused an inconvenience and apologised, but the man grinned and said he was happy to provide people with a choice. He added that he was glad that Doran hadn't chosen the drink with the rotting tooth in it, because it took weeks to make.

Several men began to dish out food. There was a fabulous array of dishes: fish, meat, vegetables, rice – anything that could be found or grown nearby.

'It's a rather splendid occasion!' said Jolwin Madsley. 'Splendid indeed! Does anyone want some sprouts?'

‘No fanks,’ said Milson with a full mouth. The food was very filling, but Milson managed to eat everything on his plate. After everyone had finished eating and were pleasantly chatting to each other, Cudombate called out ‘We will go to the outside fire now and play music.’ No one was speaking quietly, but everyone heard his voice, because theirs were, comparatively, whispers. The villagers and visitors followed him outside, and sat themselves around a fire that one of the men had started. Declaring that he was too tired, Milson went to the Investigation Team’s accommodation, which had been allocated at the back of the village.

Milson walked through the door of the hut with the rest of the team – they were all tired too – and chose a bed on the far side of the hut. He climbed inside the sleeping bag on the bedroll and quickly fell to sleep.

*

Next morning, Cudombaté promised at breakfast that he would take Mr. Inkwell and his team to the place where the rebels had been sighted. Shortly afterwards, they were on their way to the place, in a group including ten or so of the villagers and the rest of the Investigation Team. Cudombaté strode forward at the front, much faster than the rest. After him came the villagers, carrying spears and provisions. The majority of them had joined the trip to defend the team and their Chief. Behind tailed the research team, who were carrying basic provisions for their trip – first aid and food for lunch.

‘Do you think there really are rebels here?’ asked Sashlea.

‘Cudombondy seems to think there are,’ said Milson.

‘*Cudombaté*,’ corrected Doran.

‘Whatever,’ said Milson. ‘As I was saying, it would seem a bit stupid to bring us all the way here for nothing, wouldn’t it.’

‘Perhaps they were mistaken,’ said Conrad Madley, the cook. ‘I’ve heard they can be quite jumpy when they see people they don’t expect to. They might have seen someone on holiday.’

‘On holiday? In this part of the savannah?’ said Sashlea. ‘This isn’t exactly a tourist spot. And would someone come here – this is the middle of nowhere! Anyway, how could anyone mistake a tourist for a terrorist?’

‘Perhaps an explorer,’ said Conrad, becoming less sure of his theory.

‘There wouldn’t be any explorers here,’ said Jolwin Madsley. ‘That’s the whole bally point! This *is* nowhere.’

‘It’s somewhere,’ said Pom Thukru. ‘Actually I think it’s very nice. How you say… scenic.’

‘Much peace of mind can be found here,’ said Ani Buhrokk. ‘Meditation is a key part of Eastwood life.’

'Maybe they only saw an animal,' continued Conrad, now almost certain that his theory had no hope of going anywhere.

'I jolly hope not,' exclaimed Jolwin. 'Don't tell me we came all this way just to see an animal!'

At the front, Cudombaté addressed the team and the villagers. 'It not far now,' he said. 'We'll get there in about ten minutes. We call the place "Mabé-mabé" – probably the equivalent "boom-boom" in your language.'

Up ahead, Milson could see a rocky mound surrounded by a large, flat area of savannah, unusual for this hilly part of the land. So far, they had walked up the hill from the village and then down a short way further. After that it had been flat, dotted with clumps of trees and the occasional boulder. One old tree grew atop the mound, gnarled and twisted with age. Beside it sat a boulder, larger than the other small rocks that surrounded it.

'We will stop now,' said Cudombaté, sitting on the ground. 'And I will tell you what we saw when…'

There was a noise behind him that made him turn around and listen. Suddenly, something small and round, about the size of a pebble and blue jumped out from behind the rock on top of the mound. It landed and hissed at them.

'What is that?' said Doran. 'Funny animal. Why's it still hissing like that? How long can it hold its breath?'

'Dunno,' said Milson, as the hissing grew louder.

'HIDE! QUICK!' yelled Valisar Uma suddenly.

'Eh?'

Mr Inkwell deliberately fell off the grassy bank he was sitting on onto dirt, hiding behind it.

'IT'S GOING TO BLOW UP! HIDE!' roared Valisar Umu, hiding alongside Mr. Inkwell.

'Blow up?' said Doran. He shrugged and hid behind the bank, along with everyone else.

'Any moment,' said Valisar.

BOOM!

The grenade had exploded, and Milson realised that, had he stayed where he had been, he would have been in various places by now.

Slowly and cautiously they crept around to where they had been and looked around. There was a small crater on the ground, and the grass was burnt within a radius of ten metres. They didn't notice the rock slide back into place on top of the mound.

'How did you know it was going to do that?' Doran asked Uma. 'I've never heard of a small, blue animal which hisses and explodes!'

'It's not an animal,' said Valisar. 'It's man made. I think it's called a bomb. They use the same substance that's in fireworks, and it, well, explodes, killing anyone in its immediate vicinity.

'I thought they used starfish dust for fireworks,' said Conrad.

'Starfish dust!' said Milson. ''Pon my word, 'tis but a children's tale, m'dear fellow!'

'But how did these rebels invent such a terrible thing?' wondered Mr. Inkwell.

'No idea,' said Milson. 'Let's get back to the village for lunch. It's not safe here.'

'Wait a minute,' said Mr. Inkwell. 'Am I in charge here, or you?'

'Sorry sir,' said Milson. 'I suppose it's your choice.'

'It is indeed. I vote that we stay on here, although if the majority want to go back…'

The majority did. They hastily returned to the village, where Cudombaté promised them that they would have a most satisfying meal as compensation, as both Taka Rujeketa and Sampané Buhrokk were still slightly in shock.

At least they now knew enough to tell the Emperor that yes: rebels did exist – at the place that the locals called 'Mabé-mabé'.

*

Milson awoke in the night, and at first he didn't know why he had. But then he began to hear sounds; explosions, yells and ear splitting bangs from outside. As his eyes adjusted to the light, he saw Doran standing beside his bed. Milson was puzzled. Why would Doran wake him at this time?

'What is it,' said Milson, sitting up in bed as a scream came from outside, followed by several more bangs and an alarming explosion.

'Milson!' shouted Doran urgently. 'Milson! The rebels are attacking!'

Chapter 14
The Prediction

It was Chauday, and Gybes Fiddles and Chleosa were visiting Hillside Riverton. Approximately two thousand people from the surrounding area had congregated for this once-a-year gathering in the large open area on the south side of the village. This was the 'Other Tsabian Festival', as it was often referred to as. It happened in many places all over Tsabia, always on Potiton the 13th.

Many children had gathered in a game-playing area on the edge of the forest, walled off by a few ropes. There were almost thirty in all, including not only Gybes and his two best friends, but also Trudge and Mystica. Everyone was sat on the dry ground, observing a short, balding, man in a green poncho, who seemed to be in charge. He was sitting on a bench, his backdrop the rainforest.

'Gather round, children,' he said, before realising that they already had. He donned his glasses.

'I am in charge of you for this morning of game playing, where we shall play several different Tsabian games before the morning is done. We shall begin, if there are no objections, with make-a-meal.'

'Why, how uninventive!' complained a boy at the back who, to Gybes, resembled an educated gerbil. 'Could not we alter the schedule?'

'I'm afraid the schedule is firmly set, son,' said the man wearing the green poncho.

'Then I'm afraid I'm inclined to play no part in this,' said the boy. He stood up and departed, nose skywards.

Make-a-meal was an 'educational' game for two or upwards players, but was best done in a large group, although it was quite unpopular. You were required to run around in the forest, (but not aimlessly) searching for and collecting different types of food; fruit, nuts, roots, mushrooms; anything edible. After half an hour, you had to return with your load, and you then had another half an hour to live up to the title of the game. The person who produced the best meal was deemed the winner.

The man in the green poncho told them that the winner would receive a luxury bar of chocolate, which was rare in Greenworld, as only one company made it, and they were based in Tuvak. Once the meals were cooked, you were allowed to eat it, provided it was suitable for consumption.[1]

'Are we ready?' asked the man, once everyone knew what they were doing. 'Yes? Well, get ready; I'm timing you. Ready, steady… GO!'

---

[1] Minimum requirement: edible.

Gybes ran into the forest followed by Chleosa and Kicker. He knew he would have to split away from them in order to remain in the competition, because Kicker would undoubtedly assault Gybes once they were out of sight of the town. He continued along the same path as Chleosa for a short time, but stopped shortly, noticing some nuts that she hadn't, and collected them.

A little further he came across some edible leaves and a tree with several fruits hanging low enough for him to pluck. He picked them and placed them delicately in the bag alongside the leaves and nuts. Noticing some tree mushrooms on the back of the next tree, he added them to his trove.

Although the sun did not reach Gybes as he searched for reptile eggs in the undergrowth, he knew it was a very hot, dry, sunny day. The fruit was, however, still ripe, and the mushrooms were also suitable for eating, or he hoped they were. It was overdue for bird eggs, but some reptiles still had nests of reasonably good eggs. Finally Gybes came across some unguarded snake eggs and very carefully added them to his bag.

Soon time was up and Gybes returned to the village, narrowly avoiding having his collection stolen by Skidder, Kicker's sidekick. The others were already gathered in a semicircle around the man in the green poncho, who was inspecting everyone's impressive and not so brilliant finds.

'Well, young sir,' he was saying to Alfid. 'You've got a very good collection of food here.'

'Cut the talk,' said Alfid arrogantly. 'Just say I've won, or I'll… I'll make you… hurt, I will.'

'Now, calm down, young Master. I'm sure that after a short period of cooking this food will…'

'Hell! Are you gonna say we've gotta *cook*? That's what stupid girlies do, and, like, nerds and stuff, y' old git!' He swore loudly at the man, who immediately disqualified him for intolerable behaviour. To everyone's surprise, and to some people's amusement, Alfid spat at the man's face. As he stormed away, several of the local children attempted to hold him back, but Alfid, in a mad rage, punched one of them in the face, who fell to the floor, clasping his nose. Sensing the commotion, the Tsabian Searchers, who were guards-come-secret-agents-come-police, came over to the scene and restrained Alfid.

'Sorry about that,' said the Chief Searcher. 'He's a bit of a delinquent – his dad's an alcoholic because his wife was presumed dead, and he didn't bring up his son properly. You see that's why his mother killed herself, when she came back and found both her husband and son in the state they are, which just made the situation worse, of course.'

'I am not a delinquent!' roared Alfid in protest. 'I 'ate my dad! I'd kill 'im if I 'ad the chance!'

Ignoring his yells, the Searchers took him away to a corner of the village, where they attempted to converse with him.

The man in the green poncho continued to look at the children's collections of food. When Asila came out, the girl whom Fiddles fancied, he followed her as if he were an entranced dog.

'What are you *doing*?' said Gybes incredulously.

Fiddles turned to see Gybes and Chleosa laughing along with most of the other children.

'What *was* I doing?' he asked innocently.

'You were following Asila out!'

'Oh!'

Asila gave him a 'you-don't-deserve-me-and-you-know-it-but-I-want-you-to-carry-on-because-it's-funny-and-good-for-my-popularilty' look, or at least that was how Gybes interpreted it.

When it came to his turn, he walked out to the man and showed him his bag.

'Very good,' was the immediate reply. 'And what's your name, young master?'

'I'm Gybes, or Wizz' said Gybes. 'Wizz is my nickname. All my friends call me by it.'

'Well, I'd say that's rather good, Gybes. We'll see what you can make of it.'

Trudge's bag contained a lot of mud. His appearance was noticeably different from the other children in that he had only one trouser leg and his shirt was ripped, revealing part of his large stomach. His bare leg was plastered with mud, and his face was filthy.

'Ah!' exclaimed the man in the green poncho.

'Er…'

'Well?'

'I sort of slipped. I sort of, kind of, y'know, fell in the mud…'

'Ah. Well… we'll see what you can make of it all the same. Woodlouse pie?' The man laughed.

'I'll stick to the old mud cakes, thanks,' said Trudge, his sleeve falling to the floor as he wandered off.

The man stood up and addressed them. 'Now let us see what we can make of our *fabulous* collections. I see that most of us have attained food sufficient to cook a meal. I, Laberius Piksim shall judge your masterpieces. This game is especially good for learning how to cook well, and I hope you all enjoy it. Good luck!'

Trudge stared dejectedly into his bag and looked longingly at everyone else making their meals out of a wide variety of forest foods. Gybes began to make a mushroom stew with the tree mushrooms he had picked. Everyone had a small fire with an assortment of pots to choose from. Gybes picked the smallest cauldron-shaped pot and placed it on the flames with some water with which everyone had been provided. After a short time, he had cooked what could pass as mushroom stew.

He took the pan off the heat and cut the fruit up into bite-sized portions. He placed them in a ring around a shallow bowl. He poured the stew into the middle and placed it aside.

Moments later Laberius announced that their time was up, and came to inspect everyone's meals, including Trudge's respectable mud cakes.

'I shall now decide who is the winner of this game, and they will receive the bar of chocolate, imported all the way from Tuvak,' he declared. 'It's worth ten goni! Who here has enough money for this?' Two people put their hands up. 'See?' said Laberius. 'Not many.'

After a short while he stood up and announced the winner. 'Dagtan Unthies of Lavos village!'

Fiddles didn't care that Laberius had said his real name. He rushed up to collect his prize, managing a stuttered 'thanks.'

Everyone clapped, including Asila, although it was obvious that she was not very enthusiastic. Gybes saw him stare at her, and she gave him the 'you-don't-deserve…' look again. He shrunk into the safe refuge of the crowd of children, hoping that he was inconspicuous.

'So,' said Laberius, 'we have all made our meals, and fairly and justly the prize has gone to master Dagtan, "Fiddles" as you know him. So now we will continue with the games. The next one,' he said, staring around at everyone, 'is an international sports game. Can anyone guess what it is?'

A girl's hand shot into the air immediately.

'Yes, young miss?'

'Kickball, sir.'

'I am sorry,' said Laberius, 'but we do not have adequate facilities for kickball. The game is actually rockthrow. And can anyone tell me who the world champion is?'

'Is that 'im wot's called Mister Noddy?' said a young boy with a Wesport accent.

'Yes. Can anyone tell me his real name?'

No one put their hand up.

'No?' said Laberius. 'Well, his name is…'

'Snozčeskow Çeskowice,' said the boy who had left earlier, walking past at a distance and throwing the name away as though it was an everyday saying that five-year-olds were familiar with.

'Well done!' exclaimed Mr. Piksim. 'Would you like to rejoin us?'

'I have more profitable ways to occupy my time,' replied the boy, his nose as upturned as ever.

Everyone made small noises of bewilderment at the rockthrow champion's name, apart from a boy with glasses and parted hair, who muttered, 'I *knew* that' in a distinct accent Gybes recognised as one from the Dûrglav Basin.

'Well, we'll begin the game anyway,' he said.

After several games of rockthrow, and a game of hide in the jungle it was time for lunch, and everyone headed off to the various portable food stands, some eating their own creations. Gybes, Fiddles and Chleosa headed off to find some kind of attraction while they were eating Fiddles' food, which he had cooked, and afterwards, his bar of chocolate, which he kindly shared.

'Let's not go back for the afternoon's games,' said Fiddles. 'I want to see what's going on elsewhere.'

Gybes and Chleosa agreed with Fiddles, and they mingled with the other people, meandering around and observing the various happenings going on around them. At one point, they saw Alfid struggling against six Searchers, one of them saying: 'You really *are* in trouble now!'

The afternoon drew on, and soon became evening. The other children, including Trudge, came out of the games area and filtered through the crowd. Gybes, Fiddles, Chleosa and Trudge sat together for the evening meal, and when they had finished, they looked for entertainment of some kind. As it began to grow dark they headed towards the southern end of Hillside Riverton, where there was apparently going to be a musical performance.

They arrived in a large, open, grassy area, to find that it was very crowded. There was a stage erected at the back, where musicians were doing sound checks on the new, magical instrument called the rock ghittar, a magical lowsound or bass ghittar and a 'kit-of-drums'. Gybes was sure he recognized one of them, and a bunch of long-haired, drunken, pointing men certainly did, as well as a group of screaming girls.

A young man stood up from a bench of VIPs and began to speak.

'I am very grateful to all of you who have turned up at this annual gathering. Today I have the honour of presenting to you the most popular band in the whole of Greenworld, playing in their hometown for the first time ever! Yes it *really is* them! Ladies and Gentlemen, please give it up for… The Catapults!'

The crowd broke into tumultuous applause and the band waved and gave everyone the thumbs-up. The lead singer, who had long, dark hair, stood up in front of the 'Phony Mike' and introduced himself.

'Yo, dudes and dudesses,' he said, his voice booming incredibly loudly out of Gesirasiretraphones, or 'getty-louder-thingys' as most people called them, large, black boxes stacked to either side of the stage. 'My name is Down Dude Bob, and I'm lead singer of the most up-to-date, sophisticated and advanced band in the whole world, The Catapults! Ain't that right Brigg?'

'Baddest band you'll ever find, Bob!' agreed a man at the back.

'Are we the most totally cool, wicked and far out band in the world?' Bob asked the crowd.

'Yes!' came the chorus. There was a pause, punctuated by screams.

'Right on!'

Down Dude Bob struck a powerful, distorted chord on his ghittar, which resounded around the clearing. 'Last week, someone gave us the chance to play in Goodport for the festival, but instead we came back to our own town to celebrate with *you*!' Everyone cheered and Bob started the first song.

'Onetwothreefour!'

The music blasted out over everyone, cheering some people up and astounding others, while Bob half-sung, half-yelled the lyrics.

'I wonder why they call it "rock music",' wondered Gybes aloud.

'It sounds like rocks, I suppose.' said Fiddles.

'That's why they call those instruments rock ghittars,' said Chleosa.

'As long as you enjoy the music, it doesn't matter about technical details.' said Gybes.

'Some people are a bit daunted by it,' said Chleosa.

'Trudge is certainly enjoying it,' said Fiddles.

Trudge was dancing enthusiastically near the edge of the crowd, or more accurately, wobbling, while chewing a half-cooked sausage. His Mother was watching him closely.

'If you want to go to dancing lessons, I'll have them organized for you, Djok,' she said.

Trudge immediately spat out his sausage and stood still, refusing to dance. He looked at his Mother in an innocent way and wandered off on a quest to buy another sausage.

The music continued for most of the evening, until about eleven o'clock, when Down Dude Bob, Brigg 27, Bad Boy Billo and Jak the Snak bowed to an enormous and enthusiastic applause and excessive amounts of screaming and left the stage. A thin mist was beginning to form, and some people were leaving. Another VIP, a very old man with wispy hair, stood up from the bench and addressed everyone who was still around.

'Ladies and gentlemen,' he croaked. 'The penultimate event of this once-a-year festival is, as you may already know, the half an hour procession before midnight. Then, at midnight, a seer will tell of the fortune of Hillside Riverton and the surrounding area. The procession will begin in fifteen minutes, so please make yourselves comfortable.'

By the time Gybes, Fiddles, Chleosa, Trudge and Mystica had found somewhere to sit, it was time for the procession to begin. They watched as about sixty men and women, all dressed up in fancy costumes, paraded up and down in front of them, followed by a decorated serpent carried by ten or so men, weaving it's way amongst the crowd. Some were dressed as ancient tsabian gods, such as Tlalcloctl and Axlticac, and others as animals, famous people and a wide array of other popular figures. The time went very quickly, and after what seemed like only a few minutes, the procession suddenly stopped and parted. It was midnight, and the prediction was about to be made.

Through the parting in the procession's participants a woman walked, dressed in black cloth. She was quite plump, and appeared middle-aged. Gybes didn't need Fiddles to tell him who it was.

'Wizz! It's the Librarian!'

The fog grew thicker, and seemed to be concentrated around the Librarian.

'Now!' said the same man who had stood up before the procession, 'the Seer, Asgella Counír, will be telling of the future of our surrounding area in a moment. I will now retire and hand the evening to her.'

Asgella bowed to the crowd and began to speak. 'I am glad to be here tonight, as an important seers meeting in Goodport was postponed. I am therefore going to inform you of the futuristic properties of this area.'

She pulled a crystal-ball-like object out of her pocket and stared into it. She began speaking slowly, pausing between every sentence. 'The world is full of yellow,' she said. 'I see a great man – he has just won a prize. But now his heart is changing. He sees red. Now he is dead. No – he has three lives. He searches – searches but does not find. Now he sees it. He is close to it; dangerously close. I see now. There is darkness.'

She put the crystal ball away and addressed the crowd. 'I do not understand what I have seen,' she said. 'It is not relevant; so do not govern your lives by it. I am afraid it has nothing to do with his area at all.'

As she turned away, to marginal applause, another VIP, who seemed to be even older stood up and said, in a voice like gravel, 'It is now time for us all to leave. Thank you for attending, it was a wonderful day, and I would like to say especial thanks to The Catapults, Asgella Coonír, Laberius Piksim, the Chief Searcher, the Mayor of Hillside Riverton Jyle Gasney and all the participants of the procession. Good night.'

With that he turned and left the clearing. As everyone began to leave, a letterman came over to Gybes.

'You Gybes Marronon?' he asked.

'Yes,' replied Gybes.

'Letter for you,' said the man, handing him a scroll.

‘What is it?’ asked Fiddles as the man left.

‘Dunno,’ said Gybes.

‘Well open it then!’

Gybes opened the letter and stared at the first line, reading it over and over again to make sure he wasn’t seeing things. His jaw dropped.

‘What?’ said Chleosa inquisitively.

‘Congratulations,’ he read. ‘You have won a trip to L.C. Clark’s laboratory!’

Chapter 15
Empty

It was about ten in the morning, and a man on horseback was riding up to the gates of Tuvakmahan, the palace of Emperor Alu IV. The gates swung open gracefully as the two guards pulled ropes attached to them and the rider dismounted in front of the main door.

'What are you here for?' grunted a well-dressed guard.

'I would like an audience with the Emperor,' said the rider.

'Impossible!' replied the guard. 'He is currently engaged in a very important meeting, and under no circumstances whatsoever may he be disturbed!'

'This is more important,' said the rider. 'I have news of the rebels.'

'The rebels?' said the guard, surprised. 'Very well. Follow me.'

The rider followed the guard through the door into a hall, full of needlessly extravagant decorations: sculptures, engravings, animals' heads and rare artefacts. There were several doors leading off from the hall, all of them richly engraved with pictures of previous Emperors and ancient battle scenes. Directly ahead were double doors, leading through to the Emperor's Throne Room. The Emperor was sitting upon the throne, asleep, snoring quietly and absent-mindedly stroking his short, grey beard. Advisors flanked him.

The guard approached him. 'Your Majesty…'

'What is it?' the Emperor grunted.

'A man is here to see you about the rebels,' said the guard. 'I told him you were in a meeting.'

The Emperor jerked suddenly awake and stared expectantly at the man standing in his doorway.

'I have news of the rebels in the Green Savannah,' said the man, walking towards the throne. 'My name is Solomus, and I am the scout you sent out to follow the Research team, if you'll remember. They were attacked at the village of D'neru, and all of them were taken captive. Four men and two women were killed and the Chief was wounded.'

'I'll have an army sent immediately,' said the Emperor decisively. 'I shall see to it that they are destroyed.'

'Perhaps you would like to call a meeting…' began one of the Advisors.

'I know what I'm doing,' said the Emperor defensively.

Feeling no longer needed, Solomus turned and left the room, mounting his horse and then speeding off into the metropolis of Tuvak.

*

Sarmon looked ahead of him. There were dunes in the distance, and the smell of the sea wafted through the warm Tasean air. The land around him grew sandier as he walked purposefully towards them, money in his pockets from the horse he had sold. He hoped to catch a ship to Warfelt on the west coast of Tsabia from any port he could find.

He reached the dunes and ascended one of them towards a vantage point. The sand slipped underneath his feet, and the hot sun beat down on the tropical beach. He reached the summit and observed what was in front of him.

An expanse of water made up most of his view, and on the horizon he could see the long, unbroken, dark ribbon that was Tsabia. The sea was very calm, and there were a few fishing boats bobbing on the water not far from the shore. The beach however, was empty. It was wide and sandy, with several protruding rocks. An abandoned fishing net was lying in the mud at the very bottom of the beach, where small dark shapes, perhaps crabs, could be seen rushing to and from the sea. Far to the right Sarmon could see a coastal town, clinging to the side of a rocky peninsula jutting out into the Strait of Tsabia.

He began to walk along the top of the dunes towards the town, Gospruma as he remembered it being called, hoping to catch the first vessel that set out, perhaps the twelve o'clock ship, if there still was such a thing. The sand to either side slid away, and Sarmon found it hard to keep his balance. After about two miles, he realized how far away the town was. It was still about five miles, and it was nearly eleven o'clock. Even walking quickly, he would take till past twelve, and miss the ship. As far as he knew, as he had been there ten years ago, the next boat was at three o'clock. His only hope was that the timetables had changed. He didn't want to hang around when Tombhadi was on his tail.

He scrambled down to the right, away from the dunes and began to walk in a sheltered hollow, noticing a small abandoned shack in which he could shelter, as the wind was beginning to pick up. It was almost as though he *knew* he had to go into the shack... He entered the shelter, and before he knew it, the ground had fallen away beneath him.

He fell onto a hard stone floor along with a small amount of sand and saw a figure in front of him.

'Did you really think you could outwit me with my powers of wizardry, my dear Sarmon?' said Tombhadi.

*

Tents.

There was a sea of them. Most of them were cuboid in shape and green, with triangular prism roofs. Four hundred of them in all, and they were all made to accommodate ten soldiers. There was one in the very centre that was larger than the rest. It was red, and extremely conspicuous among the ocean of green. There was a noticeable, orange-coloured cloth door on one side, decorated with gold thread.

Inside the tent, Military Commander His Grace Sir Munsern Arnalson of Sector Nine of the Imperial Army of the Greenworld Empire was conversing with General Ki and General Haschmerchanti.

'I want the entire army surrounding the mound by noon,' he said. 'I'll make an announcement, and if they don't come out, we'll kill 'em all!'

The generals saluted and departed to organize the attack. Commander Arnalson sat back and took out his diary. He began to write in it when there was suddenly an explosion from outside. He jumped quickly up off his seat and rushed out of the tent.

'What the hell's going on?' he demanded the closest private.

'We're being attacked, sir!'

'By the whiskers of the Emperor!' yelled the Commander. 'But what was that explosion?'

'Some strange weapon, sir.'

Grumbling, the Commander got up and ran between the tents, stumbling slightly as he tripped on a tent peg. When he got to the scene the attackers were running off, and being pursued by about five hundred men.

'Call them back!' yelled Commander Arnalson to General Ki

'But sir…'

'Call them back!'

The men, hearing the call of their General, abruptly ceased their pursuit of the enemy and immediately headed back towards the camp.

'We will assault them immediately!' bellowed the Commander in a monstrous voice. 'And I mean *immediately*!'

As soon as he had said this, a relay of yells conducted the information to everyone in the camp. All the soldiers who had been involved in the retaliation headed back to their tents to get ready. They packed ropes, nets and grapples, and carried with them their weapons; swords, bows and arrows, shields and a few other essentials such as first aid and penknives.

They assembled just outside the camp, all four thousand of them, ready for battle. They were all of them wearing helmets and armour.

'Forward!' yelled Commander Arnalson. The men marched onwards in lines. The noise of them trudging was almost mechanical. The men moved as though they were robots, as though they were being controlled and regulated by some power other than their own brains. This was the legendary efficiency of The Imperial Army.

The mound could be seen drawing closer, something surprisingly conspicuous for a secret base. The soldiers didn't stop marching until they were at the very base of the mound.

It began to rain.

'Form a ring around the mound!' yelled Arnalson. The soldiers, as one, immense organism, obediently manoeuvred into a circular formation, ringing the small hill.

'I want exactly thirty-seven men to explore this mound!'

As soon as he had said this, about fifty men climbed the mound. Thirteen came back down the mound and the rest began to search it. Their inadequate footwear meant that they slipped on the rubble on the sides of the mound. At the very top of the mound was a single, withered tree. It seemed so old that, for all they knew, it could have been the oldest in the entire of the Green Savannah.

A man called Private Noggs bent down and felt it. 'Strange feel,' he said. 'But – what the…? Aa's soul! It's *plaster*!'

'By the whiskers of Zog!' shouted one of the recruits from Westport called Private Migton, running up and touching it. 'You're right! 'S plaster!'

Private Noggs knelt on a rock at the base of the fake tree.

It moved.

As soon as this happened Noggs jumped back in shock, accidentally knocking the rock completely out of place. An opening about the size of a manhole appeared. Fifty-degree steep steps led down from the hole into a dark room. Not much could be seen of the room beneath, although a desk was visible, with a flag stuck in a hole on the corner of it.

Both Generals sent twenty men in as a scout party. The forty units walked swiftly into the room beneath and half filled it up. To the left was a locked wooden door. There was no one to be seen.

The leader of the scouts commanded them to knock the door down. Three men with axes started violently to dismantle the entrance. As soon as there was a small hole a man stuck his hand through and unlocked the door.

The scout team burst in through the door into a wide hallway, about thirty metres long. As soon as they were through a door opened at the side and one suicidal man holding a blue grenade ran out.

BOOM!

Everyone in the army outside heard it.

'Forward Legion One!' shouted Arnalson.

About one hundred men shot up into the mound and poured inside and found a hole in the floor, half the scout team dead.

'What is this new devilry?' asked the Legunsa, the head of the one hundred men.

‘It is a “grenade”,’ said Private Jackerholds, who was an expert on weapons. ‘It was recently created in the Noscosi District in Myen to repel the Emperor’s army, but these rebels must have found the designs too.’

‘Look!’ said another Private, pointing to a flag on the wall. ‘The Zamin crest! It’s the symbol of Myen!’

‘These must be Myan rebels!’ exclaimed the Legunsa. ‘No wonder they knew about these explosives!’

They explored the rooms to the sides of the hall. The last room they came to was full of weapons: grenades, pistols and muskets. They were stacked up in piles in the corners – enough weapons to supply a small army.

‘Take one of the muskets each,’ said the Legunsa, once Jackerholds had explained to him what they were. ‘And the surviving scouts men take… *granddes*.’

‘Don’t hold it too long after pulling the pin out,’ warned Jackerholds.

Three men tried to burst through the next door with axes, but it was too strong.

‘How do we get into the next room?’ asked the Legunsa. ‘It seems impregnable!’

‘We could use the grenades, Sir,’ said Jackerholds.

‘Of course,’ muttered the Legunsa. ‘*I* shall use one. Stand back!’

He thrust a grenade at the door. As soon as it struck, it exploded and left a gaping hole in the door. Through it could be seen a large room, decorated with the same wall hangings as the hall that they were in.

As soon as the hole was made several men on the other side started firing muskets. The Imperial soldiers retaliated, and seven rebels fell dead. To the surprise of all present, there were only three left. They surrendered and sixteen men, including the Legunsa, walked through into the hall.

It was the banquet hall. A table stood in the middle, or at least, a table *was* in the middle, but it didn’t stand, because it had collapsed. The floor was stone, and the walls were dirt behind the hangings. There were no other doors leading off from the hall as far as any of the soldiers could see.

‘Get up against that wall,’ said the Legunsa to the three remaining rebels. ‘Who are you? Why are you rebelling?’

‘I ain’t tellin’ you nothin’,’ said the tallest of them. ‘It’s obvious why we’re rebelling! You’re trying to conquer Myen!’

‘We were in a group called…’ began the second rebel, who had a short beard.

‘Shut up!’ shouted the tall rebel.

‘It’s my choice if I die or not,’ said the second rebel.

'It's not your choice,' said the tall rebel. 'It's mine!' He took a pistol from his pocket and shot the bearded rebel in the chest, who fell to the floor lifeless.

The Legunsa immediately shot the tall rebel, who looked suspiciously like he was about to shoot the third. The final rebel had short, black hair and was relatively small. He backed against the wall, shaking with fear.

'You know that you face a long time in prison without trial for terrorism,' said the Legunsa. 'Under these circumstances, however, the penalty may be more severe. For instance: death. How does that sound, little man?'

'I ain't doin' no terrorism,' said the rebel. 'I'm just doin' me job. I'm jus' Lumbos the Guard. They promised me lots o' stuff, an' stuff! An' I didn't know they were really gonna be fightin' the Empire. Honest! I thought that they weren't stupid 'nough to try!'

'I can't trust you, Lumbos,' said the Legunsa. 'But if you tell me what this terrorist organisation is, then I'll free you from this sentence.'

'Very well,' said Lumbos. 'It's much, *much* more than you think! The name is 'Black Dragon' and it's led by…'

His sentence was cut short. A dart had hit him in the back and he stopped in mid-speech. He fell over sideways and hit the floor.

'Is he dead, sir?' asked the scout leader.

'I think not,' said the Legunsa, 'but if we do not quickly take him to medical help, he will die. Take some of these guns and grenades up, too. They may interest the Emperor.'

'Where on earth did this come from, sir?' asked Private Jackerholds, holding the dart that had been used to shoot Lumbos.

'No idea,' said the Legunsa. 'What I'm wondering is: who is the leader, and where is he? And where are the rest of the rebels? There *must* be more…' He shrugged and headed for the door, which was still smouldering. His men picked up some of the scattered weapons and began to follow him out of the hall.

Behind them, a crack in the wall closed with little noise.

Chapter 16
The Black Bridge

The walls and floor of Sarmon's small, underground chamber were rough stone; it appeared to be an artificial cave carved out of the rock. He sat on a rotting wooden bench in the corner of the cavern and wondered why Tombhadi hadn't killed him. It didn't make sense. The last time they had met, Tombhadi had been about to shoot Sarmon just before he escaped, but this time, he had been imprisoned for almost a week, and Tombhadi was still keeping him alive for apparently no reason. Sarmon knew he had been drawn into the trap, the shack, by Tombhadi's powers of magic, and he knew that Tombhadi was going to visit him privately this very evening.

His prison was a strange place. Sarmon had been led ten miles or so inland at night from the sea to higher grounds. The prison was built high up on a cliff; in fact it was *in* the very cliff itself, with a window to one side, invisible to anyone on the ground without the aid of a telescope. The only positive thing that could be said about it was that there was an excellent view, of the rolling hills, sparse forests and tropical grassland of Tasea. The grassland was almost devoid of settlement, and the closest road Sarmon knew about was ten miles away, where lay the coast. Behind Sarmon, although he could not see it, lay the beautiful and scenic Sespak Hills, which were composed of deep, forested valleys and steep meadows, with dizzying cliffs and rock faces. He was just wondering whether he'd ever get to see them, when he turned to the barred window to gaze longingly eastwards. He almost fell backwards with shock.

Someone was outside it.

*

Over the next few days, all that occupied Gybes' mind was the trip to L.C. Clark's laboratory. He, Fiddles and Chleosa had completely forgotten about the Librarian's prediction, and the root reading 'Te B'ardkos uoth Krethak' lay just as forgotten in Gybes' pocket.

Finally, the day of their departure came. It was Tsuday the 19th of Potiton. They were to be taken by cart to Goodport, where they would board a ship for a voyage to the northwestern headland of Tsabia, where L.C. Clark resided.

Gybes was helping his Mother with the washing outside their hut when he heard the slow trot of hooves and the trundle of wheels. As he peered around the corner of a nearby building, he saw a man standing beside a carriage drawn by two, fine horses. It was huge – fit for the Emperor himself – and was full of hangings. There were rolled-up curtains that could drop down as a protection from the wind. It had a flat, wooden roof, which was held up by four, sturdy corner poles.

'That's the man coming to collect you,' said Gybes' Mother. 'You'd better hurry. Have a great time!'

'I will!' said Gybes. He headed off, giving his Father a goodbye wave. Now to find Fiddles and Chleosa, he thought. He tried both their houses but he only found Chleosa's mother asleep, and Fiddles' Father getting ready for work. He swept half the village before finally found them playing rockthrow with Trudge, who had begun a diet three days ago and was trying to find other means of recreation aside from food.

'Fiddles, Chleosa, it's the man to get us!' he cried as he spotted them.

'Get us for what?' Fiddles.

'The trip to L.C. Clark's! It's that man over there in the red and blue top!' Gybes pointed

'It looks blue and yellow to me,' said Trudge.

'Maybe you need glasses,' said Fiddles, laughing. Gybes tried to imagine what Trudge would look like in glasses. It was almost disturbing.

'It says *Goodport City* on it,' said Fiddles.

'What's that?'

'Kickball team, I think,' said Chleosa.

'I support Sclodwell,' said Trudge.

'I support Aurawey UTD,' said Fiddles.

'Come on, let's go!' said Gybes. 'Who cares who supports who? We're about to embark on a journey of a lifetime!'

After saying goodbye, they headed over to the man, who was standing waiting for them with his hands in his pockets.

'Hey, you're that guy who sold us the paper,' said Gybes, noticing for the first time that it was the same short beard, straw-like hair and kickball top. He looked, he realised, like a younger, less-educated version of Sir Fawning.

''S right,' he said. 'Name's Liggo Napkin, innit, 'n I'm 'ere to transport you lot to good old Goodport, where you get a boat to the Laboratory.'

'L.C. Clark's?'

''S right. 'S an amazin' place. Hop in!'

Gybes Fiddles and Chleosa clambered into the luxurious cart and settled themselves on cushions in three corners.

'So, what's your usual job?' asked Gybes as the horses moved off.

'Well, I recently got a job in newspaper distributing,' said Liggo. 'Y' see, I got a degree in the study of Current Affairs at the Royal Institute for Social an' Political Matters in Tuvak. After goin' to the Royal Institute of Printers an' Publishers for a year I got a job in newspaper publishin' in Tuvak. But a couple o' months ago, they set up The Rural Distribution

Department in Tsabia, an' I'd been dreaming of goin' 'ere all me life, the rainforests an' all that, so I got a job for the Hillside Riverton area, an' here I am!'

'Intriguing,' said Fiddles dully. 'The Royal Institute for Social and Political Matters must be really *fascinating*.'

'Stop being sarcastic,' said Chleosa.

'As a matter of fact, I wasn't being sarcastic,' Fiddles lied coolly. 'I was expressing my… fascination.'

As trees and bushes passed by, the three friends searched the things they had packed and talked about the time ahead, wondering what sort of creatures L.C. Clark might have created, apart from the Mayothan.

'Maybe he'll have some kind of snake that can fly,' said Gybes.

'Maybe he'll have a flying pig,' said Fiddles. 'Then chocolate would be good for you and war would be right and peace would be wrong. And aliens would rule over the Emperor,' he said with a side-glance to Gybes. 'Like what you said someone said to someone once…'

'I was only joking,' said Gybes remembering the occasion. 'Aliens rule over Sonchād and Greenforest. It's mutants from the year three thousand that rule over…'

'I've heard that he's created this creature called a Crogphar.' interrupted Chleosa.

'What's it like?' asked Gybes.

'I don't know,' said Chleosa. 'I just saw it in the latest paper my Mother bought.'

'In Westport, my Uncle says they call Mothers *Mums* and Fathers *Dads*,' said Fiddles.

'Weird,' said Gybes.

'It's good for speaking quickly,' argued Fiddles. 'And it's easier for babies to learn.'

'What do they call children?' Gybes asked.

'Kids.'

'What? Baby *goats*?'

As the minutes ticked by, the sun rose higher. They had turned off from the main road as they were talking, and were now on a smaller, single-track road with passing places. They were taking this road as a shortcut to Goodport, via the Tudian Gorge, which Liggo said they would reach at about four o'clock.

They came across a small forest clearing, containing a large pond and scattered palms. They hopped out and walked to the edge of the lake, where they sat beneath one of the palm trees to eat their lunch.

'When do you think we'll reach Goodport?' Gybes asked Liggo.

''Bout eight o'clock,' said Liggo. 'Still seven hours or so to go yet. 'S a long way to Goodport.'

'I bet the Tudian Gorge is *cool,*' said Fiddles. 'I've never seen it before, but my Mother says the crossing's really scary, but I think that's just her. My Father says it's "totally wicked".'

Soon they were off again, trundling along at a reasonable speed. They were travelling downhill now, after going up a shallow slope for the last few miles. The ferns on either side brushed the cart, and there were fewer and fewer passing places, but they met no one coming the opposite way and they came to no settlements, save the occasional hut or two. None of the wildlife was scared of them, as most of the wild animals were not used to many humans. A cheeky monkey even leapt in and fled with the last of the sandwiches. The scenery of the forest grew more and more colourful, and the trees were bedecked with blooming vines. The ground alongside the track was carpeted with brightly coloured flowers visited by vivid butterflies and beetles, and alarmingly large bees.

'How far is it to the gorge?' asked Gybes.

'Cor, s'ages yet,' said Liggo. 'We's on'y been goin' for 'alf an hour. We'll reach the River Tudian soon.

Sure enough, not five minutes after Gybes had asked, they came to a thin, fast-flowing river. There were many sets of rapids as they continued, and several times the river passed over small waterfalls.

After nearly two hours of travelling down the river valley, they came to a small gate in a high fence where an old, battered sign read 'Native Reservation 06 – Tsabian District Council Restriction Zone – Please Close The Gate.'

'Why do they need to keep Natives in places like this?' asked Chleosa.

'Dunno,' said Liggo. 'They don't *need* to. Them natives should 'ave their freedom if y'ask me.'

They travelled for a couple of hundred metres and came to the small settlement. This was a native Tsabian village, on the edge of the river Tudian. The natives wore a fabulous array of colourful clothes and sported elaborate hairdos. Some women were cooking while one, who Gybes presumed was the chief's wife, was watching over them. She spotted Liggo and walked over to the carriage.

'Where do you go, travellers?' she asked.

'We're on our way to Goodport,' said Liggo.

She smiled. 'Would you like to stay and eat, or are you in a hurry?'

'No thanks, we've had our lunch.'

'Very well. Not many people come this way and we rarely leave – we're rarely allowed to.'

'Well thank you for offering us food,' said Liggo, 'but we'd better be on our way now.' He took the horses' reigns and they began to move forward. Several villagers looked up and waved. Gybes waved back, and was joined by first Chleosa and then Fiddles.

They continued down the road, and the River Tudian grew faster and faster, rushing over rapids and waterfalls. They were going downhill slowly, following the river's path. Not long after they had left the village, Gybes heard a roaring sound from ahead.

'Is that the waterfall?' he asked.

'Yeah, 's right,' said Liggo. 'Goes straight down into the gorge, it does. Never seen it before though, mate. It's said to be the biggest spectacle in the 'ole of Tsabia.'

They rounded a corner and Gybes saw what Liggo meant. It was the most dramatic sight Gybes had ever seen. It was not a rocky gorge as such, as it was as wide as it was tall, and the sides were covered in forest, but that wasn't what was so awesome. Gybes' eyes were immediately drawn to the waterfall, cascading over the edge of a cliff and plummeting two hundred metres to the bottom of the gorge, which was shrouded in billowing mist out of which a stunning rainbow grew. Gybes was speechless.

'Wow!' said Chleosa, awestruck.

'That is one hell of a sight,' said Fiddles.

The horse-drawn carriage continued along the top of the gorge and Gybes' eyes strayed from the waterfall to the river, rushing along the bottom of the gorge and glinting in the sunlight like a ribbon of silver rippling in the wind. They passed a flight of stone steps zigzagging down the slope to the river, where the Tsabian natives went to fish. Not long after they came to a bend, and turned it.

Ahead was a bridge. It wasn't a fancy bridge, and it certainly wasn't new. It was old and spindly, and only just looked wide enough for the carriage. It spanned the entire width of the gorge, a long, dark line against the green slopes.

'Tha's what them calls the Black Bridge, it is,' said Liggo. 'We's gotta be careful crossin' that 'un.'

Gybes considered asking if there had been many accidents, but decided against it.

It took a while to reach the bridge, as it was much farther away than it looked. When the path turned a final bend and met it, Gybes could see that it was wider than he had first thought, but no more stable.

'Now over you go, 'orsies,' said Liggo. The horses didn't move. It was obvious that they were petrified. 'Now, c'mon,' he said, more sternly this time. 'There's nuffink to be scared of.'

'Nuffin' to worry 'bout,' he said to the children. 'Jus' the 'orsies. They's scared, they is, 'coz the bridge ain't too safe lookin'. But it is safe, promise ya.'

'Er…' began Chleosa uncertainly. That was as far as she got. Fiddles bent down so that he couldn't see over the top of the carriage's sides.

Finally, Liggo managed to persuade the horses to move onwards. They stepped nervously onto the wooden bridge and walked slowly forwards. The bridge swayed slightly as they moved, and they slowed down cautiously.

Gybes closed his eyes. The bridge began to creak, and the horses neighed. After a few, terrifying seconds, Gybes opened his eyes. They were nearly at the other side. The suspense was incredible.

Suddenly he heard a cracking sound, and looked over the side. He watched in horror as one of the planks fell away and shattered on the rocks at the bottom of the gorge. Chleosa screamed, and Fiddles, as though it helped, ducked and covered himself with a cushion.

One of the horses' feet was stuck in the gap in the bridge, and it was struggling to get it out.

'Whatever you do, don' panic,' said Liggo, in a voice that Gybes was certain was full of it. 'The 'orse as jus' got 'is leg stuck in it. 'E's fine.'

Even though Liggo didn't sound too sure about this, he was right. The horse freed its leg, and both of them bolted to the opposite side.

'This is crazy,' said Fiddles, who, now that they were relatively safe, looked like he was enjoying it.

''S jus' the 'orses,' said Liggo, who was trying to slow them down. 'We're OK now.'

The horses ceased panicking and Gybes could see what was around him. The scenery had changed again, and the trees were taller and less colourful. The vines bore fewer flowers, but many insects, mostly flies, buzzed around the ferns and amongst the undergrowth. To the right, Gybes could see a hill range: the beginning of the Aurig Highlands, which were a small range of hills in the centre of eastern Tsabia. They reached another fence and gate, which Gybes presumed was the end of the reservation.

'How far is it to Goodport?' he asked, almost forgetting that they had come near – he didn't know how near – to plummeting to their deaths.

''Bout twenty kilometres,' said Liggo.

Gybes thought the situation through in his mind. Goodport was only about an hour away. Tomorrow, he, Fiddles, Chleosa, and the other winners would be on a voyage to L.C. Clark's Laboratory, where they would be discovering the amazing things the Professor was renowned for.

Gybes had no doubt about it. They were in for a very good time.

Chapter 17
Backalleys

'*You*!' exclaimed Sarmon in utter surprise.

'Me,' said his Brother. 'It's been a long time, Sarmon. At last I've found you.'

'But *how*, Bromon?'

'It was difficult. I will tell you later. But you must come quickly.' He spoke urgently. 'I am suspended on a rope attached to a peg stuck in the ground not far back from the cliff ledge, which we can climb up… hopefully. Come on, before your captors notice that we're here.'

'Who's "we"?' asked Sarmon as he helped Bromon to cut the metal bars on the window, and climbed out. There was a rope hanging down just beside him, with knots tied in it, which Bromon was climbing onto. He grasped the rope tightly and, without looking down, began the strenuous climb upwards.

'You'll see,' said Bromon.

Sarmon found it hard to keep his balance on the thin rope. He was a reasonably good rope-climber, but he still found the ascent extremely exhausting. He looked down, and wished he hadn't. The bottom of the cliff was about four hundred metres below him, and it looked so far away that it seemed like a different world. He looked up again and struggled up the last ten metres of rope to the ledge at the top of the precipice.

He crawled over the top and onto the safety of solid, grassy ground, and looked around. There was his sister, Eridia, and her boyfriend Tacius, both of them straining to stop the peg attached to the rope from flying out of the ground. They looked up, and gave relieved smiles as Sarmon stood unsteadily. He stumbled away from the cliff edge and embraced both his sister and brother. He shook hands with Tacius, who he had only met once. They exchanged brief greetings before Bromon took the situation under control.

'Now we must get out of this accursed place,' he said.

'You must have a long story,' said Sarmon. 'Why don't you tell me on our way? We should head towards the coast.'

'Only after you have told us yours,' said Bromon.

Sarmon gulped. He realised he dreaded telling them what he had done – how he had served Tombhadi. But, as he couldn't keep it a secret forever, he started talking.

*

It was the morning on which the ship to L.C. Clark's Laboratory was to leave, and Gybes, Fiddles and Chleosa were outside in the streets of Goodport with six other children on the trip. Mr. Dawnley, a gaunt-faced man with short black hair, was there to replace Mr. Inkwell, who had disappeared along with the other members of the Investigation Team at the rebel base. The ship was not to set sail until two o'clock, so he had kindly decided to show the winners around central Goodport.

They were in a part of Goodport that seemed to consist of old fashioned, ornate buildings and statues. The incredibly steep, rocky, forested Hill of Goodport was constantly watching over them as Mr. Dawnley showed the party of nine around the works of art.

'…And this is the statue of Sir Puckwather of Goodport, second Lord of the state of Tsabia, 1578-1643,' he was saying. 'He was assassinated at the age of sixty five by a man in a black cloak with a mask over his face.'

'Was that Baron Von Causmenhauter?' asked a pretty, black-haired girl.

'It is suspected that he was the culprit,' said Mr. Dawnley. 'Although some say that it was his brother, Baron Von Zechstein. Both were accidentally killed in the 1645 massacre after the battle of Doomba Alimbo.'

They moved on to a large, gold-painted statue that looked like a grossly overweight pig who just happened to be in the possession of a sword. 'This is Sir Sir Snofflington, the current Duke of Kappleham,' said Mr. Dawnley. 'He is the fourteenth Duke, following the fairly recent resignation of Sir Sir Fawning, whose son is currently applying for the position of Vice-duke of Goodport. Of course, the first Duke of Kappleham was S.S.S. Sir Sir Kappleham, who had the most knighthoods anyone has ever had in Greenworld, five.'

After what seemed like aeons, but by Gybes' timepiece was twenty minutes, they had finished looking at the statues. They began to wander the streets, for Mr. Dawnley had said, 'You can explore Goodport for a little yourself, as long as you can find your way to the docks by two o'clock, and at all costs, you must *not* enter into the Backalleys.'

*

It was awe-inspiring to see the Great Palace of Tuvakmahan in all its splendour against the orange, gold and pink of sunrise. The rising sun cast golden rays of light across the side of the Palace, causing it to look mystical and forbidding on the calm, clear day. The great spiralling tower was silhouetted against the lightening sky as, a ladder to the heavens.

As the sunlight spread out across the grass of the gardens, a handsome, stately man accompanied by two bodyguards strode up the path to the door of the Palace. The guard bowed to him and opened the door to admit him into the official residence of the Emperor. He walked swiftly down the entrance hall and knocked on the double oak doors leading to the Emperor's Throne Room.

It was opened by one of the Emperor's guards, who let the Ambassador walk in.

'What brings you here, Dakaras?' questioned the Emperor.

'This a full and detailed report of the incident at the rebel base, produced by the Royal Institute of Secrecy, Department of Information Concealment,' said the Ambassador, taking a piece of paper from his pocket and holding it up.

'Is there perhaps one especial piece of information you wish to inform me of?' asked the Emperor.

'As a matter of fact, there is,' said the Ambassador. 'I would advise you not to inform the public, as it is strictly confidential under the orders of the Institute.'

'And what is it that you wish to tell me?'

'We couldn't help noticing how easily the Rebels found the Team, and knew exactly how to attack them, and at what time they were least aware,' said the Ambassador. 'We came to the conclusion that there must have been an insider.'

*

Gybes, Fiddles and Chleosa were in a street a little away from the Statue Ground when they heard someone calling from behind. They turned to see the black-haired girl running up from behind them.

'Hey!' she shouted. 'Is it all right if I come with you three? Only I don't have any friends with me.'

'Yeah, you can come with us,' said Gybes.

'My name's Anassa,' she said. 'None of my friends wanted to come on the trip, so a couple of other boys came from near Aurawey came instead.'

'I'm Fiddles,' said Fiddles, 'and this is Wizz and Chleosa.

'What strange names you two have,' said Anassa. 'Are they nicknames?'

'Yeah,' said Gybes. 'Don't you have one?'

'No, we don't have them in Bayside,' said Anassa. 'The trend never got that far. What are your real names?'

'I'm Gybes, and this is…'

'DON'T SAY IT!' yelled Fiddles so suddenly that Anassa jumped backwards. 'I hate my real name. In fact I *detest* it.'

'OK… I'll just call you Fiddles,' said Anassa timidly.

‘You can call me Gybes if you want, though,’ said Gybes as they began to walk.
‘Wizz suits you way better,’ said Fiddles.
‘Why don’t we explore this way?’ said Chleosa, gesturing to a road leading uphill.
‘We’ve got maps,’ said Gybes. Mr Dawnley had given them to them earlier, as a precaution against getting lost.
‘So we do,’ said Fiddles, producing a small piece of paper from his pocket. ‘Except… this is a brochure advertising furniture.’
‘Well, I’ll be damned, so’s mine,’ said Gybes. ‘But Goodport’s not *that* big. We should be OK.’
‘As long as we don’t end up in the Backalleys,’ said Anassa. They began to make their way up the small, cobbled road that Chleosa had suggested. It went slowly uphill, bending slightly, amongst old shops and cafés. Most of the shops sold cheap, touristy items, and they tried to avoid those. Instead, they searched a few of the small jewellery and spiritual shops. One had an amazing bracelet that Chleosa longed for, but it cost nearly thirty goni, something only the daughter of an extremely rich man would acquire. Anassa, however, managed to buy a special necklace worth fifteen Goni.
‘Where d’you get all *that*?’ inquired Gybes.
‘My Father’s a professional rockthrower,’ Anassa explained. ‘He gives money to charity, too, and we’ve got a big house in South Bayside.’
‘I live in a hut,’ said Gybes. ‘But it’s nice,’ he added. ‘In my village, most of the buildings are mud-stick huts.’
They came a bend to the left, and Gybes saw a sign reading, ‘Welcome to South Wryley’.
‘Do you think we should go back?’ asked Fiddles. ‘We might be getting close to the Backalleys.’
‘Don’t worry,’ said Gybes. ‘If we see a sign which says “Back Alleys”, we’ll turn around and go back.’
‘I’m not sure there would be a sign,’ said Anassa. ‘Like Poortown in Tuvak. They don’t want you to know it’s there, so there aren’t any signs.
They continued down the road and turned left. Gybes saw a bar, and was about to suggest that they could go in for a sit down and a drink before he saw the sign which said ‘no under-18’s’. He turned his attention to the junction ahead, where he could see that they were about to meet a main road.
‘Let’s go left,’ said Chleosa. ‘I like the look of some of the streets down that way. They look… interesting. And I’m sure they’re not the Backalleys,’ she added.
‘Good idea,’ said Gybes. They turned left along a road, which, despite being wide and straight, was relatively empty. There were one or two

carts parked at the side, and a few horse-driven vehicles moving past them, but almost no pedestrians.

The road met another, and they turned left, to head back towards the sea. It began to slope downhill slightly, and, when Gybes looked up, he could practically see the whole east half of Goodport.

'Let's just go down here,' said Anassa, pointing to a sharp right turn. 'Just one last street. I've got a bit of money left, and there's some nice-looking shops down there.'

'Very well,' said Gybes. 'But you were the one who wanted to keep away from the Backalleys. And we need to be quick.'

'It's perfectly safe,' said Anassa, as they headed down the narrow street. 'As you said if we see a sign, we'll avoid it.'

'But you said…'

'They'll have a sign,' said Anassa.

They walked along road for a short distance, and turned a very sharp left along a street that was so narrow that it was like a kind of wide alley. There were lots of interesting shops to either side, but none of them were ones Anassa was interested in. The street turned slightly to the right, and something caught Gybes' eye.

It had caught Anassa's eye too. 'Let's have a quick look in that one,' she said. 'I like mystical things.'

'So do I,' agreed Gybes. 'Let's go in.'

It was called 'The Shaman', and Gybes could see that it was full of dream catchers and crystal balls. There were also a few gems and some strange looking rods, which were glowing blue. Gybes pushed open the door, and the four of them walked in.

It was a small shop, but it was crammed with all sorts of things. The smell of incense filled his nostrils as he looked around. To the left were the dream catchers, made with feathers and seashells dangling from them. The to the back of the shop, behind the counter, were the crystal balls. To the right were the gems and rods, and some strange stones that were black with green and orange lines, which seemed to swirl on the surface, like flailing whips or slithering snakes.

At the counter sat an old man. He had long, grey hair and a slender, shaven face. He wore three necklaces and was looking into a small polished screen on a stone, which had the same moving orange and green lines on it as the stones on the shelf. His skin was dark, and he looked to Gybes like a native of the North Steppe.

'What are these?' asked Gybes, holding one of the rods and feeling it's cold, smooth surface.

'Ah, you have a fine choice, young man,' said the man at the counter, taking the cylindrical object from Gybes. 'This is a Durioú rod. It glows red when danger is near, and yellow when someone close to you is dead.

If it glows green, then your goal is near, and orange means that there isn't a soul within a mile of you.'

'What about blue?' asked Gybes, noticing the current colour of the rod.

'That means that there's magic in the air. Purple means that there's even stronger magic around.'

Gybes decided to buy the rod. It was quite expensive: seven Goni, and nearly all the money he had with him, but he decided it was worth it. Chleosa bought a dream catcher, and Anassa, with the last of her money, bought a necklace with a tiny diamond set in it, which the man behind the counter said was made by the Nanachu tribe of the North Steppe.

They left the shop with significantly less money and headed back the way they had come. They turned onto the road and headed to the right, the way they had been going when Anassa had suggested they went down the smaller road.

'What's the time?' asked Fiddles.

'Half past twelve,' said Gybes, looking at his timepiece.

'We've still got an hour and a half,' said Chleosa. 'If we're later than that, we'll miss the boat, but we should probably head back now.'

Up ahead there was a large crowd, grouped around some kind of band. Gybes could see lots of people of all ages, and even two of the other boys on the trip.

'What's going on here?' asked Fiddles.

'I don't know,' said Anassa. 'Where's your bag, Gybes?'

Gybes rolled his eyes. 'Give it back,' he said.

'I didn't take it!'

'Then who…'

'Look!' shouted Chleosa. 'That man over there in the red jacket! He's got it!'

'Hey!' shouted Gybes, spotting a man nonchalantly walking away. 'That's my bag!' The man glanced back, open mouthed, and began running. Gybes sprinted after him. He could hear Fiddles, Chleosa and Anassa trying to keep up with him behind. The man was no faster than Gybes, but he wasn't gaining on him.

They turned a corner to the left and Gybes ran onto a long street, which bent out of sight to the right. The man was still running with the bag, though Gybes wondered why he didn't just drop it and escape without being found.

'Give that back!' panted Gybes. He hadn't noticed the sign that told him which part of Goodport he was now in. He had followed the thief right down the street, oblivious to anything other than the man he was chasing.

Gybes turned a bend to the left and saw the man run into a narrow street to the right. He followed him, and it bent to the left, and then to the left again. He saw the man standing at a dead end about ten metres ahead of him.

''Ere,' he said. 'You 'ave yer bag. 'S pointless me havin' it. Nothin' but a stupid shiny thing in it. But I bet you can't find yer way back to where you came from. You're in the Backalleys, mate.' He gave a high, maniacal laugh.

It was true. Gybes turned around to see the dark, cobbled, empty street, looking more sinister than ever. He turned around again.

'But what should I…' he began, but the man had gone.

Just at that moment, Anassa, followed by Fiddles and Chleosa, came running around the corner.

'You've got your bag then,' said Chleosa. 'But where are we?'

'We're in the Backalleys,' said Gybes.

Anassa and Fiddles both swore. It would have been comical if it had been the same word.

'Then let's *go*,' said Fiddles.

They turned back the way they had come, but Gybes stopped. He could hear laughter coming from ahead. 'Let's go the other way,' he said. 'There was a turning just there before the dead end, and it might lead out. I don't like the sound of that laughter. It sounds like drunken men.'

'At this time of day?' said Fiddles, as they walked swiftly back to where the turning was. 'Are you sure?'

'This is the Backalleys,' said Gybes. 'It's notorious. Anything could happen here.'

They turned under an archway into a separate street; slightly wider, but still overshadowed. It was cobbled, and small, alleys ran to either side. The air felt cool, and the light of the sun seemed dimmer. It was almost silent, apart from footfalls and the occasional yell or malicious laugh from one of the numerous side alleys. One man was standing at a stall selling what looked suspiciously like human hands, and Gybes thought he saw a man down one of the side alleys holding a knife. Many of the windows were smashed, and there were notices above the shop doors such as 'Dave's Drugs: Stuff To Take When You're Feeling Low' and 'John Barr's Knives'. One pub was called 'The Slaughterhouse', and another 'The Killing Spree'. What looked like a bundle of blankets lay on the cobbles below the wall, and Gybes would have taken it for granted had it not been that two feet were protruding from one end.

'I don't like the look of those side alleys,' said Chleosa. 'They're too dangerous looking. We've got to find a way out.'

'We've only got forty minutes!' said Anassa. 'It's twenty past one!'

'We'll have to take one of the side alleys,' said Gybes, staring at the wall not far ahead. 'The road ends. It's a *dead end*!'

They looked around for an empty alley, but all of them seemed to be occupied by people, shadows moving about in the dark. None of them seemed at all safe as exits.

'This alley looks empty,' said Fiddles. 'If we've got to *get the hell out of this place*, this is probably our last chance.'

They turned off on the alley to the left that Fiddles had suggested and began to creep along it, looking ahead cautiously and trying to make as little noise as possible. The dark alley consumed them as they walked deeper into it.

Gybes heard something to the left and stopped suddenly. 'Nothing,' he said, and they began to walk off again.

Suddenly, a burly man jumped out of a doorway and blocked their progress.

'We're just… passing th…'

'Hand over all your stuff,' he said in a husky voice.

'Try and get us!' said Fiddles.

'Just hand it in,' said Gybes seriously.

'You're not getting my stuff,' said Fiddles.

'Fiddles, *no*!'

The man grabbed Fiddles by the throat and threw him against the wall. Fiddles looked petrified.

'Give me everything you've got in that bag or I'll kill you,' he said.

'Leave him!' said Chleosa.

'Shut it!' yelled the man.

'Stay away from my friend!' said Gybes angrily.

'Little jerk,' said the man, advancing on Gybes. 'If you don't want him to die, it'll cost you all your things, and I want to at least beat 'im up!'

'No way!' said Gybes, backing away.

'Then I'll beat you up, an' if you die, 's your fault.' He raised his fist threateningly.

WHAM!

Suddenly something came rocketing out of the sky and into the narrow alley at a tremendous speed and hit the man on the stomach, bowling him over. Gybes hardly had time to come to terms with what had happened before he saw that it was a man wearing a blue cloak, with brown hair and a short beard. Someone he recognised.

And that wasn't all. He was sitting on a broomstick.

Chapter 18
The Blackfire

'*Porloke*!'

'Who?' said Fiddles. He looked up at the man on the broomstick. 'Who *are* you?'

'He's my Uncle!' said Gybes. 'He's a wizard!'

'Gybes!' exclaimed Porloke. 'What on earth are you doing in the Backalleys? Are you completely out of your mind? That guy could have killed you…' He sounded worried, but not angry, and after a few seconds of ominous silence, his face broke into a wide smile. 'Great to see you!' he said. 'Aa knows how lucky you are that I saw some trouble down here. I tell you, I was just on a leisurely cruise on this fine broomstick…'

'You're really a professional wizard?' questioned Anassa.

'That's right!' said Porloke. 'I trained at the Royal In…'

'Not *another* Royal Institute!' said Chleosa. 'How many are there?'

'My Father says there are three hundred and thirty-seven,' said Anassa. 'Are you part of the International Wizard's Union?'

'Sure,' said Porloke. 'But I believe that you have thirteen and a half minutes exactly to get to your ship.'

'My timepiece says we've still got half an hour,' said Anassa.

'Well it must be slow,' said Porloke. 'So, hop on!'

'What, *on the broomstick*?' said Fiddles.

'Sure! It's a five person one. Picked it up in the Wizards Supplies Mall in Riso. A fine specimen! Cost me, though.'

The four children clambered onto the broomstick behind Porloke; Chleosa at the front, then Fiddles, Anassa, and finally Gybes at the back. It shot off into the air, and Gybes nearly fell backwards. Anassa cried out as he had to grab onto her shoulders.

They soared out of he alley and up into the air nearly four hundred metres and as Porloke steered the broomstick near to the top of the Hill of Goodport, they saw the whole of Goodport laid out beneath them. To the left, it stretched a short way to its western edge, and to the right lay the eastern half: Wryley. The Backalleys were behind them, tucked away in a valley behind the hill. Ahead lay Central Goodport, and Gybes could see the sea spread out, a vast blue savannah of rippling blue grass. He could see a small sailing ship in the docks up ahead, almost ready to leave, and they spiralled down towards it, holding on to each other's shoulders like a conga line. They landed lightly just around the corner from the ship, in a thin, dull street, so that they would not be noticed.

'Well, goodbye,' said Porloke. 'Must be off. Can't miss the Wizard Union's Congregation. Hope to see you again at L.C. Clark's – I might be working there for him for a while.'

They bid him farewell, and walked out of the street on to the seafront. Up ahead was the ship, lying in the water of the dock. The sea was glittering in the sunlight, and there wasn't a cloud to be seen in the sky.

'Ah, there you are,' said Mr. Dawnley, spotting them from where he was standing at the end of the gangplank. 'I was wondering when you four would turn up. You certainly cut it very short. Come on, the Blackfire's about to leave!'

Gybes scrambled up the gangplank along with everyone else, and onto the deck of the ship.

'Cast off there!' yelled a man who looked like the Captain. He was middle-aged, and had short, greasy, brown hair and legs that ended in knee-high leather boots. The boat moved slowly out onto the sea as the ropes were rolled up on the deck, and Gybes looked out to the northwest. He could see a strip of land on the horizon, presumably the Tsabian Headland. On deck, the crewmembers were about their tasks and Mr. Dawnley was speaking to the Captain.

'Well, Wickerworth,' he said, 'when shall we be arriving on the east coast of the peninsula?'

'Maybe tomorrow morning, or a little later perhaps,' he said hurriedly in a voice that sounded like it could go all over the place. 'But, ah, you see, it depends…'

'Depends on what?'

'Well, you know what the weather's like,' he chuckled. 'Forecast's good, though. No rain until tomorrow afternoon, according to the meteorologists. It might even warm up, if it can get any hotter! But they say there is a storm brewing, out past Gonithea to the east, and it may be heading our way.'

'I've organised some carriages for our arrival,' said Mr. Dawnley. 'I was just checking they'd be there at the right time. A nice couple has agreed to keep them safe.'

'I've got a couple of chariots folded up in the hold,' said Wickerworth. 'I would be perfectly willing to lend them to you, if need be.'

'That's very kind of you,' said Mr. Dawnley. 'But I wouldn't want to cause any inconvenience.'

'It's none at all,' said Wickerworth. 'I'll have horses ready for you at the other end.'

'No, I've already organised transport, as I said,' said Mr. Dawnley. 'It would be confusing to try and reorganise.'

The other children; Poddy, Silver, Squidge, Lunger and Crack, were exploring the ship. Gybes, Fiddles, Chleosa and Anassa joined them.

'Bunkbeds!' yelled Squidge, who, despite his nickname, was quite thin.
'I get a top bunk!' said Silver, whose unusual hair was the derivation of her nickname.
'Lunch is ready!' yelled a sailor whom most people apparently referred to as Sandwich. Another sailor, whose nickname was Rabbit, showed the children to the Dining Room, where Mr. Dawnley sat alongside Wickerworth and eighteen members of crew. One old man had a wooden leg, and another, an eye patch. Once everyone was seated, (Gybes squeezed between Fiddles and Anassa on the wooden bench) Cookpot the Chef came in with the meal; salmon, pasta and green sprouts. Poddy wouldn't eat his, and Wickerworth added them to his plate. By this point – not for that reason – Gybes had come to the conclusion that the Captain was distinctly odd. He seemed strangely nervous for someone in a constant position of authority.
Afterwards, Wickerworth stood up and addressed everyone. 'Crew, guests,' he said, 'now we have set sail, we can experience the gusts of wind and white-crested waves of the sea. But I have a few rules that I wish to lay down.
'Firstly, I would be most grateful if you were to keep out of the way of the crew, especially in the corridors, where it is very hard for them to get around quickly if they are constantly being blocked. Secondly, I would advise you not to get in the way of the cook, he's got a very bad temper when he's disturbed.'
The cook chuckled and grinned. 'Right you are, sir,' he said. 'Don't mess with Cookpot, or that's where you'll be bound for!'
The Captain acknowledged the Cook's remark with a nervous smile and continued. 'Thirdly, I would be very grateful if you were too keep *away* from the hold. It is a matter of your… well, safety, really. I would not deprive you of the freedom to explore this ship, but please, *keep out of the hold*. That is all.'
Wickerworth picked up his goblet of wine and raised it in the air. 'I propose a toast to a thoroughly enjoyable voyage!' he said.

*

After lunch, Gybes ventured out onto the deck with Fiddles, Chleosa and Anassa. They sat on the side of the boat and watched the seagulls fly above them. Several dolphins swam beneath them alongside the boat, splashing in and out of the water. The sun was still shining brightly, and there were almost no clouds to be seen, only the tell tale wisps of cumulus along the coast of Eastwood, a couple of hundred miles to the north. The breeze was crisp and the sea a dark aquamarine. Small waves rebounded off the sides of the ship, and the white sails propelling it slowly over the rolling swells.

Gybes moved from where he was standing to make way for a member of crew who was on his way to do a job. He turned around and saw Mr. Dawnley speaking to Wickerworth by the cabin door.

'It's a wonderful day,' commented Mr. Dawnley.

'Certainly,' said Wickerworth, 'though if it carries on like this, we'll be for ever getting to the peninsula!' He made a fake laugh and darted a look sideways to the sea. Gybes thought he looked as though he was scanning the horizon.

The day wore on. Slowly the ship made its way across the sea, heading away from the coast at an angle, bound for the Tsabian headland. The sun was still shining, though lower in the sky. The wind had picked up now, and clouds were beginning to form on the eastern horizon.

At six o'clock a member of the crew came around giving out newspapers to those who wanted them.

'Shall we take one?' asked Anassa. 'They're free!'

'Good idea,' said Fiddles. 'We can find out the latest on the Tombhadi story.' He glanced sideways at Gybes.

Fiddles walked up to the man and asked for a paper. The man handed one over enthusiastically, thankful that someone had finally taken an interest. 'It's not often that people of your age are interested in what's going on in the world,' he said. 'They're not usually old enough to get paranoid.'

Fiddles brought back the paper to Gybes, Chleosa and Anassa and Gybes looked at the main headline. 'You were right, Fiddles,' he said. 'It's about Tombhadi.' He felt an odd sensation in his stomach, and realised he was worried.

Across the top of the front page, below 'Reporting Greenworld' were the words 'Tombhadi sighted by villagers?' Gybes began to read the article aloud.

Today, at eight o'clock in the morning, Vini Osacha of the village of Stombritum, in eastern Tasea, reported sighting the supposedly dead Tombhadi when fishing on a nearby stream. An exclusive interview was carried out to find out just what Vini supposedly saw. The translation is this:

'It was early in the morning and I was out fishing on the river with my new rod. From out of a patch of trees a rider emerged; a man dressed in a cloak with a strange-shaped weapon protruding from its pocket. I then saw several other riders, perhaps about fifteen, emerge from the bushes. They

were also wearing cloaks. At this point, I began to be wary, and I backed away from the river and hid behind a bush.

'All of a sudden, I heard one of them call him "Tombhadi". At first, I thought that this must be his nickname, but I couldn't help noticing that his face was almost completely covered in shadow, save for the tip of his chin, which I could only presume meant magic. Of course there are no available pictures of Tombhadi without the hood that keeps his face hidden. I could not understand it, as I was sure that I had read somewhere in a paper nearly five years ago that he had died. They were talking about something strange, and I distinctly remember the word "doom" being used. They also mentioned Tsabia, and something to do with going there. They then disappeared into a field of corn, and I saw no more of them.'

This story may be a hoax, but Vini Osacha sounded genuinely terrified when he first reported his tale, and two practical jokes, one from the Tuvak and another from Tasea a couple of hundred miles away seem unlikely. As a precaution, six galleys are being stationed along the coast of Tasea to patrol the waters, and thirteen Searchers are on his trail. Even if Tombhadi is alive now we are sure that he cannot possibly succeed in whatever he is attempting to do, despite whatever powers he may or may not hold.

Jakid Slemabot, 'Reporting Greenworld'.

'More nonsense!' said Fiddles abruptly, though he sounded less sure this time. 'It's as much nonsense as that legend about the Apple of Doom. And that's saying something!'

'It's no nonsense!' said Gybes. 'The legend is true. Otherwise why would they have bothered telling it?'

'And the root proves *that*,' said Chleosa.

'If I found a root in the forest, I might write my name on it,' said Fiddles.

Gybes nodded. 'Of course Fiddles. A man called The Apple of Doom *just happens* to be on a stroll through the Tsabian rainforest, and it suddenly decides to carve his name into a root. Now *that's* a likely story!'

'It might have been written *because* of the legend, as a practical joke,' countered Fiddles

'But the problem is, the Apple of Doom might have something to do with Tombhadi!' said Chleosa.

'I thought that *ages* ago,' said Gybes.

'Then why didn't you say?'

'I…' Gybes trailed off. He wasn't sure what to say. He hadn't wanted to cause anyone to worry? But that would just make it worse…

'Neither exist, as far as I'm concerned,' said Fiddles.

'Be reasonable: there *is* a chance,' said Chleosa

'Let's just lay it off, right?'

'The Apple of Doom is too close to us,' said Gybes. 'It could be a danger to us all. And it *does* exist.'

Fiddles didn't argue. He was gazing over the sea towards the distant eastern horizon. The clouds were drawing closer, a black mass hovering over Gonithea wondering whether or not to make Tsabia it's next stop. The birds were flying back towards the shore, or landing on the mast, and the dolphins had disappeared in search of fish elsewhere. A man was ringing the bell for dinner.

As they walked towards the dining room, Gybes looked at his timepiece. It was half past six. Only a couple of hours until the sunset, and plenty of time to still do things on the deck. The four friends made their way down the corridor to the dining room and walked in through the door.

Anassa spoke for the first time since before they had bought the paper.

'I wasn't really listening to your conversation, so I didn't understand much of it,' she said. 'I may have been mistaken, but did you mention the Apple of… *Doom*?'

Chapter 19
The Galleon

'What amazes me,' said Bromon, 'is how you fell for Tombhadi's tricks.'

'I know, I was very foolish,' said Sarmon, still surprised how horrified his brother wasn't. 'But he lured me in. He promised me a reward such as I had never seen. And I thought of how poor we had been, and thought it a wise thing to do. Risky yes, but at the time it almost seemed sensible. And he has magical powers beyond anyone I've ever known.'

Bromon didn't comment. Sarmon recounted Bromon's story again in his head: how he, Eridia and Tacius had noticed Sarmon's continuing absence, and questioned his friend Jakkio, who said he had gone with a suspicious stranger into the Green Savannah. They had followed his trail, and when Bromon found an article about a break-in in the southeast, they had suspected something. A local wizard had told them, at a high price, that he could sense Sarmon in eastern Tasea, and sent them in the right direction. He had told Bromon that there was a noticeable interference – which meant a great wizard – although he said that whoever it was had been cleverly disguised. Tombhadi's powers of magic were perhaps even greater than Sarmon had feared.

Last night, they had slept a couple of miles towards the sea from the cliff. Only now, walking with Bromon across the low hills and hillocks of Tasea, towards the sea, could he appreciate just how immense it was.

Eridia and Tacius had gone northeast to the nearest village, Gurum, where they hoped to find horses for the four of them. Soon the cliffs were three or four miles behind, and could be seen in the distance only as a thick brown-grey line. The brothers crossed a meadow to the right of a forest, on a hill that was gradually sloping upwards towards a grassy ridge.

They reached the crest of the hill, and Sarmon stared at the land in front of him. The land stretched out in smaller hillocks for the remaining six miles, right down to the ocean. He could see the dunes where he had been captured almost straight ahead, and slightly to the right there was a river valley, beautiful and grassy and radiant with light in the summer sun. A winding snake, the river, ran down the valley towards the sea, where there was a marsh and a bay. Where it met the bay, a headland jutted out to the right, rising to a rocky summit, higher than anything for a few miles around it. The left half of it, the north side, was covered in buildings, the port that Sarmon had been heading for. He could see several ships heading out from the bay; their sails fully out in the light breeze. Atop the hill was a large building that appeared to be a castle. Sarmon saw the road heading inland from the port and then bridging the river and winding northwards among the small hills like a tapeworm. Another road split off to the south and followed the coast past numerous resorts to the distant horizon.

'What an amazing view,' he said. 'Look – you can even see Tsabia in the distance. That green line over there, see?'

'That's our destination,' said Bromon. 'But what will we do when we get there?'

'Well, first of course we must try and stop Tombhadi,' said Sarmon, as they began to make their way down the hill. 'That is our primary goal. He will succeed if we don't warn them all.'

Bromon nodded his head solemnly and said, 'But why not stop him now? Why not warn the Taseans?'

'We need official help,' said Sarmon. 'And that is impossible outside the Empire – we have no passports.'

They reached the bottom of the hill and found that there was a track running along the base. To the right, it wound around a corner and disappeared behind a hill.

'It looks like it's heading for the sea,' said Bromon. 'We should be able to follow it and we'll end up at the port.'

They followed it for a short while, and it bent to the right and met a larger road. This must have been an expressway, as it was paved and there were signs. One pointed to the left and said; 'Gospruma 5'.

'That's where we need to head for,' said Sarmon.

'We are still only halfway to our goal,' said Bromon. 'And the sun is low. We might not get there until it is dark.'

'We may need to be under cover of darkness,' said Sarmon. 'They may have gates – and walls. And we look like common travellers. They probably won't let us in.'

'Worse, they might think we're spies,' said Bromon. 'I've heard they've got very strict laws about foreigners and passports and that kind of thing, so any foreigner who doesn't have one is potentially a spy or a terrorist. You can even get done for treason for not having one.'

'I would have thought spies *would* have passports,' said Sarmon. 'You'd think they'd be good at justice, Taseans, seeing as it's a whatsemy… democracy.'

'Tasean politicians are pretty empty-headed, when you get down to it,' said Bromon. 'Examine their brains and you'll find four sections: non-stop argument, irrational logic, self-interest and an empty space big enough to fit a clenched fist in.'

Just as he finished the sentence, Sarmon heard the sound of hoof beats. Looking back, he could see four horses galloping towards them, two of them ridden by people.

'It's Eridia and Tacius,' said Bromon.

‘Hello!’ greeted Tacius, as he halted his steed. ‘We found the best horses we could afford, and they’re pretty fast! We should be able to reach Gospruma by sundown easily – we could get there in fifteen minutes.’

‘Do we know when the last ship sails?’ asked Sarmon.

‘I asked at the stables, and the man reckoned the latest one was about eight o’clock.’

‘We should be able to find a ticket before sundown, then’ said Eridia.

‘Not without a passport,’ said Bromon. ‘They’ll think we’re up to something. We’ll have to stow away.’

Sarmon and his brother mounted the other two horses and they began to trot along the road. The trot soon became a gallop and they found themselves speeding along the cobbled expressway. They passed little other traffic, and they had the entire width of the road to themselves for most of the journey. They were travelling through grassy, farmed hills, with cottages dotted around the hillsides. The hills weren’t very tall, but the landscape was still quite steep in places.

After little more than a quarter of an hour, the town of Gospruma loomed ahead of them. Sarmon saw that the town had no gates, as he had feared, but was, in fact, completely open to any outsiders, which relieved him.

They entered Gospruma, and cantered along the cobbled street. It followed the coast of the peninsula, with the sea to their left. On the right there were lines of buildings, mostly old houses, some of them made out of wood. The others were stone, and mostly white-walled. They all had small back gardens, which went back to the next road, behind which was another row of houses. Sarmon noticed how many palm trees there were and hotels. They were everywhere. This was obviously a tourist resort, although the apparently lax security surprised him for a country with a justice system like the Tasean Court and Searchers more efficient than any others in Greenworld.

‘We’ve got a little time,’ said Eridia. ‘Why don’t we stop in a bar for a drink?’

‘Good idea,’ said Bromon. ‘Let’s try that white one on the right just there.’ He pointed to a large building to their right. ‘But we’d better be careful: I’ve heard they’ve got undercover Searchers who can ask foreigners to see their passports whenever they want.’

They stopped the horses and left them tied up outside the bar. A sign above it read ‘Da Seafront Bar’. The door was wide open, and they walked right in.

The atmosphere was somewhat smoky. The room was dimly lit, and somewhere in the back of the bar there were people dancing to music. They walked up to the bar.

'Ah,' said the barman, who was a large and dark skinned man in a colourful t-shirt with dreadlocks. 'What do you want?'

'Could I have a pint of... a pint of... whatever you sell here,' said Sarmon.

'I 'spect you'll like dis beer 'ere,' said the barman. 'It's called 'Big Momma'. Finest beer dere ever was, man.'

'Er... yeah,' said Sarmon. 'One of those. Sounds good.'

'I'll have one too,' said Bromon. 'What about you two?'

'I'll have a small glass of tequila,' said Tacius. 'What about you, Eridia?'

'Same for me, please,' she said.

'You from Tuvak, eh?' asked the barman.

'Arrow Downs,' said Sarmon. 'We're just...'

'On holiday,' finished Eridia.

'You like dis place?'

'We've only just arrived,' said Bromon. 'But yeah, nice place. Good music, too.'

'Nah, you is 'eard nothin' yet, man. Wait 'til you hear da ruggie.'

They walked away from the bar and sat down in the corner by the window, where the last of the sun shone in through the window onto them. Most of the other people were sitting at the back of the bar, where there was the music and dancing. There were ships out on the bay, mainly fishing boats, and a few couples, probably on honeymoons, were wandering the promenade, or sitting on wooden benches looking out over the sea.

'Nice place,' Bromon repeated. 'But we've got to be going. Come on.'

They went up to the bar and paid the barman for the drinks, and then left 'Da Seafront Bar'. The sun was on the horizon as they walked along the front street and the fishing boats were beginning to come in from the bay. They rounded the corner at the end of the peninsula, and there at the end of the town were the docks. The last building on the left was the ticket stall, but the four travelers avoided this, knowing that they needed to stow away on the last transport boat, and if they were asked for their passports, anything could happen.

Sarmon noticed the other vessels on the water. There were a few luxury boats owned by rich business-types and a few fishing boats. But what caught Sarmon's eye was the boat to the far right. It was large and it had large, hollow, black cylinders mounted on two wheels at the front. The sails were being hoisted and men were already beginning to get it ready for sail. Sarmon could tell it was a galleon, and there were archers aboard it. He still wasn't sure what the black things were, and it puzzled him why it would set to sea when there wasn't a war on.

‘That’s a galleon, but what’s that black thing?’ wondered Eridia, echoing Sarmon’s thoughts.

‘I think it’s a cannon,’ said Tacius. ‘They use gunpowder. Same stuff that’s in fireworks.’

‘For destructive purpose?’ said Sarmon.

‘Yes. The explosion fires a stone or metal cannon ball out of the end of the cannon. It can sink ships if the ball hits beneath the waterline.’

‘But can it propel… humans?’

‘It has been put forward as a new form of execution,’ said Tacius knowingly. ‘But I don’t think the Emperor’s too impressed. He’s a bit reluctant to support it, in case the whole cannon blows up. The trebuchet method of execution is much more popular, especially in the north, I hear.’

A man walked down the gangplank and strode over to where they were standing.

‘Whadda you thinka you doin’, just standing around staring atta ma boat?’ he asked in quick Tasean

‘Nothing,’ replied Bromon. ‘We were just wondering why there would be a galleon around at this time. Not a war on, is there?’

‘No, just rumours,’ said the Captain, trying to speak more clearly. ‘I don’t believe half of them, but there you go.’

‘What rumours?’ asked Sarmon in shaky Tasean.

‘Don’t you read the papers? Haven’t you heard of all these stories about Tombhadi being around?’

‘No… I mean yes!’ said Sarmon desperately, suddenly switching to Tuvakian, not caring if the man knew he was a foreigner. ‘He’s going to Tsabia and… and… just get some kind of security! We’ve got to do something!’

‘Goodness me!’ exclaimed the man in clear Tuvakian. ‘You don’t seriously mean…’ His sentence was cut short as an arrow struck him in the heart.

‘Quick!’ Sarmon called to the others. ‘We’ve got to get out of here!’

Just at that moment Sarmon saw a figure walk out from behind a cart further down the road holding a crossbow. Whoever it was, they were wearing a cloak and you could hardly see their face.

‘It’s Tombhadi!’ said Eridia in a panicked whisper. Tacius grabbed her arm and all four of them dived behind the wall that ran along one side of the jetty. The transport ship was just along a bit further, only twenty metres or so. And there was no one guarding it.

‘It’s our only chance!’ he yelled. They ran up to the edge of the boat and up the unguarded gangplank. The deck was empty, but to reach the hold, Sarmon had no idea what they would encounter. The hatch was closed, but Tacius was able to grapple with the catch until it swung open. All four of them tumbled into the room below. They closed the hatch.

Tombhadi came round the corner of the wall.

Chapter 20
The Golden Coin

Gybes lay awake in bed, the top bunk above Fiddles. It was nearly midnight, but his mind was too filled with thoughts for him to get to sleep. He could hardly believe that he was on a trip to the laboratory of one of the most influential men in Tsabia. But what was puzzling him was whether or not Tombhadi was alive, and if he was, as it now seemed, what was he doing, and how dangerous was it to the world in general? It was evident from the previous day's newspaper that if he was around, he was heading towards Tsabia and… and the Apple of Doom? Gybes couldn't come to terms with the worst possible. He tried to reassure himself that the worst possible *wasn't* possible.

He heard someone walking in the corridor. They stopped a moment outside the door, which stood ajar. He could now tell that it was not one, but two people, and they were talking to each other. He could hear that one was Captain Wickerworth, the distinct, mumbling, stumbling voice was unmistakable, but the other voice was unrecognisable.

'It's all ready, then?' asked the other man, who had a well-educated voice.

'Indeed it is, yes,' said the Captain. 'It's all there exactly as you ordered it, sir.'

'Hidden?'

'Of course, of course, sir. It's in the hold. You know, in the secret…'

'I know. Shut your clumsy mouth. There might be someone listening.' The man paused. 'I want it cheaper than the price you have set.'

'Ah, well, you see, I am a bit low on…'

'I will have it at half price.'

'…cash at the moment. I just lost out in a deal with…'

'It is not negotiable.'

'…a certain man, who…'

'Shut up!'

'All right, half price,' finished Wickerworth in an exasperated voice. 'I'll be off then and, er, I'll see you when we're at the shore.'

'Good,' said the man, and from the sound of it, turned around in the corridor and walked up the ladder to the deck. Gybes thought he heard the sound of paddles splashing in the water, but he wasn't entirely sure, because the wind had picked up a little, and it could have been waves striking the side of the ship. But he was sure that Wickerworth was up to something.

'Fiddles!' he said in a hoarse whisper, once he was certain that the Captain had left. 'We've got to go down to the hold!'

*

It was midnight, on the Tsabian Channel and the transport vessel was travelling across the rough waves. The breeze was strong on this side of the island, and the sails were waving in the breeze.

In the hold sat four travellers. They carried little, and were not eating for the whole trip. They were on their way to Tsabia secretly, as stowaways.

*

'Uh?' grunted Fiddles.

'I'm sure the Captain's hiding something there! I just heard him talking to a dodgy-sounding man outside the door! He said something about "it's all ready" and "you'll get it at the shore" or something. The man wanted whatever it was at half price, and Wickerworth said it was in a secret part of the hold!'

'Whatever,' said Fiddles sleepily. ''Snothin' to do with us.'

'Yes it is,' said Anassa, who was now wide awake, and sitting up. 'If he's hiding something it's up to anyone and everyone to find out what.'

'I'll go, if you two are,' said Chleosa.

'Oh, *all right*,' said Fiddles. 'I'll join you three hooligans, but you get the blame if there's nothing and we're caught.'

'Whatever you say,' said Gybes. 'Let's go.'

They crept down the dark passageway by the light of a white candle, which had been in their room. No one was up, and the Captain was presumably up in his cabin. It was dark up ahead, though Gybes could distinguish the closed hatch that led down into the hold from the wooden floor. He was the first to reach it, and he opened the hatch climbed down the ladder into the gloom beneath, holding the candle. Anassa followed, and then came Chleosa and finally Fiddles. He held up the candle. He was a little scared, but excited. Maybe they were about to foil the plan of a major criminal…

The hold was small and full of crates. They were towered in piles everywhere, and most of them seemed to contain fruit. There was seemingly nothing sinister about the contents of the hold.

'See?' said Fiddles. 'Nothing! I was right!'

'But Wickerworth nearly spoke of a secret place!' said Gybes.

'What do you mean, *nearly*?'

'He said, "they're in the secret…" before the man cut him off.'

'Well, look around then,' said Chleosa. 'It must be visible.'

They looked at the two end walls of the hold, checking for latches or keyholes, but they could find nothing. Gybes was disappointed in a way; he had wanted to find something interesting. But at least they hadn't been caught

'It's not as if nothing else interesting has happened,' said Fiddles. 'The trip, remember? That's why we're here!'

'I just wanted to be like one of those people in books, like *The Sunny River*, where those kids find a load of stolen gold – and then they got some of it,' said Gybes

'Wishful thinking,' said Anassa. 'Like there's going to be gold *here*.'

'Wait!' said Gybes, looking downwards at the straight, well cut floorboards and spotting the irregularity. 'There's a trapdoor on the floor!'

'So there is!' exclaimed Chleosa in surprise. 'I didn't think there could *be* a lower part to the ship.'

'Well, there is,' said Gybes. He reached down and poked his finger into a small hole. He pulled, but it wouldn't move. 'I think it's locked,' he said.

'Well *obviously*,' said Fiddles. 'But can you open it?'

'I wish I had a hairpin,' said Chleosa. 'That's how they always pick locks in stories. Like *The Sunny River*…'

'You read it too? That bit was really great, when Seela Toothkey took a hairpin and…'

Fiddles was already using something out of his pocket. The lock clicked open immediately.

'What's that you're using?' inquired Anassa.

'It's a skeleton key.'

'Where did you get it?'

Fiddles didn't answer. There was a clicking sound and the trapdoor opened. Gybes could now see what the captain had to hide.

Drugs.

'I don't believe it!' yelled Fiddles. '*Wickerworth? Drugs?* Never! He looks like someone who wouldn't even smoke or drink!'

'Thasprune, Lispetrine and Torethune!' exclaimed Anassa.

'Eh?'

'What?'

'And Wacky Whizhead?' hazarded Fiddles.

'They're different types of drugs,' explained Anassa. 'My Father told me – he used to be a Searcher, before he started playing rockthrow. But why would Wickerworth be selling them? You'd think he's rich enough anyway.'

'I don't…' began Gybes. He stopped. 'Hey, look!' he said. 'What the…'

He had spotted something glinting on the floor in the candlelight. It was round and golden. He picked it up and discovered that it was a coin. It had a dragon embossed in the centre, surrounded by engraved flames.

'What does that mean?' asked Anassa.

'I've no idea,' said Gybes. 'All I know is that we've got to report Wickerworth.'

Gybes closed the trapdoor and it locked it again. 'Let's go,' he said. 'He pulled a box over the trapdoor and stood up.

Wickerworth emerged from the shadows.

'Now children, you know you shouldn't be down here, especially at this time of night. Now, come on and go back to bed, it's nearly one o'clock.'

'But you're a drug smuggler!'

'Ah. Well, I'd be very glad if you didn't mention that. You might think I'm rich, but I'm very low on money. My Grandad pulled me into the business and now I can't get out of the trade. I'd lose everything. You don't say anything, and I won't mention that you came down here.'

Gybes could tell the panic in Wickerworth's voice was false.

'If you mention a single thing, I can still cancel the trip for you. I have the power. And you won't catch me. If I were you, I'd just get back to bed and forget all about it.'

'We'll do no such thing…' began Chleosa.

Wickerworth pulled a gun out of his pocket and aimed it at her. 'Now, go back to bed,' he said. 'And if you tell anyone…' He drew his hand across his neck.

They had no choice but to accept.

*

It was three o'clock in the morning. Sarmon was sitting alone at the bottom of the boat. Bromon, Eridia and Tacius had gone up to the deck to try and find a boat to escape in; Sarmon was taking care of their bags.

The hatch in the roof opened and a stepladder descended. Eridia came quietly down the ladder into the hold.

'We've found the boat,' she said. 'If we're lucky, we'll get to the shore in a couple of hours, maybe by five o'clock.'

'You'll be lucky,' came a voice from behind Eridia.

She looked upwards. The ship's Captain and seven of his crew were holding onto Bromon and Tacius, who were struggling to get free.

'Come with us,' he said. 'And don't bother trying to resist.'

*

The sun shone in the bright and clear morning sky of the northwestern peninsula of Tsabia. Dark clouds still haunted the eastern sky, and the wind promised to bring rain. The rainforest was anticipating this after the long dry spell, and the animals of the forest were getting exited about the coming water, even if the people weren't.

On the east coast, on a picturesque cove under the clear, blue sky was a small cottage. On the sandy beach beneath it, a man was attempting to remove a lobster from a lobster pot, while his wife observed from the top of the rocky slope.

'Watch what ye'r doin', Higgit,' she squawked. 'Them lobsters ain't 'alf got big claws.'

'But Nansy, I can't get it out, without bein' nipped, y'know,' said the man in the same Westport accent.

After a few curses and yells on Higgit's part, he finally removed the lobster and ran up the rocky slope and in the front door into the kitchen to drop it in a pan of boiling water on the stove. He returned to his wife's side, looking and feeling exhausted.

'Wossat over there?' said Nansy, pointing over the sea.

'Well, some people, not all min' you, call it the sea. Others call it the ocean and some even…'

'No, you stupid wallaby, I meant that boat!'

'Well, I suppose it's probably a boat.'

'Is it 'eadin' for 'ere?'

'How should I know?'

'Well, It's getting' closer anyway,' said Nansy. 'Like what things does when they's 'eadin' towards ya.'

Sure enough, the ship was coming towards them. It was bound for the small harbour at the base of the slope on the north side of the hillock on which the cottage stood. Behind, the rainforest trees creaked in the harsh wind beginning to blow in from the east, the forewarning of a storm. The clouds were building up over the eastern end of Tsabia, and were rapidly heading for the west.

The ship put down an anchor, and seven boats set out across the rough water towards the harbour. They came up to the sides of the small pier and a well-dressed man hopped out of it.

'Who are you?' asked Nansy suspiciously.

'Sorry to be any bother,' said Wickerworth. 'I'm just dropping off these people for the trip to L.C. Clark's Laboratory.'

'Oh, well, that's fine,' said Nansy. 'I'd forgotten they was comin'. I thought you were tax collectors or somethin'.

'What, coming by sea?' said Higgit, surprised at his Wife's assumption.

‘I was speaking *politically correct* so as not to offend them,’ she said. She lowered her voice so that only her Husband could hear her. ‘I meant *Pirates*.’

‘Ah.’ Higgit paused. ‘Eh?’

Most of the crew, apart from Wickerworth and two other men, began rowing back to their ship. Mr. Dawnley stood up and addressed Nansy and Higgit.

‘It may be that the carriages that we ordered will take a while to get here, so…’

‘You can come in fer lunch, if you want,’ said Nansy.

‘We would be most grateful for that,’ said Mr. Dawnley, glad he didn’t have to ask.

‘So… I’ll just go, shall I?’ said Wickerworth. It was obvious to Gybes, who was standing not far behind Mr Dawnley, that the Captain wanted to leave as quickly as possible, before he could be revealed.

Before Mr. Dawnley could answer, Wickerworth was on the boat bound back for his ship. Higgit led them into the house, with Nansy bringing up the rear. They didn’t notice that Wickerworth landed fifty metres up the coast and met someone there.

Soon the party was seated around the old, dusty table in the kitchen ready to be served a vegetable stew that Nansy was cooking, with some of the lobster that Higgit had caught.

‘Go an’ feed the cat, Higgit,’ demanded Nansy.

‘No,’ said Higgit firmly. ‘How many times does I ’ave to tell you, I don’ want to feed no cat. I got pussyphobia or somethin’. ‘It all scratches me an’ stuff too.’

‘Thay wouldn’t scratch you if you ‘andled it more, like, careful,’ scorned Nansy.

‘I do!’

‘Wot, like pickin’ it up?’

‘Cats is meant to be picked up!’

‘*Not by the tail!*’

‘Oh, *not* by the tail! Well, that changes everythin’!’

‘Sorry to intervene,’ said Mr. Dawnley, ‘but how long will this stew be. It’s only, the carriages will be arriving in half an hour or so, and we’ll need to go as soon as they do.’

‘Don’ worry,’ said Nansy. ‘It’ll only be five minutes or so.

After the meal, Anassa began a discussion with Gybes and Fiddles.

‘So, what do you think L.C. Clark will have at his place?’ she said.

‘He might have flying camels for the Imperial Army,’ Fiddles hoped.

‘I don’t think he’s really into military things,’ said Gybes. ‘Listen, that’s the carts coming. We’d better get going.’

The short-lived discussion ended abruptly, and they walked out the door with everyone else, to where two carriages awaited them, joined together by a metal bar. Mr. Dawnley stood at the front of one of them.

'Hurry up,' he said. 'We've still got a big day ahead of us!'

Chapter 21
The Underground Home

It was now early evening. Sarmon, Bromon, Eridia and Tacius were confined in the Searcher Station in the small town of Warfelt on the western coast of Tsabia. Since they had been apprehended in the hold of the transport ship, they had been handled roughly by members of the Tasean Navy and confined to a room in the Searcher Station.

The door to the waiting room was unlocked and opened. A man walked in.

'Come with me,' he said. 'The Chief Constable wishes to speak with you.'

Sarmon followed him out of the room, his three companions behind him. They tailed the Searcher down the corridor and up to an office door.

'In you go,' said the man. 'Chief Constable Briggs is waiting for you.'

He left them, and they walked in through the door to the Searcher Chief's Office. The Constable twiddled his pen in his hand and looked up at them.

'Take a seat,' he said. Once they had sat down, he began: 'Now, I'm afraid it has come to my attention that you stowed away illegally on a transport ship from Gospruma. Is this true?'

'Yes,' said Bromon truthfully.

'If that is so,' said Briggs, 'then no further enquiry is necessary. I'm afraid a small fine will be necessary, but no more than that. But tell me, why did you do it? The tickets are not extortionate.'

Bromon sat silent. Sarmon knew that if he told the truth, they could, as his brother had said earlier, be arrested for spying, even treason, and if the Chief Constable handed the case to the Tasean Court of Justice, anything was possible. Bromon thought for a moment and then answered.

'We had no money,' he said, hoping that Briggs didn't check him for it, there was a wallet with over two gold coins in it in his left jacket pocket. 'We merely wished for a method of transportation to reach our relatives in Barrentown.'

'Well, may I see your passports?' asked the Chief. Sarmon froze. By the look of it, so did his companions. They had no passports – none of them.

'May I see your passports please?' repeated the Constable.

Sarmon said nothing.

'You have none,' said Briggs, his stare seeming to penetrate Sarmon. It wasn't a question. 'You're in *real* trouble now.'

*

Gybes, Chleosa Fiddles and Anassa climbed into the back carriage, which was attached to the front one by two metal bars that met like a trailer would join to a tow bar. The other five children climbed into the front carriage and Mr. Dawnley sat at the very front. The carts were not far along the track when it began to rain. Tremendous drops of water bounced off leaves and started to form small puddles to either side of the track. Soon the dry earth on the thin track had become glutinous mud, and the carriages rocked in steady winds coming from the east. After twenty minutes, everything outside the protection of the carriage was absolutely soaked. Thunder rolled over the sea to the east, and the wind picked up to almost gale force.

'Summer! *Huh*!' said Fiddles agitatedly. 'You can't see the views!'

'What views?' said Gybes.

'There *aren't* any views, unless you've got eyes that can see through trees,' said Chleosa.

'Wizards have got something that can see into humans,' said Anassa brightly. 'They call it "ecks-ray", or something.

'Yeah, Porloke said he did one of those once,' said Gybes.

In the distance, back towards the coast, lightning lit up the sky, violently striking some far-off tree. A huge crash of thunder followed and the wind picked up speed again and fiercely rocked the unsteady cart. The clouds grew closer, and the light began to fade. The sun was blacked out, making it feel like night. Gybes had never experienced anything quite like it.

He heard Mr. Dawnley bellowing something from the front, and just caught the last few words.

'...Norgstorm. We'll just have to carry on.'

'*Norgstorm*?' said Fiddles incredulously. 'Never! They only happen every fifteen summers or something.'

Gybes was amazed too. Norgstorms were notorious for turning up prior to especially hot summers, and they were one of the most violent storms in Greenworld.[1] This was the first time he had ever experienced one. In fact, Gybes had rarely been in a thunderstorm – sometimes they would rumble over the mountains to the southeast of his home, but seldom did they pass directly over Lavos.

To pass the time, Gybes, Fiddles Chleosa and Anassa talked about what would have happened if the King Vornost had overtaken the Empire in

---

[1] The worst Norgstorm that there had ever been in the known history of Greenworld was supposedly around 4000BD, when one of the first great civilisations, the Kurdus, had dwelled in Eastwood. The legendary city of Talmor supposedly fell prey to this vicious storm and most of its population was killed, and the rest fled. Although the ruins were barely more than humps of grass and leaf-litter, many historians knew exactly what city and its people were like from 6000-year-old word of mouth and a single brick with a burn mark on it. Or at least they liked to think they did.

1555 and introduced his fascist regime, and jokingly plotted outrageous ways of embarrassing Alfid that got more unrealistic as they went on.

As the time went by, it seemed that the eye of the storm was gradually drawing closer to them. The wind was even stronger, and they began to worry seriously about the stability of the carriages. But they stayed upright and continued to move onwards. Gybes had to reach for the tarpaulin rolled up at the back of the carriage and let it down to stop the lashing rain from soaking them.

'We now approach the Barrier Mountains and the pass below Mt. Cendor,' bellowed Mr. Dawnley from the front. Sure enough, the track was beginning to head uphill, winding its way up a thinly forested slope that soon opened into moorland. There were very few trees, as here the soil was very sulphurous due to the nearby volcano, Mt. Cendor. 'Cendor' meant 'bad ground' in the old Tasean language, as, in the short time in which the Taseans had once occupied Tsabia, they had found that near the volcano they could not grow crops or feed their animals on the pathetic, sub-standard grass.

The carriages wound towards a thin valley between two very steep slopes, the pass. It always looked as if it ended just ahead, but the journey drew on for nearly ten minutes. They came out with the whole of the headland on which L.C. Clark's laboratory was situated in view. The slope rolled straight down to the flat rainforest, where Clark's land was towards the end of the headland on the south side, although Gybes couldn't tell this.

As they were now heading downhill, the horses were very speedy, although Mr. Dawnley had to try and slow them down due to the dangerously muddy ground. Shortly they reached the flat, forested ground and began to trundle along the track towards the Laboratory, now only a couple of miles away.

'Aren't there any other settlements along here?' said Gybes.

'It doesn't seem like it,' said Chleosa.

A flash of lightning and a rumble of thunder almost at the same time told them that the centre of the storm was relentlessly pursuing them. The rain was cascading down, almost a solid waterfall, running into gullies at either side of the track and turning dry forest floor into a swamp, with water reaching a foot deep in a few places. This was certainly a very bad Norgstorm.

A sudden calming in the wind meant that the eye of the storm was now over them. The rain had also stopped, and if it hadn't been for the overcast sky, you could have mistaken it for a nice day. However, the tranquillity didn't last for long.

There was a sudden ear-splitting *CRASH* and a blinding flash of lightning just to the right of the path. Mr. Dawnley shouted something but it was drowned by the very loud creaking noise coming from the tree that had been struck.

Not good… thought Gybes.

The tree fell with an almighty crash, narrowly missing the back of the carriage. A branch flailed out and smashed into the wooden roof, crushing part of it and making one of the four corner poles crack in half and fall into the mud behind.

Fiddles ducked speedily out of the way of the collapsing pole and flung himself to the opposite corner – straight into Chleosa, who yelled out in pain. The roof collapsed into the corner where Fiddles had been only moments ago.

'What the…' said Anassa. The carts had suddenly started to fling wildly about, flying nearly a foot off the ground.

'The horses are panicking,' said Gybes. He tried not to, but it was difficult.

'Ow!' yelled Fiddles as he was thrown roughly off Chleosa and onto the floor. At the front they could hear Mr. Dawnley yelling at the horses and trying to slow them, but they still belted onwards. The other carriage was not at all damaged, but one of the wheels on it was beginning to fall off. The horses rounded a corner and there was the Laboratory.

It was nothing like they expected.

Gybes wondered whether they were at the wrong place. It certainly didn't *look* like a laboratory.

'A hut!' roared Fiddles as the horses reared in front of it and managed to stop. The back carriage nearly hit into the one in front. 'We came *all this way* just to see some old gramps in a dirty mud cake like this!' He swore as loud as he could without Mr. Dawnley hearing it and spat on the ground.

The children clambered out of the carriages and were immediately soaked by the torrential downpour. They followed Mr. Dawnley to the door and everyone tried to bundle against the wall to be sheltered from the rain. Gybes failed to, and the rain soaked very quickly all the way to his skin. Mr. Dawnley knocked three times on the door and Gybes heard footsteps hurrying.

The door opened. A wild-looking, elderly man, with a tangle of white, shoulder-length hair and a long, black cloak stood in the doorway. He had bright blue eyes and looked in need of a shave. He didn't have that many wrinkles, he just looked old with experience, although there was a glint of something else in his eye. Perhaps it was sadness.

'Come in, friends,' he said. 'I've got a warm welcome for you.'

Gybes couldn't quite see what he meant by a 'warm welcome'. He couldn't quite imagine the hut to be at all *warm*. But all the same, he was glad to get in out of the waterfall of water.

The room was tiny. Gybes wondered whether they would all fit in. There were three chairs to the left and a very small coffee table to the right. Apart from that the room was bare. The walls were made out of panels of wood, protecting them from the strong wind.

The old professor walked across the room and reached up to a panel in the wall, which slid aside to reveal a lever. Clark pulled it and, to everyone's surprise, a floorboard juddered and moved aside, revealing a hole with a ladder leading down to another room. L.C.Clark spread his arms as if to say *voíla*, then bent down and began to clamber down the ladder and Mr. Dawnley waved his hand to tell the children to follow him.

Apart from Mr. Dawnley, Gybes was the last person down the ladder. They found themselves in a dimly lit, stone-floored chamber. Crates littered the floor and were piled up around the walls. Candles on top of some of these boxes produced the only light in the room. There was a door to the right, but apart from it and the crates, the room was completely bare. The only sound was the offbeat sound of water dripping to the floor from the visitors' drenched clothes.

Clark produced an old, brass key from his pocket and thrust it into the lock on the door. He turned the handle and slowly pushed open the door.

Gybes stared in awe at the room they had now entered. He had never seen such a warm and inviting place in his life. His hut had a stone floor and stick walls and hardly any furniture at all. He could see that the others were amazed too, and were gazing admiringly around the room. In front of him there was a sofa and two armchairs facing the opposite wall, upon which hung a tapestry of the Great Tsabian War of 1603. The L-shaped room continued left, and then bent round a corner to where a funky, wooden dining table sat. Directly to the left was a desk, set up against the wall and underneath a painting of Clark, beneath which, in loopy letters, was written; *Professor Lanran Carpsid Clark, Son of Elfis Bronstrum Clark, thirty-second Mayor of Mayberryville. Great Inventor and Biologist, born 3rd Glomoton 1629 in Southers, Tuvak.* Gybes glanced to the right of the desk, where the wallpaper ended and the stone walls of the dining area began. Looking directly upwards, he noticed that the ceiling was ornately carved, with birds and leaves and beetles. To the right, a corridor ran onwards with four doors on its right-hand side, the side that Gybes could see.

'Welcome,' said L.C.Clark, 'to my home.'

Before Gybes really had a chance to take it all in, the Professor spoke again. 'Now, if you would follow me, I will show you your rooms,' he said. 'I am sure that you will be most comfortable here. You'd better change out of your wet clothes, too.'

He led them to the right and then turned left, down the corridor to where he showed them the first bedroom, on the second doorway to the left, with two bunk beds and one single bed. A small table occupied one corner and a painting of a ship hung on the wall.

'Mr. Inkwell paid for these rooms to be organised,' said L.C. Clark. Gybes could see a glint of sadness in the professor's eye. 'But of course, he disappeared with the rest of the Investigation Team in the Green Savannah. And a good friend of mine he was too. Some of you will sleep in here,' He walked to the door and led them out. 'But the rest,' he said, opening the next door 'will sleep in here.'

This room was slightly narrower, with two bunk beds and a small table. The walls were bare, but there was a shelf set into the wall between the two beds. L.C. Clark led them out of the room into the corridor.

'The next room down is my room,' he said. 'Mr. Dawnley, I have organised the first room on the left for you; I hope it is adequate. If there is anything else you require, merely ask and I will do all I can to provide.'

'Everything will be fine, thank you,' said Mr. Dawnley.

'Very well, then,' said Clark. 'I suppose you'll be wanting to change clothes?'

Everybody did. Luckily, everyone had packed an extra set, and were in and out of the bedroom very quickly. As soon as he came out, Gybes saw L.C. Clark standing at the end of the corridor, waiting.

'Come this way,' he said. 'I have prepared a meal for you. If you will follow me back to the dining room you may enjoy some of the best food this place has seen in years. In fact, my new friend and temporary assistant Porloke is setting it up right now.'

Chapter 22
The Tunnel

'*Porloke*!'

'Yes, of course,' said L.C. Clark. 'Why, do you know him?'

'He's my Uncle!'

'Ah, right. He didn't tell me he had a Nephew. But I suppose we've only been working together for a few hours.' The old man chuckled. 'Poor old Bundis, my previous assistant wizard died a couple of weeks ago, and Porloke is filling in for the time being.'

'Now I come to think of it,' said Gybes, 'he did say he might see us here.'

'Well, I've got a real meal for you lot tonight,' said Porloke as they turned into the dining room.

'Is it nearly ready?' asked Poddy.

'Sure!' said Porloke.

'You *always* say "sure",' said Anassa. 'Sure!'

Porloke grinned and disappeared into the kitchen to the left at the end of the stone walled dining room. The prizewinners seated themselves around the wiggly funky wooden table and awaited the food. The table was laid with two enormous platters and twelve plates. There was one large candle set in the centre between the two platters, adding light to that provided by the chandeliers above on the ceiling.

'Before the meal,' said Clark, 'I'd like to know all your names.' He looked along the bunch of children. 'You,' he said to Silver, the girl with straight, silver hair, 'what's your name?'

'Cisslona,' she said. 'My friends call me Silver.'

'I hope you enjoy your stay, Silver,' said the professor. 'What's your name, young man?' he asked Poddy, who was a heavily built boy with short black hair.

'Me?' he said. 'Adhen, and don't ask how to spell it. I can't even spell 'it'.

L.C. Clark gave a small laugh and turned to the next boy, who was short and stocky with light brown hair and freckles. He looked a little like an overgrown rat.

'Lunger,' he mumbled, when L.C. Clark asked him his name.

'But what's your real name?'

'Dunno,' he said dully. 'Never though 'bout it.'

'What about you?' said Clark, looking at a thin black-haired boy with long arms.'

'Salato.'

L.C. Clark repeated the procedure for Gybes, Chleosa and Anassa, and finally reached Fiddles who stared into space, apparently not noticing the staring Professor. L.C. Clark who realized this and spoke. 'What's your name, young man?' he asked.
'Me?' said Fiddles. 'Oh, Fiddles. Fiddles.'
'Curious,' said Clark. 'What is your real name?'
'Fiddles is my name!' exclaimed Fiddles, almost desperately. 'My Mum called me it because… I used to fiddle a lot with… things… when I was a baby… Er…'
'Well, if you *really* hate your real name, you can get it changed,' said the inventor. He winked at Fiddles and turned away and looked at the kitchen entrance, where Porloke was standing ready with a tray on wheels holding all the food.
'Where?' asked Fiddles, almost ecstatic. But L.C. Clark wasn't listening. Gybes turned his attention to the tray heading his way. There was some kind huge meat pie, steaming from a cut in the centre, and vegetables of all sorts around it. There were roasted, spiced dock spuds, still sizzling in the oil and an ocean of gravy in a massive bowl. As soon as it arrived, Porloke began to dish it out.
'Come on then!' said L.C. Clark. 'Tuck in!'

*

Sarmon stared sullenly at the cell wall.
'There's nothing we can do now,' said Bromon. 'Tombhadi… there's nothing we can do,' he repeated in a depressed voice. 'Look…'
'We've got to do something,' said Sarmon, still staring at the wall.
'We can't!' said Bromon. 'We're in this cell until the ship from Tasea arrives. Then we're in another cell until our trial. There's no window in this room. We should have told the Searcher about Tombhadi there and then!'
'He's right,' said Eridia. 'We're trapped. I suppose if we're sentenced to death, we'll never be killed by the Tasean Government, because Tombhadi….'
'He's bound to kill *us* though,' said Tacius. 'It's just our fate. There's no escape.'
'We *will* escape,' said Sarmon definitely.

*

The ship was off course. Tombhadi was enraged. The Norgstorm had blown it right up into a tiny cove on the coast of northern Tasea, and it wouldn't be until next night before they reached the northern peninsula of

Tsabia. The wind had died down now, and it was about midnight. The stars were beginning to appear as faint pinpricks in the thinning cloud.

Tombhadi strode restlessly up and down on the deck. He'd waited so long – a short while longer was no problem. He'd get there; it was only a matter of time.

*

Gybes couldn't tell what time it was when he woke up, there was no light, but he was underground, so that didn't mean anything. Fiddles, Chleosa and Anassa were already up. He donned his clothes and got out of bed, picking up his timepiece from the table and slipping it into his pocket as he did so. He left his poncho off, instead putting on a thin, brown shirt. He left his hat beside it on the bed.

After Gybes and the rest had breakfast, L.C. Clark instructed them to follow him to the corridor. Once they were there, he addressed them.

'I will now be taking you to my Laboratory,' he said. He laughed slightly. 'That sounds slightly ominous, doesn't it? Who knows what experiments I will do to you there?' At the look on Mr. Dawnley's face he added, 'No. It's perfectly safe. I'm sure it will interest you greatly.'

The children and Mr. Dawnley followed the professor and the wizard down the corridor to the end, past the four doors to the right to the very last door ahead. L.C. Clark took a bunch of keys out of his cloak pocket and swiftly opened the door.

The smell of chemicals was wafted to Gybes' nose as he peered through the door. He was met with the sight of a spacious room with a high roof and three tables standing in the centre. It's floor and four walls were all of stone; the floor was paved with polished granite and the walls were sandstone blocks. The ceiling was too dark to see properly, but it looked to Gybes as though it was made of wooden beams. On the table on the left stood three or four jars of what looked suspiciously like blood, and beside them was a funnel leading into a pipe that disappeared into a hole in the stone wall to the left. The second table hosted a bag of some strange white powder and a jar containing a runny green substance. On the table farthest to the right was a weighing bowl and a board with loose straps hanging over the side. There were no chandeliers in the room, only a few candles occupying holders on the walls and standing on the tables.

'This is my laboratory,' said the professor. 'As you all know, I create new species of animals by a type of magic, and a little drop of ingenuity I like to call inventiveness, although "inventor" is a fairly inaccurate title for me. First I will show you the procedure for the creation of the new species themselves.' He crossed to the table on the right. 'This is where I strap down the animals and…'

'That sounds cruel,' interrupted Anassa

'I do give them a sleeping draught,' said L.C. Clark. 'And I work quickly. They don't feel anything.'

Satisfied, Anassa let the Professor continue.

'Now, this is what I call a pippento,' he said, holding up a thin glass instrument. 'It is a simple pipette with a needle fitted to the end, to withdraw blood from the animal. Exactly two millilitres of blood, in fact. I then drip it into a jar, of which I have four at the moment.' He walked along to the next table where he picked up the bottle and the powder, which had scrawled on a label, 'Transformation Enhancer'. Clark then moved along to the last table with the children following like puppies at his heels.

'This should interest you,' he said as they reached the last surface. 'The boys most of all, in my experience. These jars contain blood.' He picked up a particularly red jar. 'To create a different creature I have to pour some of this blood – that which I earlier extracted – into a beaker with a small amount of the Transformation Enhancer, one of my earliest inventions, and this green liquid, which helps to stop the moisture from evaporating. I then tip it into this funnel here, which takes it through the wall to the next room, where it is injected into another animal. Sometimes I use a liquid – one which unfortunately is not here today – to increase or decrease the size of the animal in question, but that takes very powerful magic. If I had none of a Wizard's magic, nothing could happen.

'After that, it's so complicated that the most intellectual person in Tsabia couldn't work it out.' He sighed. 'If only *I* knew how it worked. But magic is beyond the range of human comprehension. We know how to perform it, but not *why* it happens, or how. Such big questions are not there to be answered, but to remain a mystery. That is why we call it magic.'

'It's to do with cells,' said Porloke. 'Not prison cells,' he added, noticing the expressions of confusion on everyone's faces. 'Cells are tiny parts of all living things. We see them through magical minutiscopes. They use them in medical research now, too. Of course, we haven't developed a way of explaining it, it's just there as a fact.'

L.C. Clark leant on the table and launched into a monologue about his achievements. 'I can invent many different new species by simply incorporating the genes of two separate animals. Originally the wizard Gombrey and I would only mix fly with beetle or worm with slug, but as I grew more confident I began to develop them into more complex mixtures. But those early creations had no specific intention; they were merely new species never before seen in Greenworld.

'Later, however, I managed to create a new species of mice which would squeak very loudly to alert their owner of any danger, although I found that they would often squeal excessively, especially within large groups of people, so therefore I could no longer advertise them as reliable, and the profit was no longer sufficient for me to make a living from.

'When Gombrey left, I befriended another wizard named Bundis, who was much more skilled at his art than Gombrey. With this new asset, I began on larger creatures in 1675 at the age of 46. With the 1676 invention of the Feledun, my profits shot up again. The Feledun, as some of you may know, is a mixture of the felecrim, the dog from the Arrow Downs with acute hearing and the bold and vicious ponodun from the Katak Lands. The Feledun also has a sixth sense, the sense to recognise untrustworthiness. It was to be used to ward off muggers and thieves. It worked. And now many thieves still live with the fear of being confronted by a Feledun in someone's back garden, especially in the Arrow Downs and Field East.'

'That's still a while ago,' said Squidge.

'Ah, yes,' said Clark. 'Well, later on I discovered that the population of Thans was dropping rapidly, and they were in desperate need of some kind of saviour. So, I invented the Mayothan, which was simply a Than with the tameness rare burung otter. Unfortunately, both creatures are now extinct, and now I only have twenty-three Mayothans. Or at least, I did have them until they escaped a fortnight or so ago…' He trailed off. 'Since the Mayothans, there have been so many inventions that it would take me an hour to tell you. But of course, you would like to see the real things?'

Everyone nodded.

'Then follow me!'

The group followed the aged professor through a door on the other side of the laboratory. Through the door was a long corridor, with three doors on the right and four on the left. L.C. Clark strode purposefully down the hallway to the last doorway on the left. He took a bunch of keys from his pocket and opened the door.

It revealed a dimly lit stone tunnel with walls crudely cut from the bare rock. It was far colder than the warm corridor, even though the climate outside was tropical. In the centre of the tunnel ran two parallel metal bars. Upon them stood two wooden carts, the wheels fitting precisely onto the metal of the track.

'Step in!' said L.C. Clark. 'Five to the back and four to the front!'

Gybes, Fiddles, Chleosa and Anassa stepped into the back cart with Porloke, followed by Crack, or Salato, as was his real name. The other four got into the front cart with Mr. Dawnley and the Professor.

'Ah, hello,' said Porloke to Crack. 'I didn't catch your name.'

'I'm Crack – or Salato,' he said. 'None of Anassa's friends wanted to go, so I was really lucky to come. We live down near Cour, and my Mother forced me to take my big brother, Lunger. He's got a memory like a sieve with very large holes. He doesn't even know his own real name.'

'Do *you* know his real name?' asked Fiddles.

'Funnily enough: no,' replied Crack.

Gybes noticed Porloke wave his hand as the carts moved off.

'How do you do that?' he asked, amazed, as the carts shot round a dizzy bend to the left.

'It's just magic,' said Porloke, stroking his beard. 'No one knows how it happens. But you have to train to do it, master to apprentice. What I did there was very simple in terms of all the magic there is. I'm still an amateur really, and I've been fully trained for over five years. It all comes with experience, and the best Wizards are normally the oldest. Wizardesses are getting more and more uncommon these days – people say wizarding is a man's thing – but anyone can do it. All it takes is perseverance.'

The cart rocketed around a corner to the right and slowed down to where it finally stopped in front of a stone platform. A door stood at the end of the tracks, straight ahead.

They all clambered out of the carts and Clark took a separate, singular key from out of his pocket and placed it into the lock with little force. The door swung open with ease.

Chapter 23
The Crogphar

As soon as he opened the door, Gybes was confronted by a bare chamber very similar to the one beneath the hut. Numerous boxes and candles occupied the room, and one ladder fell from a trapdoor in the roof. The room was much less used to visitors, and was not kept presentable; glaringly obvious muddy footprints were easily noticeable in the dim light, and the walls were dirt-ridden.

L.C. Clark ventured forwards and clambered up the sturdy ladder. The trapdoor opened up into the fresh air and the professor emerged out into a grassy clearing in the forest, followed by Mr. Dawnley and then the children, with Porloke bringing up the rear. Dazzling sunlight blinded Gybes after the dim chamber as he scrabbled out of the hole. To the right was a small rectangular wooden building; Gybes guessed that it was for storing food, or maybe tools.

The rainforest trees were short and stunted; the temperature was cooler here than on the rest of the island. Birds squawked and chattered, while strange rasping noises emanated from the right and distant roars rolled in from far ahead, sounds that couldn't be mistaken for waves. The scent of salt rode the cool, penetrating wind. The water from the Norgstorm had dried up, yet here and there it's legacy remained; several trees lay derelict across the dirt track leading ahead, their strength tested beyond the limit by the ravenous gales.

'Well, as you can see, we're approaching my creations – my inventions, if you like,' said the Professor. 'I hope they will interest you.'

There was a murmur of excitement from the children.

Gybes watched something fall to the ground from L.C. Clark's pocket. 'You've dropped one of your keys,' he observed.

'Ah yes, thank you Gimbers,' said L.C. Clark.

'Gybes,' corrected Gybes. The old man bent down to pick up his key. Gybes observed that, even though the aged inventor seemed to be healthy, if not fit, underneath he was old and feeble, just like most other seventy-six year olds. Everyone, he thought, had to die one day.

'Ah, this is my key to my watch tower up north,' said Clark. 'That reminds me; I've got to go up there this evening. I feel like jogging up…'

Gybes doubted his previous assumption. Professor Clark still had a good few years in him yet.

'You're lucky it didn't get struck by lightning,' said Mr. Dawnley.

'It did. That's why I've got to go up there.'

The Inventor led the children along the path, talking to Porloke and Mr. Dawnley at the front. The forest began to thin out, and fences bordered the track to either side, obviously to stop animals escaping.

To the left, Gybes noticed the beginning of a dirt track, about the right size to be an animal track, leading to a stile that crossed the fence into an enclosure. Beside it was a sign that said, 'Oxelope'.

'In here,' said Clark, 'are creatures which harbour immense pulling power and staggering speed and agility. The Oxelope is basically an antelope from the Green Savannah mixed with a few brown ox genes, such as its tremendous strength and its calm attitude towards humans. Yet very little of its appearance has been modified, for it must still keep its stamina as well as having strong muscles.'

He led them into the enclosure and along an animal path in between the trees. There were fewer forest ferns on the ground in here; it appeared that they had been eaten.

They now approached a circular clearing, containing several fallen tree trunks: the ever-evident aftermath of the Norgstorm. The grass was short, and there was a spot in the centre that looked as though food of some kind had been placed there many times. In one corner stood a wooden trough, which was definitely more than just beginning to rot.

L. C. Clark gave a short sharp whistle and from out of the trees on the far side ran several bulky antelope, muscular and strong, but with long, thin legs. Although they were not as slim as normal antelopes, they still looked very fast. Their tails were short and stringy, and their heads were slightly wider than that of an antelope. They flicked their ears at the biting prayer flies and mosquitoes, constantly present in the Tsabian Rainforest.

The Oxelope halted just a few feet in front of L.C. Clark. The professor patted one of them, and sighed. 'These creatures are sure and faithful, but so long as it still has the spirit of an antelope, the wild touch the original was born with shall remain. However, before I speak for too long, I'm afraid we must move on to the next creature – there is no time for us to dawdle.'

The Inventor turned his back on the Oxelope and lead the group of children towards the edge of the pen, yet the creature at the head of the group followed doggedly behind its creator.

'Your creature is too loyal perhaps,' Mr. Dawnley chuckled.

'He is as loyal as any servant to me,' said L.C. Clark. 'And that includes obeying me.' He pointed to the clearing and said, 'Go! Go back and nibble the grass so that you can keep up your special strength!'

His faithful Oxelope turned and sped away back to its regular grazing pasture. Everyone followed its designer to the stile and back onto the main path.

Gybes, who was at the front of the group, overheard the end of the conversation of the three adults.

'I suppose it would be dangerous if the creature were to escape back to the wilds,' said Porloke.

'If that were to happen, I fear it would become an easy hunting target,' said L.C. Clark. He fell silent, and they continued to walk onwards. All this time Gybes had not spoken a single word, and he chose the momentary absence of conversation to raise a question that he had been waiting to ask for some time.

'Professor Clark,' he addressed the man, 'what is your most *recent* invention?'

'Ah, well,' said the Inventor. He turned around and raised his hands to stop the group. 'Gimbers here –'

'– Gybes –'

'– has questioned me, "What is your most *recent* invention?" This I shall not divulge until we reach it, but be assured, you will like it!' He began walking again and looked around at Gybes.

'Sorry I keep getting your name wrong,' he said. 'Gybes. I'll try and remember it. You did like the Oxelope, though?'

'Oh yes, that was great,' said Gybes, meaning it. He rarely even came close to an ox in Lavos, and he had only seen paintings of antelope.

Gybes heard Fiddles mutter 'Jolly splendid, Gimbers,' just behind him.

As the path continued, the forest returned to being just the same to either side as it had been when they had emerged from the underground tunnel. L.C. Clark addressed the group just as they reached a new enclosure. Gybes supposed that they would go down the other side on the way back, but he also suspected that the first enclosure on the right had been labelled 'Mayothan'.

'Here we find the Cardopeggan,' Clark said. 'Many of you may not believe it possible, but what I have created is a rabbit-pigeon-hedgehog.'

Most of the children including Gybes and Fiddles, laughed out loud. Gybes thought he must have been having them on.

'It's real!' exclaimed L.C. Clark. 'It has no real purpose; I was really just messing around. In fact, I was drunk at the time I came up with the idea nearly twenty-five years ago.'

'It's still my favourite,' said Porloke. 'I love the way it flies about three metres and collapses. And then flies off again. And then collapses. It's really like a kind of over-extended jump.'

'I say it has no purpose,' said the Professor, 'but it's adorable. I get loads of people requesting it for a pet and wanting to cuddle it.'

To everyone's astonishment, the Cardopeggan really did exist. How in Greenworld it survived was a mystery to even Porloke, who said it defied the laws of magic.[1] The Cardopeggan had long, brown fur, with traces of feathers in it. Some of the hairs had developed into spines; Gybes supposed this was the hedgehog part. Its ears were slightly shorter than a rabbit's, and it's snout more slender and quite bony. The weirdest thing was that it actually had stubby wings sprouting out of its back. Although it looked quite pathetic, it was still able to get around reasonably fast with its short flights, and when Lunger made a bit too much noise, it fled without any difficulty. Apparently, it attracted much attention from all over Greenworld and was a popular mascot for the international game of kickball. It had even featured on the flag for Westport United team, which was famed for its success up until the point at which it adopted the flag.

Afterwards, L.C. Clark led them to the other side of the path into an area that was not enclosed. 'There would be no point enclosing it,' he told Gybes when he asked. 'If they wanted to escape, the Nuu Birds could easily fly away. I have to keep it here by feeding it and providing them with accommodation'

The Nuu Bird, as it turned out, was an enormous Pelican, with a wingspan of nearly four metres and a beak so massive that it probably could have swallowed a cat. Gybes was speechless.

'I am working on the Giant Nuu Bird, but it could well be a few years before it comes in to being,' said Professor Clark to the group as they stood beside one of the enormous beasts. 'Enlarging an animal as well as modifying it takes a lot of work, and Porloke's magic isn't quite advanced enough. The Imperial Army have asked if I can breed some for them. I have agreed that they shall have two hundred, if I ever breed them, although they will have to train them themselves.'

'I am practicing' said Porloke. 'I only trained for five years under the Wizard Fauzel and even with my experience it will take me a while to be good enough to double the creature's dimensions. Anyway, I may only be here temporarily.'

They left the birds with high spirits, wondering what other amazing creatures the Inventor had in store for them. They continued to be surprised by the complexity and impossibility of the creatures they saw as they made their way along the straight path. They stopped to have lunch at one point, and then continued onwards, visiting the creature that had made the strange rasping noise, which was a giant lizard with an extremely long and extremely dangerous barbed tail.

The path seemed to never end, constantly twisting through the forest. They had travelled at least three miles when they finally emerged into the open. In front of them was the end of the peninsula, and there was the final pen in front of them.

---

[1] Despite the fact that he knew magic had virtually no laws.

It must have been enormous. The fences stretched all the way to the sea on either side, which must have been a mile away at least to the left and further to the right. The part of it that was directly in front of them was forested, and there was a wooden walkway on stilts disappearing into the trees, a flight of steps leading up to it.

'In there is my latest creation,' L.C. Clark said, answering Gybes' question. 'It is named the Crogphar, a mixture of the deadly crogor of the Forest of Shadows and the Western Border Mountains, and the numonphar, or kengero as it is often called, the leaping marsupial which inhabits Wangoolie and the eastern half of the Desert of Death. It has the head of a crogor, and its body is a mixture of the two, as are its arms. It stands upon its hind legs, which end in long, thin feet like the numonphar's, but also sport vicious claws. Not only is it a vicious and persistent predator, it can also travel at terrific speed using its hind legs to propel it along in huge bounds. There is only one in Greenworld and you are to be the first people to see it apart from myself, Porloke, Bundis and a few other wizards.'

There were awed gasps from the group as they followed him up the steps onto the wooden walkway, and began to walk along it. It was quite high up, about five metres or so above the forest floor, and it wound between the trees until finally they came to a wooden observatory with a sloping thatched roof. Below them was a small clearing, empty but for a few wild birds pecking at the floor where meat had previously been thrown. There was nothing to suggest that an enormous creature had ever been there, though Gybes was sure that it must have been the Crogphar's feeding place.

'I have this observatory here for safety reasons,' said L.C. Clark. 'As the Crogphar can be extremely dangerous at close quarters and is very strong, please do not provoke it, or we'll be down there in a pile of wooden ruins before you can say "whoops".'

The Professor crossed to the corner and picked up a bucket that contained a rather large piece of seemingly rancid meat. He tipped the bucket sideways and thrust the meat into the clearing, where the birds began to cluster around it.

There was a rustling sound far off in the trees, and the birds panicked and scattered, squawking wildly. The bush that bordered the clearing on the other side shuddered.

And then the Crogphar burst forth. It was even more impressive than Gybes had imagined, with a glossy brown coat and bright, sharp eyes. It was over two metres tall, not counting its tail, and its claws were terrific, As it lowered its head to swiftly gulp down the meat it had been given, they glinted in the sunlight. The meat was gone in seconds, and before the children were able to observe it properly, the Crogphar had bounded back into the bush.

'That's an amazing creature you have there,' said Mr. Dawnley.

'Thank you,' said Clark. 'Alas, now that it has eaten it will not come back. It is wary of others.'

After a pause he said, 'Now, I think, it is time for us to head back to my home.'

The group of children, disappointed at not having longer to see the creature, walked back along the elevated walkway until they reached the boundary of the enclosure. As they headed back along a separate path, which was thankfully a shortcut, the afternoon sunlight radiated from the blue sky. The wind brought the smell of the sea, and a few small cumulus clouds were breeding in the north, floating gently across the sky.

When they reached the clearing, they sat down for a moment to catch the last of the sun they would see that day. Some of the children began wandering around, and Gybes, Fiddles, Chleosa and Anassa crossed over to the side of the clearing where began chatting quietly.

'It was amazing, that mon… that Crogphar,' said Chleosa.

'It was jolly splendid,' said Fiddles. 'That's my new… thing that I say.'

'That's what *Sir Fawning* says. You have to think up your own.'

'What rule says that?'

'Who's Sir Fawning?' asked Anassa.

Gybes' eyes wandered to a particularly dark part of the forest, where he noticed a wooden trapdoor in the rainforest floor, half covered in vines.

He walked up to where L.C. Clark was conversing with Mr. Dawnley about alternative accommodation. 'Excuse me,' he said. 'I was wondering what that trapdoor over there was for.'

'Ah, well,' said the Professor. 'You aren't really meant to know, but as you've seen it, I'll tell you – as long as you promise not to tell no one. *No one*. Understand?'

'I promise said Gybes, eager to know what Clark would want to keep so secret.

'It is a special place I go to, a kind of study,' he said. 'It is also the beginning of a tunnel which leads to the edge of the sea, just a mile or so to the southwest. Only I, and a few of my friends, know of it. My old friend Zemphanian did, but he died in the Dark Forest over ten years ago. You must promise to tell no one. I know I can trust you.'

He stopped speaking, and at that instant, Mr. Dawnley began. 'We have a change of plan,' he said. 'We are to sleep tonight near to the north coast beside one of L.C. Clark's watchtowers. Not the one that was struck by lightning,' he added. 'Why, you may ask. Why? Because Mr. Clark is organizing a surprise for us.'

The children began to mutter excitedly amongst each other as they walked back to the ladder and through the dark room to the rail carts, wondering what the surprise could be.

Chapter 24
The Raid

They camped beside L.C. Clark's wooden outpost, in a large clearing adjacent to a rocky beach. The accommodation was comfortable; the circular tents packed full of excessive amounts of cushions. What little baggage the children had with them was stored in one tent at the far west of the encampment, and there was a separate tent for Mr. Dawnley. There was also one slightly larger tent in which guest artist Vetrum Lavoni slept, a tent containing quantities of cushions to rival all the rest in the encampment put together. Everyone had been surprised at his sudden appearance; he had virtually materialised the previous night, explaining that he was there to… paint a picture, funnily enough.

Gybes had rarely actually been to the sea before, and he, Fiddles and Chleosa took the chance to go swimming in the warm water. Gybes knew how to swim – he practiced in Lake Forou – but he had never had the chance to swim amongst seaweed and sand.

They had been splashing around for nearly an hour when Mr. Dawnley called them out for the Artist to portray them in a picture for the next newspaper.

'We asked the Wizards for a kammara that they use for foghtoes, but the IWU charged one hundred goni, and I decided; no, that would be a waste of money,' said Mr. Dawnley.

'IWU?' questioned Squidge, whose knowledge of the world at large was very limited.

'International Wizards Union,' said Mr. Dawnley wearily. 'Now, if you would form two lines right here… If you, Gybes, and Anassa would go at he back, er… yes and you, Kemen and… er…'

'Lunger.'

'…*Lunger* would stand there also, and the rest can stand in front.

The children obeyed. Gybes thought that either Fiddles didn't find his real name funny any more, or he felt that laughing was not permitted in the presence of Vetrum Lavoni. He was certainly very solemn, and every time he looked at them they saw deep furrows of either concentration or grumpiness on his bald head.

'Now, stay still,' he said sternly. 'I can't paint you otherwise. No moving!' he snapped, and Salato stopped twiddling his fingers and looked up suddenly, staring forwards innocently. 'I want you all looking this way,' finished Vetrum.

Gybes was sure it was going to be tedious.

*

It had been a successful escape, much to the surprise of the other three. They had waited until four guards had come to take them and Sarmon had hidden behind the door. Swiftly, with the help of the other three (for, at some point in his eventful life, Bromon had trained in martial arts), all four were knocked out and their suits were taken. After convincing a thankfully gullible Sergeant that the commotion had been nothing out of the ordinary, they had left the jail unnoticed, and had bought a small sailing boat with the last of their money – one that could be controlled by one person – as Sarmon was sure no one would look for them at sea. Sarmon had dropped his siblings and Tacius off on the coast not far to the north of Warfelt, insisting that he pursue Tombhadi alone. His boat was bound for the Tsabian Headland; he knew his foe would be heading there also. As he drew nearer he became increasingly anxious. He must get there before Tombhadi – everything depended on it.

*

It was well over an hour later that a relieved Gybes walked away from where he had been standing uncomfortably for that time, free at last from the piercing gaze of the artist. It was a good painting, he confessed, but he was not entirely happy with how stiff he was once Vetrum Lavoni had finished.

'I wonder who that Zemphanian bloke Clark told us about is?' said Gybes as he, Fiddles, Chleosa and Anassa sat down on the grass.

'Who?' said Chleosa.

Gybes suddenly remembered that he had promised the Professor he would tell no one about the trap door. 'Oh, just someone L.C. Clark mentioned,' he said, and shrugged.

'I'm sure I've heard of him,' said Anassa. 'He was a young Wizard who won loads of prizes – astonishing for his age. He was the heir of Schazakia, a small country that the Empire swallowed up recently, on the north side of the Revel Valley, I think. He was really famous for about a year, and then he died in the Forest of Shadows. Nobody knows how it happened.'

'Pity,' said Gybes. 'We need a brilliant wizard to sort out the world.'

Their discussion halted as Vetrum Lavoni began to speak. 'There are papers, if anyone would wish for one,' said the artist, standing up. 'I brought several of them up from Goodport. They're free,' he added, seeing no one interested. 'Also, I must inform you that we will not be going back to Professor Clark's tonight, for the surprise will take a little longer to organise.'

'What authorisation do you have for this?' said Mr. Dawnley gruffly.

Vetrum held up a telegram. ' "By the order of L.C. Clark, the group currently lead by Mr. J. Dawnley must remain encamped for a further night at my watchtower due to certain unforeseen problems. They will be resolved as soon as possible. " '

Mr. Dawnley took the letter and read it. 'Very well,' he grunted. 'Children, we will not need to pack up today!'

'We could get a newspaper,' suggested Gybes.

'Boring,' said Fiddles.

'I think we should get one,' said Anassa.

'So do I,' said Chleosa. 'I want to know what's going on. It's three on one, Fiddles.'

'Whatever.'

They walked over to the pile that Vetrum had left on an outside table and Chleosa picked up the top one.

'The main headlines are; "Pirating 'Mad Sharks' Target Small Farming Village",' read Chleosa, ' "North Steppe Bids for Freedom", and "Empire Withdraws Last Troops from Myen, and… look at this!'

'Tombhadi Story Declared Hoax,' said Fiddles, a superior smirk spreading across his face.

Gybes was puzzled. 'Let me see that,' he said. Chleosa handed him the newspaper and he read:

> *Today several men of the Green Savannah have made a sensational and relieving discovery. They found what they say is the grave of the villain Tombhadi, whom we now know died in the Forest of Shadows after all. It is a small Tombstone set in the ground some thirty miles west of the town of Egaduné, and is dated 3rd of Talisoton 1698, thirteen days after he died. Presumably someone had found his body and decided it best that it be buried. We can only guess that native fisherman Vini Osacha must have been mistaken. It has been speculated that he was worrying that every stranger he saw could be Tombhadi, or that someone dressed up and pretended to be Tombhadi as part of the joke.*
>
> *This, and more evidence, as yet undisclosed, means it is a near certainty that the Tombhadi story was an elaborate hoax.*
>
> *Jakid Slemabot, "Reporting Greenworld."*

‘Well that’s that then!’ said Fiddles, still smirking. ‘Who’s the stupid one now, eh Gybes? It’s all nonsense, just as I knew all along.’

‘I suppose so,’ said Gybes.

‘You suppose so? It’s a certainty!’

*

Sarmon pulled the miniscule sailing boat ashore and got out of it.

There were several other, much larger boats on the beach.

He was too late.

*

The four friends were wandering in the forest. It was early afternoon, and they were just south of the camp, a kilometer or so away. The sun was still relatively high in the sky, although a cool breeze was rustling through the parts of the rainforest where trees grew sparsely.

‘I wonder why this ‘surprise’ is taking longer to organize,’ said Gybes.

‘I suppose that means it’s pretty good,’ said Fiddles.

‘We’re not far from the laboratory here,’ observed Anassa. ‘The track’s just down there.’

‘Well, we don’t want to find out what the surprise is,’ said Chleosa, walking back down a small slope towards the camp. ‘Come on, let’s go.’

‘We could…’ said Fiddles. He stopped.

Someone was yelling.

‘NOOOOOOOOO!’ The sound resounded eerily through the forest and caused them to turn suddenly. Gybes shivered. It wasn’t a pleasant sound: desperate and enraged, yet despairing.

‘It might be the Professor!’ said Chleosa.

‘We’d better go and look,’ said Gybes, against his instinct. ‘In case he’s hurt, I mean…’

They ran up a slope and onto a small hilltop. As they came down the hill, they saw a man standing, head in hands on the track in front of the laboratory’s entrance hut.

Or at least, where the hut should have been.

Instead they saw the crumbled wreckage of what was once a hut. The wooden floorboards were ripped from the ground, and where the trapdoor had been was a gaping hole. There was no sign of the Professor Clark, or Porloke

Gybes, Fiddles, Chleosa and Anassa rushed down to where the man stood, or more accurately, kneeled. He had short, brown hair and wore a long cloak, which was grey with expensive-looking golden fastenings. He appeared to be sobbing.

'What on earth has happened?' asked Chleosa. 'Who are *you*?'

'I'm too late!' the man wailed, getting to his feet and turning to face the four children. 'It's all hopeless!'

'What is?' asked Gybes. 'What are you on about? Who *are* you?'

'My name is Sarmon,' said the man, his voice urgent. 'It's Tombhadi. He's after the Apple of Doom and there's no way of stopping him!'

'But how do you know this?' said Gybes, trying to keep his fear at bay. If what the man was saying was true, it was everything he had feared. 'And why did he raid L.C. Clark's home?' he added.

Sarmon pulled himself together. 'The second question: I do not know,' he answered calmly. 'It looks as though he was searching for something, but what – I have no idea. As for how I know what I know, I will have to tell you. I was once in his service, but realized what an awful thing it was I was about to do, and that I had been bribed and pulled into a trap, so I escaped. He was going to kill me, and has nearly done so on many occasions, but this time he's going to kill a lot more people than just me.'

'But that's terrible,' said Anassa. 'What can we do?'

'It's terrible multiplied by tragic and with ladles of doom,' said Sarmon, despair conquering him again. 'As to what we can do, nothing.' He sunk to his knees. 'Nothing,' he repeated. 'Just sit and wait. Or try to escape, at least.'

'I knew it all along,' said Fiddles, seeming to come out of a trance. 'I *knew* it!'

'So why did you try to pretend you didn't?' asked Gybes.

'I didn't want to believe it,' replied his friend. 'I tried to convince myself it wasn't true.'

Gybes stared at he ground. Then he looked up in the direction of where the hut had been. 'We could at least check L.C. Clark's home,' he said.

'I suppose we could,' conceded Sarmon, gradually standing up again. 'It's not going to stop Tombhadi, but it'll pass the time, and we can look for something to escape in, though I expect he'll track us down. He's a wizard, and a powerful one at that. We've no hope of hiding.' He stood up and began to walk to the derelict building, followed closely by the four children. 'How do you know about the Apple of Doom?' he asked.

'Book,' replied Gybes simply.

They had to jump into the bare room, as the ladder had been torn down. Numerous boxes were lying broken open on the floor, and to the right the door hung off it's hinges, revealing a dark doorway into a pitch black room. Sarmon took a tinderbox from his pocket and set alight one of the candles. He held it aloft as they walked into the room, so that they could see.

Gybes was horrified with what he saw. The place felt like a dungeon. It had lost its entire former atmosphere, as if it had been scoured of all humour and happiness with a razor-sharp knife. Every piece of furniture had been overturned, every painting on the wall ripped from its place. The carpets had been torn and burnt, and the hearth had semi-collapsed. As they walked carefully through the wreckage towards the dining room, Gybes saw that the priceless wooden table was broken in half, and through the kitchen door he could see that broken plates, cutlery and cups were littered on the floor, and the wood-burning stove was lying on its side.

'All the beds are overturned,' said Sarmon. 'And the study is full of paper. The library's no better – there are books littering the floor, some of them ripped and torn. But the laboratory's the worst. The tables are smashed, and everything breakable is in pieces all over the stone floor.'

'But… why would Tombhadi do this?' asked Anassa.

'I have no idea,' said Sarmon.

'And how did he get here without being noticed?' said Chleosa.

'He must have got past the fence around Clark's land,' said Gybes. 'The tunnel!' he said suddenly. 'Remember that tunnel he told us not to tell anyone about? He must have used that!'

'What tunnel?' said Fiddles.

'I… oh, nothing,' said Gybes, feeling guilty. It wasn't necessary to reveal the Professor's secret.

'And now he's going to take over the world,' said Sarmon. 'Let's go. We can use my boat to get back to Tasea.'

'But what about our families?' asked Gybes as they clambered with difficulty back into the sunlight. 'As far as I know, the Apple of Doom is a couple of kilometres from my home village.'

'Then they'll be dead. There's no way we can save them.'

'But…'

'Come on! He'll kill loads of people, and then build statues of himself, and order palaces to be constructed. He'll be an absolute dictator – ruthless and insane! He won't spare lives! He won't have mercy!'

'I suppose you're right,' said Gybes. 'But you don't have a family to worry about!'

'What do you mean? I've got parents! They're vulnerable too! And my brother and sister were heading for Aurawey – they're getting closer to the danger with every passing minute.'

Gybes felt in his pocket, and sure enough, there was the root. 'It all comes back to this,' he said, holding it up in his hand. 'And this root is part of the prophecy. "It is said by certain seers that one root of that tree has upon it an inscription, and when that root is snapped danger is near." Remember?'

'No,' said Fiddles 'How did you remember that?'

'I... don't know.'

'What about that magical rod you bought in Goodport? Have you still got it?' enquired Chleosa.

'Right... here,' said Gybes, taking it out of his other pocket. It was glowing a luminous, ominous red.

There was a sudden rumble of thunder from behind them. Far off to the southeast, Gybes saw a dark cloud forming.

'Not *another* thunderstorm!' exclaimed Anassa.

'That's no ordinary storm,' said Gybes. It's... OW!'

He dropped the root in alarm. It had just burnt his hand, and now it was lying on the ground amongst the leaf litter, the inscription glowing scarlet.

A look of despair crossed Sarmon's face. Gybes knew what it meant.

'What is it?' asked Chleosa.

'It's too late,' said Gybes, his eyes still fixed on the root. 'Tombhadi must have the Apple of Doom.'

Chapter 25
The Storm Grows

Everyone stood silent, none of them were able speak. Finally Fiddles said, 'Well, that's it then.'

'I told you there was no hope!' wailed Sarmon. 'It's too late! It's all over!'

Gybes' glance wandered to where the wreckage of the hut was. There was something else amongst the rubble, something he recognized immediately.

'That's Porloke's five-person broomstick!' he yelled suddenly. A sudden, rampant thought charged wildly into his mind. 'Do you think it could last until Lavos?' he said.

'You don't seriously mean… no… you *can't*!' said Sarmon. 'Go after the one thing we want to be running away from? You're mad!'

'You're the person who's so distressed!' yelled Gybes furiously. 'Those are real people back there! And some of them are my family and friends.'

'If you are going, I shall come,' said Sarmon. 'I will have to keep you safe from Tombhadi… and from your insane bravery.'

'Go ahead,' said Fiddles. 'What are we going to do when we get there?'

'Something,' said Gybes definitely.

'No way am I coming,' said Fiddles. 'I'm not a… a *lunatic*!'

Gybes sighed.

'I will come,' said Chleosa plainly. 'All the ways I can see out look black, so I'll have to choose one of them.'

'Then I too will join you,' said Anassa, 'even if it leads to certain death.'

Gybes climbed onto the broomstick, ready to go. It hovered.

'Don't you think I'd best drive?' said Sarmon. 'It could be pretty bumpy –'course, none of us are wizards, but…' he trailed off. Gybes let the young man take a place at the front, and the two girls clambered on behind.

Gybes watched Fiddles standing alone in the wreckage as the broomstick took off, his friend's expression a mixture of fear, concern and guilt. He looked forwards again. There was nothing he could do to persuade him.

'Wait!'

Sarmon swerved the broomstick around. Fiddles was waving his arms in the air.

'I will come!' yelled Fiddles as Sarmon clumsily halted the broomstick in front of him. 'I've decided I was being too cowardly and self-centred.'

‘Great!’ said Gybes as they came down to where he was standing. ‘Jump on at the back!’

‘We’re all going to die anyway,’ said Fiddles as he climbed on behind Anassa. The broomstick began a dizzy ascent, shooting like an arrow higher and higher. It was being violently jolted in the wind, and the atmosphere was growing colder and thinner. Gybes began to find it difficult to breathe. He looked down, and saw the entire of Tsabia stretched out below him. Several small, wispy clouds lay beneath them, and the huge thunderstorm cloud dominated the centre of the island. Across to the right, Gybes could see the Tsabian Channel, and beyond it, Tasea and the Desert of Death.

‘Get down,’ said Gybes in as loud a voice as he could, but he could hardly hear himself.

The broomstick gave another jolt and shot downwards as steep as it had come up. The trees grew closer and closer, and Sarmon pulled off the dive just before they hit the trees.

‘What were you doing?’ asked Fiddles exasperatedly.

‘Sorry,’ said Sarmon, as he levelled the broomstick. ‘I was trying to plot our course. I didn’t know that’d happen.’

They reached a small lake. Around it, the trees grew low, and Gybes could see orogongs[1] grazing on an area of scrubland on the south side. The wind was incredibly strong as they sped along at tremendous speed, forest rushing past quicker than ever. Gybes could see that they would not be in sunlight for much longer, as the storm cloud was growing rapidly. Only now could he observe the abnormality of the dark mass; it seemed to have a vague purple colour about it, and no rain was falling beneath it.

As they carried on, the encroaching cloud became more and more disconcerting, dominating the horizon like a huge, dark mountain. Soon they were plunged them into a dull world of shadows.

After some time they came to Aurawey, a peaceful town nestled in a valley, its white houses and cobbled roads no longer shining in the sunlight and its people oblivious to the danger in the east.

‘We need to bear left!’ yelled Anassa through the battering winds. ‘I think we’re too far west.’

Sarmon turned the broomstick away from the town and was immediately sent off course by the wind. He steadied the broomstick, and they were suddenly heading straight into the wind. Both the broomstick and Sarmon seemed to be handling the wind incredibly well.

Soon they came across a lake, about ten kilometres long, and a dull grey-blue in colour, looking vast, sinister and forlorn, its surface broken with foaming waves and swells as if it were an ocean. Their reflection

[1] These were large, ungainly grazing mammals, a prehistoric species still surviving in Tsabia.

was a dark silhouette in the water, like some strange, demonic bird gliding silently into the wind.[2]

Fiddles was almost sick when the broomstick gave a sudden jolt and shot down towards the water. Sarmon managed to bring it up, but the tail skimmed the top of a wave, making the broomstick judder violently.

'What was that?' asked Chleosa.

'It must have been a sudden gust of wind,' yelled Sarmon through the gale.

'I wish I'd never come,' said Fiddles.

'Well it's too late to turn back now,' said Gybes as they reached the edge. The trees were wildly swaying and leaves were scattered on the lake, being thrown up in the turmoil of the waves. Yet the broomstick kept going with astonishing resilience.

'Five kilometres to Lavos,' estimated Gybes. Still no rain fell, but Gybes could now see that the centre of the storm was not only purple, but also red and orange, and flashing with cosmic greens, blues and yellows. Its underside was undulating, and rumbling with something that wasn't thunder, but was very close to it. It would have been an amazing spectacle had it not been so sinister.

After what seemed like seconds, Lavos was in front of them. Sarmon controlled the broomstick and brought it down so they could land. There was no sign of any life. They must all be inside, thought Gybes. Unless…

'I hope they're still alive,' he muttered. No one heard him. He hadn't intended them to.

The broomstick landed, but not very well. The point was thrust into the ground and everyone was thrown off and onto the dust of the clearing.

'Ow,' said Fiddles.

Gybes got unsteadily to his feet, rocked by the wind. The place didn't feel like home at all: it was desolate and unwelcoming. 'Hello?' he yelled. There was no answer. He ran to one of the huts and peered inside, fearing what he would see there, but it was empty. 'The village is deserted,' he declared.

'There are footprints here,' said Sarmon, looking at the ground. 'They're heading south.'

'Towards Hillside Riverton,' said Chleosa. 'They'll be safe… for a couple of hours… at most…'

'We've got to find Tombhadi,' said Gybes. 'Even if it's hopeless.'

'We can head out in three separate directions,' said Sarmon. 'We don't know where he could be. Who will come with me?'

'I will,' volunteered Anassa.

---

[2] There was, actually, such a bird. Known as the kogo, it had strange feathers that enable it to glide *into* the wind. According to Greenworld's wizards, this was magic, although it had been discovered that the bird had no magical powers.

'Very well,' said Sarmon. 'We will go north. Who will go alone?'

'I'll go west with Fiddles,' said Chleosa.

'Then that leaves me,' said Gybes. 'To go… East.'

'Good luck!' shouted Sarmon as they left. 'If we find anything, we'll come back. We'll meet back here in half an hour. Then we can decide what to do.'

They all set off their separate ways, and Gybes walked up the track towards Motherton. He hoped that he wouldn't actally meet Tombhadi face-to-face: a confrontation was the last thing he wanted, and he had a feeling it would end in his death. Still, he had a growing suspicion that he was heading right into the crogor's jaws. The wind had virtually stopped, a sure sign that he was close to the centre of the storm. He was sure that the cloud was darkest almost directly above him.

He turned left along the shortcut, the path taking him steeply uphill, but then levelling out when he reached the clearing. It seemed so long ago that he had last walked up here, but it had only been a week before he left on the trip.

He reached the road quickly and continued up it, searching for anything suspicious. He felt extremely uneasy when he realised that he was directly below the centre of the storm cloud.

Deciding to turn back, Gybes headed into the forest to his left for one last quick look before giving up hope. He took a small animal path leading into the rainforest and followed it closely, looking around nervously in the dark and intimidating growth. He traversed the hillside for fifty metres or so before he decided to head downhill again.

Then something caught his eye. Even though he had given up hope, he still couldn't help noticing a very strangely shaped rock to his right, uphill and about twenty metres away. It was conical, and had a peculiar, out-of-place sphere on top of it, of the same stone. It looked as though a giant wearing an outlandish hat had been turned to stone and buried in the ground.

Gybes moved cautiously towards the rock, and once he reached it he realised the sphere had an arrow on top of it, pointing clockwise. Not properly considering the possible consequences, Gybes reached down and twisted it the way the arrow indicated.

To his utter surprise, the whole rock swung open as if on hinges, revealing a gaping hole in the ground. Before Gybes could stop himself, he had slipped on the crumbling earth and was plummeting into blackness. The rock swung back into place without even the faintest sound.

Chapter 26
The Twelfth Member

Gybes landed flat on his feet, but fell over as he did so, onto something cold and hard. He scrambled up and looked around him. He was in a small, stone chamber, lit by torchlight casting eerie shadows across the floor. There was a passageway leading out straight ahead, his only possible means of escape.

Or it would have been, if someone hadn't been standing in front of him.

It was a woman; tall and thin with long, brown hair. She wore a hoodless, black cloak and tall black boots, which came up to meet a dark tunic. Upon her right arm, Gybes could make out a tattoo, a dragon surrounded by lightning. He recognized it, but he couldn't remember where from.

The woman strode forwards. 'Come with me,' she said calmly, as if he had been expecting Gybes. She grasped Gybes tightly around the arm, and dragged him down the tunnel. It seemed pointless to resist.

After a short time, they reached a fork. A man stood waiting, a tall, imposing, lean, blond-haired man with the similar clothes to the woman, and the same emblem tattooed on his arm. He smiled a smile that didn't extend to his eyes.

'A local by the look of him,' said the man. 'Leave him, Chomothon, I will take him to the Master.'

The woman nodded and turned down the left fork. The man led Gybes down the other tunnel. The passage was twisting, dark and dusty, and they took several turns along the way, until finally they reached two enormous double doors, giant stone slabs cut from the rock. '*Dameid Uma*' was carved across them in large, gothic capitals.

'Am I in the secret base of Dameid Uma?' Gybes queried.

'You are in what was once one of his abodes,' said the man. 'No longer is that its use.'

The cloaked man raised his hand to knock on one door, and immediately after he had done so, the double doors were both opened simultaneously by guards on the other side. What was now in front of him was a complete contrast to all that Gybes had seen so far: a much larger, much lighter cavern, with carved pillars leading to the high ceiling. The floor and walls were still stone, but they were carved, and gargoyles leered from corners. In the centre the floor was an altar, a carpet spread across the elevated platform, and a carved, wooden, throne-like chair sitting on it.

And upon the chair sat a cloaked man, with his hood up, so that you could only see the tip of his chin protruding from beneath unnatural shadow. He radiated power and exuded villainy and, upon setting eyes on him, Gybes felt, not just uneasy, but scared.

'Leave us,' the man said to the Guards, who immediately obeyed and departed, closing and bolting the doors to the chamber behind them. 'Tamethathon, stay beside the doors and see to it this boy doesn't escape.'

His head twisted towards Gybes. 'Welcome to my playroom boy,' he said. 'I knew someone might stumble upon me. But I won't let that get in way of my plans.' He cackled evilly and smiled. His voice sounded young and smooth, but unnerving; full of greed and malice.

Gybes stood rigid, too afraid to speak. This was Tombhadi. The man he had been hoping he would never meet. And he had come face to face with him.

Tombhadi gestured for him to sit down, and Gybes did as he was told, thinking of no other option. The chair was hard and uncomfortable, and lower down than Tombhadi.

'Of course, as you have guessed I am Tombhadi,' he said. 'Seeing as you are here, I will… entertain you. Let me tell you a tale, a story of my journey. I love telling everyone about me – how I came to be who I am, and how I am about to become the greatest man ever to have walked the face of this world. It won't do any harm – I shall soon master the Apple of Doom.'

Someone tied Gybes' hands behind the chair.

*

On level three of the Royal Tuvak Hospital in Ward 63, someone was awakening.

The men around him watched anxiously. The man had been asleep for almost a week now. They had presumed that he would die.

'Lumbos,' said their leader, the Legunsa, recalling his name. 'Who, and where is the leader of your organisation?'

He seemed disorientated at first. Then he looked up into the man's eyes and said, 'He is Tombhadi. He 'as gone to Tsabia after the Apple of Doom with his band of rebels, from Myen.'

'I have seen a strange cloud growing over Tsabia the last hour,' said one of the other men.

'Then it is already too late,' said another

'No! It is not,' said the General. 'His Majesty must be notified immediately. Send Sector five to Tsabia on the strongest, fastest battleships we have! This is a serious situation!'

'No point,' said Lumbos. ''F 'e's got it, 'e's got it.'

*

In the forest a little to the north of Lavos, Sarmon paused.

'What is it?' asked Anassa.

'Gybes is in trouble,' he said.

'How can you be so certain?'

'I... don't know... Go back to the village and get help with the other two.'

'Will that really be any use?'

'No. It's just something to do. Ask for a messenger falcon and send an urgent note to the Emperor. But seriously, we are the only people who can resolve the situation now.'

'How?'

'Don't ask that question.'

*

Gybes had been tied quickly, not extremely tightly, but well enough to prevent his escaping.

'The Apple of Doom,' said Tombhadi mildly. 'Such a wild imagination I must have had. But it all paid off. Back when I was about to be executed for treason, that was when I first came up with the idea. Luckily for me, I escaped, but I knew I would be followed. And followed I was. Right across Field West and through the diamond mines of the Cohen Downs. Indeed, right to the border of the Forest of Shadows, though my pursuers dared not follow me far in. They knew I would die in there, and they were almost right. But my wizard's magic was enough to repel the cursed wolves that tried to attack me. It was wolf's blood they found, boy, not mine. I left my cloak to make sure they thought I was dead.

'I stayed in the Western Border for over a year, and when I came back, no one recognized me, as many people wear a hooded cloak. Swift and unseen, I quickly made new friends. An assassin and artist, as well as a sailor and a rich young man with a notorious father. And then, of course, I found Sarmon. For he is who you have travelled here with, is he not?'

Gybes said nothing. He had no intent on revealing Sarmon.'

'You fear endangering your friends?' Tombhadi laughed. 'I know of them, boy.' He spat the last word. 'Your insignificant friends won't get away. I know it. You know it. Now it's time to face it.'

Tombhadi was staring menacingly at Gybes, so menacingly that Gybes knew even though he could not see the man's eyes. Gybes stared back at him, defiant, but his eyes quickly dropped to the floor, as if weighed down by lead.

'As I was saying,' continued the Wizard, 'I met Sarmon. And he led me to Milson, who would supply me with apple seeds. A potion must be taken every six days, three times, if I am to control the Apple of Doom, even though I am a wizard. That is why everyone else who had tried before has failed. They never did this one vital thing.'

Gybes' curiosity got the better of him. 'People have tried it before?'

'Oh yes, many. My very own great Grandfather was one of the twenty or so to try. But I knew I would be able to with the potion. Having little money at the time, I demanded the seeds at half price, which he had no choice but to accept.'

Tombhadi paused. Gybes sat perfectly still, feeling pathetic and helpless that he wasn't able to do anything to stop the villain.

'For my plan to be stable I needed loyal followers. Backup, in case of trouble. My first idea was to hire a group of assassins, but they were far too expensive. Then I remembered that it was people with a grudge against the Emperor I would need – people who would be happy to organize a revolution and oversee the Emperor's execution. My mind wandered to the current siege of Myen, with Imperial troops to the north and to the south in Sonchād. I had heard of a group of rebels based in the middle of the Green Savannah, where they were secretly planning an assault on Tuvak. The Septagons, they were called.

'So, Sarmon and I travelled across the miles of grass until we reached them, with our flag reading, "We come in peace". Of course they were fooled not by it, but by the small mind-controlling powers I possess, and admitted us, Sarmon under the name of Basron, and I under the name of Shainodari. However, although I was elected as leader, the fools would only allow me to be Military Commander, and they tried to explain that Eathon, their present leader, would be ruler once Emperor Alu IV was executed. I, of course, could not accept this, and I killed Eathon in his bed that night. I was going to do away Sarmon as well, but, untrustworthy as he is, he fled before I had a chance.

'I was certain that the 'tragic' death of Eathon would prompt the Rebels to crown me their leader, but they were less mentally tractable than I had at first perceived. They suspected me of murdering Eathon, and this made me revert to violence. I told them they would follow me or die, as did their second-in-command Panothon. Realising what they had to do, they pledged allegiance to me, and so the group "Black Dragon" was formed.

'So, with my new loyal rebels under my wing, I set out for Tsabia, tracking Sarmon as I went. I promised myself I would kill him for his betrayal.

'Also, there was the matter of the seeds. I had sent someone back to pick them up, and he caught up with us not long after we had left the base.

'I then heard that an investigation team was setting out, with the rumour that a band of rebels was plotting the Emperor's downfall in secret, somewhere in the Green Savannah. My immediate thought was to kill them all, but I managed to implant two of the friends I had met in Tuvak into the team, two who I could trust to betray the rest. The first was an assassin, who would have no killing part to play, but would have to work silently. His name was Andron Duir, although he went under the pseudonym "Arakkanid Hirstuto", which, I must admit, is not much of a name for a good impostor. However, on the third night he pretended to be drunk and ran off into the darkness. Once he realised that thankfully they were not following him, he returned and planted a gravestone in the ground, then proceeding to carve my name and a false date on it. This made sure everyone thought I was dead.

'The other man was Valisar Uma, the son of my old ally, Dameid Uma. When the Investigation team reached the native village, he slipped away on the second night and betrayed them. The remainder of my rebels then attacked the village and they were all captured.

'Unluckily for those I had left behind, the Emperor sent in his army. However, they spotted the danger in time, and fled with the prisoners. They reached me in a base ten miles from Gospruma, a port in Tasea, where I was certainly not in a good mood after capturing Sarmon by a little mind control and then losing him again. I knew he would be useful to bargain with people and to torture for any information he knew of the Emperor's plans, but he was rescued by his own brother and sister. I left for Tsabia immediately – now with over fifty rebels behind me, though that is still less than a quarter of my force.

'So, using boats stolen from Gospruma itself, I passed the guard ships unnoticed and came to Tsabia. As I was passing through, I searched Lanran Clark's home, for money he owed me from a very long time ago. I used his secret tunnels to reach his house. With the Professor and his wizard captured, I made my way here.

'But I did send two people to prevent the group lead by Mr. Dawnley from accidentally coming across me, although of course it did not stop *you*. Wickerworth, for one, the sailor, who was to watch over your progress, and the artist, Vetrum Lavoni, who made sure you got the newspaper article that dismissed my existence, and kept you away from the laboratory long enough for me to pass through. I have great pleasure in informing you that all hope for you is gone.'

Gybes' head was spinning. He had not trusted Wickerworth, but for him to be under the service of this villain… And Vetrum Lavoni may have seemed a little gruff, but Gybes had certainly not suspected him of anything.

His memory wandered back to when they were on Wickerworth's ship, the *Blackfire*. He remembered the coin – the dragon with lightning surrounding it, the very same symbol that had been on Chomothon and Tametathon's arms. Black Dragon.

'So finally I reached the insignificant village, Lavos, and found the tree,' continued Tombhadi. 'The Apple was beneath it, but of course once I had uncovered it I had to levitate it out, as I had not then taken the last potion. I have now of course!' He gave an evil laugh. 'Once I had the Apple of Doom in my possession I came here – the old abandoned base of my ally, Dameid Uma, a place still undiscovered by any authorities.

'If I may, Master,' said Tametathon, 'I would like to bring the rest before you while you take control of the Apple of Doom.'

Gybes had not noticed the man standing there, because of how silent he had been.

Tombhadi considered for a moment. 'Do not bring them all,' he concluded. 'I require Uma and Duir to be here, as well as Ovuthon, Chomothon and Derethon – and bring the twelve prisoners in as well. I want them to realise how insignificant they are. And it would be wrong not to permit them to see the face of the man who will order their deaths '

Tametathon departed. Gybes waited for what seemed like ten minutes. Surely some kind of help must be on its way now, he thought. But maybe they were all too scared. Or maybe there really *was* nothing anyone could do. Eventually the double doors swung open and in walked Tametathon, followed by three other rebels and two well-dressed men. Behind them came the ten innocent members of the Investigation Team and behind them, Porloke and Clark, who made muffled noises of their surprise at seeing Gybes there. They were all bound and gagged.

Tombhadi stood up. 'Today you will witness me taking over from the Emperor and all the other leaders in Greenworld,' he said. 'Some of you may work for me and others may die. But I will let you in on a little secret before that happens, which will, of course, no longer be a secret. This is the reason why there are no existing pictures of "Tombhadi", and I always wore a hooded cloak. You all know me by name, but I coined "Tombhadi". It is not my given name. It is not *anyone's* given name. You are certainly privileged, for I will now reveal my true identity.'

The man who wasn't really Tombhadi reached up to his head, and slowly pulled off his hood.

Chapter 27
Flame

The hood fell silently behind the villain's head. He looked surprisingly young for one who had been legend for so long. His long, blond hair was straight and his face handsome and smooth. His blue eyes shone briefly in the light of the candles, malice glinting in them. He smiled at the expression on L.C. Clark's face.

'You may know my face,' he said, 'those of you who were interested in the awards of young wizards. But none know me better than my old friend Lanran Clark, for I am Zemphanian, son of Zemorphin and heir to the throne of Schazakia, which became part of the Empire little more than thirty years ago. Yes, I did not perish in the Forest of Shadows – just as I did not the second time.'

Nobody spoke, mainly because they were not able to. Gybes looked at the face and wondered how such a person could have been drawn into such treachery and devilry.

'So,' said the man who was not Tombhadi, but Zemphanian, 'It now comes to the time I have been waiting for ten years. So, Valisar, bring me the Apple of Doom.'

Gybes suddenly felt cold. It was finally time for the man in front of him, Zemphanian, to take control of Greenworld. He couldn't quite believe it was happening.

'And remember,' yelled Zemphanian as Uma opened the double doors, 'do *not* open the carved box! Or you shall perish in most entertaining, yet disturbing way.'

The minutes ticked by, and nobody moved. Tametathon and the other four supporters of Zemphanian stood silently, grim figures at the side of the room, like statues that had been there since the dawn of time. Gybes grew anxious, anxious and terrified. Terrified that the world would be plunged into an age of darkness. Terrified that he would die.

After what seemed like an hour, Valisar Uma returned with the box – the box containing the Apple of Doom. The moment it entered the room, Gybes knew that what was inside it was of the purest evil. It glowed, yet it was not a glow of light but a glow of darkness that radiated from it. It felt as though, if the box were to be held up to a candle, the light of the candle would fade.

Valisar placed the box on a small table in front of his master, and backed away to the wall with the rest.

Zemphanian lifted the box and grasped the lid. This was it.

A sudden crash made him abruptly return the box to the table. A look of anger and amazement crossed his face.

'Someone's in the armoury!' he yelled at Andron Duir. 'How is that possible? I told you to close and lock the hidden trapdoor!'

'Sir, I...'

'You forgot to close it, fool! Go and kill whoever it is!'

'Yes Sir!'

'And don't think this'll go unpunished!'

'No Sir.'

Andron left, and began to walk down the corridor, leaving the doors open as he went. At the end of the corridor he took a right and disappeared, though the sound of his footsteps still remained.

Shortly there was a sudden, strangled, desperate yell, and then the 'thump' of a body falling to the ground. There were footsteps again, and someone appeared from round the corner. But it wasn't Andron.

It was Sarmon.

He held a sword and wore his cloak with hood up. He was striding determinedly towards the open doors.

'Close the doors!' yelled Zemphanian, but it was too late. Sarmon was through in a moment, his sword held tightly in his hand.

Ovuthon darted out in front of him, his gun drawn, but Sarmon was quick, and his sword cut the rebel's hand clean off, causing him to yell out in agony. He lurched forwards, unluckily for him, directly onto Sarmon's sword. Sarmon threw the rebel off. The body of Ovuthon collapsed to the ground.

'You haven't won yet, Tombhadi!' yelled Sarmon, wielding his sword menacingly.

'My name is Zemphanian.'

The wizard's sword met Sarmon's in a deadly clash of metal. Zemphanian grasped his weapon and swung it round full circle. Sarmon dived out of the way and staggered backwards, falling to the floor. He got up again, ready to fight, but Tametathon stood in his way.

The much stronger man ducked under Sarmon's skewering motion and grabbed him by the legs. Sarmon dropped his sword with a clatter to the stone floor and was thrown aside into the corner of the room, where he lay motionless.

'So you see, there is no hope left in the world for those who defy me!' yelled Zemphanian. 'The Apple is mine for the taking. Such a fool was that wretched Sarmon to think he could take on the might of Zemphanian, the greatest wizard of all time!'

Tametathon moved towards the unconscious man, a sword in his hand.

'Leave him,' said Zemphanian. An almost gruesome grin grew on his face. 'I want to dispose of him in a more... interesting way.'

Gybes felt the anger against this man well up inside him. His right hand found his pocket and he felt within. There was something there.

'Now is the time when I shall triumph over all!' Zemphanian bellowed. 'I am the greatest man ever to live! No man has ever come close to what I am about to achieve! This is my triumph!'

Gybes felt the thing in his pocked and pulled it out. It was the magical rod he had bought in the shop in Goodport. He lifted it out as much as he could with his bound hand, only to notice that it was cracked. He gently pressed his finger onto the crack and had to stop himself from yelling out in pain. It had burnt him; there was a red mark on his fingertip. A fleeting idea crossed his mind. He held it so that it did not touch his clothes, and a few drips of the mysterious liquid fell onto the rope.

To his astonishment, most of the rope sizzled away and the final strands snapped leaving his right hand free.

Zemphanian was holding the box again, the terrible grin still on his face. He placed it on his own lap, and opened it.

He laughed out loud and looked up at the rest of the people: Ovuthon lying on the floor, lifeless; Sarmon lying at the side of the room; his faithful rebels standing in the shadows, looking intimidated by their master; Gybes in his chair, tied tight apart from his right arm. 'This was easier than I expected. Isn't anyone going to try and stop me? Once I take the Apple of Doom, I become immensely powerful, with ten times more endurance! It would be virtually impossible to kill me. Oh, of course, you *can't* stop me. Sorry, I forgot!' He cackled

Insane as well as evil, thought Gybes. He watched, frozen, as Zemphanian lifted something out of the box. At first, Gybes didn't think it was an apple at all, because it was black, but apple it was. The Apple of Doom – the symbol of the end of freedom and justice.

'So this is it!' yelled Zemphanian triumphantly. 'As soon as I absorb its power, I am in control of the whole of this world!' He swelled with ego and stood up, holding his prize aloft.

In a last, desperate effort, Gybes threw his magical Durioú rod at Zemphanian. It flew through he air as if in slow motion. Gybes watched silently as it smashed open on Zemphanian's arm.

The wizard screamed in pain, dropping the Apple of Doom to the stone floor. As Zemphanian desperately made a dash for the apple, Valisar Uma, seeing that something had not gone to plan, fled, running down the tunnel and away.

Another scream of pain caused Gybes to look up, and saw that Zemphanian's arm was now on fire. He was desperately trying to extinguish it, but to no avail. The wizard finally reached for a jug of water lying in the corner of the room. Pouring it over his arm, the flames went out, his robe disintegrating as they did.

But one small piece of flaming cloth flew wide. Gybes watched in disbelief as it floated through the air like a feather, and then landed on the Apple of Doom.

The tool of evil exploded into a thousand tiny shards of black, clouding the air with dust. There was a sound like the roaring of a waterfall, and a jet of pure energy shot vertically from the place where the Apple had been, creating a hole in the ceiling of the chamber.

Gybes looked up in wonder, not believing what he had just seen.

*

All over Tsabia people gazed in wonder as the black and purple cloud receded rapidly and a ray of light and fire like a dragon's flame erupted from the centre of the island and exploded like a massive firework display far above Tsabia. The Apple of Doom had been destroyed.

*

Gybes finally freed himself fully from his ropes. The smoke had cleared, and Zemphanian, and his supporters, were nowhere to be seen. He turned around. Staring directly at him were the ten remaining members of the Investigation Team, Porloke and L.C. Clark. But Gybes ran first to the corner to where Sarmon lay. He turned him onto his back. Sarmon immediately became conscious and sat bolt upright.

'What the… where's the Apple… where's Tombhadi?'

'The Apple of Doom is destroyed, and Tombhadi is Zemphanian, and he's just ran off down the corridor with two other rebels!' said Gybes desperately. He stood up, ran over to Porloke, and began undoing his ropes.

'What do you mean, he's…' began Sarmon. 'I've got to follow him,' he said resolutely.

'I'm coming with you,' said Gybes, untying Porloke's gag.

'Gybes… what the… why… how did… did *you*…'

'Undo everyone else's ropes and gags. I've got to go!' Gybes wasn't sure why he wanted to chase after Zemphanian, but he was certain in his decision. He thought, adding up everthing that had happened in the last few hours, that he probably owed Sarmon his life

However, the two were hardly through the double doors when several broomsticks shot round the corner, an enraged Zemphanian seated on one, flanked by another two: one with Uma aboard it, and the third the transport of Derethon and Tametathon. All held pistols, and Gybes and Sarmon ducked as they fired. The immensely loud sounds reverberated around the stone tunnel as the broomsticks pelted past them, and then straight upwards, through the hole in the roof and off into the sky. They had escaped.

*

'Gybes!'

Fiddles, Chleosa and Anassa ran towards him and Sarmon and stopped in front of him as he reached the other side of the swamp.

'We thought you were dead!' said Anassa. 'What happened?' She paused. 'Why aren't we *all* dead?'

'Gybes saved us all!' said Fiddles

'No I didn't! I just…' Gybes couldn't think of how to word it. 'I'll tell you what happened later,' he said.

'I told them,' said Sarmon. He had run ahead when they had left the underground chamber, while Gybes had searched the forest in vain for evidence of Zemphanian and his followers.

'What's happening here?' Sarmon pointed towards Hillside Riverton.

'The Mayor's having a meal with the Investigation Team and the Professor, and Porloke,' explained Fiddles. 'You're invited too, Sarmon.'

'Half the district turned up to see what all the commotion was about,' said Chleosa. 'There's going to be a huge banquet!'

The banquet certainly was huge. When they reached Hillside Riverton, they found that almost thirty large tables had been set up in the area of grass on the south side – where the festival had taken place. How the event had been so quickly organized, Gybes couldn't guess, but he didn't really care right now. All that mattered was that the threat was over and he could relax.

There was an enormous amount of food set up on the tables, and still more was being brought, continuously. Crowds of people were wandering among the tables, chatting, laughing and generally milling around. Through the crowd Gybes spotted his Mother and Father, talking to Mr. Inkwell. As soon as she saw him, his Mother dashed over and embraced her son.

'How did you do it?' she said, tears in her eyes. 'I thought you were dead!'

Gybes' Father came running over behind her. He put his hand on his son's shoulder. 'I'm very proud of you, Gybes. What you did was…'

'Wizz!'

Gybes looked up. Trudge was running towards him, running, not waddling. Gybes was astonished to see that, in the short time he had been away, he had lost a lot of weight.

'Trudge?'

'Wizz! You're a hero! They should put you in the papers! "Wizz the invincible!"

Gybes laughed. 'I'm not *that* great,' he said. 'All I did was lob a tube at a dude!'

'Come on!' said Trudge. 'We're ready to eat at table seven. The team and Clark and your Uncle are there, and the Mayor and stuff, 's well as your Mother and Father, of course. And a few other people, and stuff. And that Sargon guy, too.'

They walked over and sat down on a rough wooden bench at the table, Gybes beside Fiddles and Porloke on the other side. Seated along the other side was the entire Investigation Team, of whom Gybes had met only Mr. Inkwell. 'And to think I suspected him of being involved!' he muttered to Fiddles.

Once everyone was seated around all the tables, the Mayor of Hillside Riverton stood up at the end of their table and banged his spoon on the surface. Once the noise had subsided, he began a speech, which he improvised on, having had no time to make cues or notes.

'Of course we all know why we are here today,' he began. There were noises of bewilderment from many people in the crowd. 'Well, in fact, most of us don't.' He gave a nervous, embarrassed laugh. 'We are here today because of the defeat of the wizard and murderer Zemphanian, who took refuge under the false name of Tombhadi. We owe this… great achievement to many, many people, but to two in particular. Firstly, to the courageous Master Gybes Marronon, who prevented Zemphanian from controlling the world, even once he had the Apple of Doom. And secondly, to the brave Sarmon, who took the children back to their home, and stood up against Zemphanian in hand-to-hand combat. Therefore I am awarding them both, with His Majesty's word, when it arrives, the Devis Grenderley Award for Service to Greenworld'

Everybody cheered, and the Mayor continued his speech.

'Today we have witnessed how dangerous the Apple of Doom truly was. We know now that it no longer exists and, about half an hour ago, I received the information that Zemphanian's broomstick was found underneath a suicide note and several people spotted his body floating in the stream from which this village gets its name. His face was identical to that described by Sarmon, sure proof that the villain is now actually dead. As said in the great Jamid Bind play, "*You Only Live Thrice*".'

The speech continued for some time, and once the Mayor's mind was empty, and he trailed off, everybody clapped politely.

Gybes felt a tap on his shoulder and turned around to see Porloke looking at him.

'Have you any idea what you're going to make of your future?' he asked.

Gybes considered for a moment. 'Not really,' he said.

'You know that your family has magic in its blood, as I am your Uncle. The only reason that you are not the son of a wizard is that your Mother and Father decided to settle down and lead an ordinary life. Of course, you might know that Eriko Gampolball, your Great, Great Grandfather, was a rather talented wizard himself. You're bright and determined, not to mention very fast. What I propose...' He paused. 'What I propose is that I take you on as my apprentice.'

'I...I...' Gybes stammered. 'I don't know what to... I mean I'd love it, but I... you know I'm not... not magical or anything.'

'Everyone has the potential to become a wizard, even those without magic in their blood,' said Porloke. 'So... what about it?'

'Yes,' said Gybes. 'Yes I will.'

'I'll take you to Tuvak one day, to see the Royal Institute for Magical Skills and Development,' said Porloke, grinning. Gybes returned the smile. He began to help himself to some of the food on the table, and watched the people around him chatting and eating. Nothing strange or unexpected was going to happen, Gybes decided. Fiddles had gone off on a quest to find Asila, Mr. Inkwell was coughing violently over a glass of strong spirit, and one, substantially bulky member of the Investigation Team who Gybes gathered was called Milson was laughing heartily at a joke... Yes, the next few weeks were going to be perfectly *normal*.

* *Epilogue* *

The next few weeks were far from perfectly normal. With the members of the investigation team still lurking around, there was plenty of fun to be had. They all participated in various games, such as gridhop and rockthrow. Pom Thukru, Milson, Doran and Sashlea even took part in children's games. Porloke demonstrated his magic to the inhabitants of Lavos, and he, the Professor and Sarmon took pleasure in being hosted in the village hall.

The thirteen visitors were given an exclusive tour of the surrounding area; Motherton, the Temple of Au Crassig and many other places besides. Gybes Father acted as guide, being very knowledgeable about the area.

Searchers were dispatched from Aurawey, and managed to find forty-five of the fifty-one rebels, not counting Tametathon, Chomothon, Derethon or Uma. Six terrorists remained elusive, but nobody worried too much about them. No one had remembered to tell them about the other supporters of Zemphanian still residing in Tasea.

Two days after the banquet, an entire sector of the Imperial Army turned up, only to find the situation resolved. Gybes and Sarmon were officially presented with their Devis Grenderley Awards, and the army departed very quickly, having important business to continue with on the northern border of Myen.

Over the week that followed, the visitors gradually departed. The last to leave apart from Anassa were Sarmon, L.C. Clark and Porloke, who still promised to take Gybes to Tuvak, to show him the Royal Institute.

Once they finally left on Caroton the 1st, the inhabitants of Lavos got back to their usual business. Gybes played games with everyone as usual, and Anassa joined in, until her parents came to collect her five days later.

Sir Fawning even turned up to congratulate Gybes, and to tell him that Tsabia would be liberated from the Empire in two-and-a-half years' time.

Gybes was still wondering when everything would go back to normal, the way it had been, playing games without a care, simply messing around with his friends. He mused about all the things that had happened, and all the things that probably would happen. He realised that in his life, there would never be such a thing as normal. He was growing up, and being thrust into the big world; and he was certain that this was not The End.